REUNION

RICHARD S ZIEGLER

July 2023

ZZZ Publishing

Cover Credits-

Photo Montage from

1969, 1970, 1971 Freedom High School Yearbooks

DEDICATION

To Young life friends:

Skip, Robin, Rod, Sheila, George, Debbie, Patty, Ron D.

To Old life friends:

Ed, Frank, Tom

To Friends and Family Past:

Helen, Dick, Cile, Carl, Grammy, Nana, Pastor Kopperman, Coach Martz

To Family Present:

Barb, Mike, Sarah, Robin

CHAPTER 1

The drive to the doctor's office used to be fifteen minutes. With two new housing developments and a new apartment complex springing up in the last two years, the drive was closer to thirty minutes and only if you hit the lights right. So far this afternoon I had been stopped at every light between my house and the medical building. I would be lucky to be in time for my 2:30 P.M. appointment. Not that it really mattered; it was rare that I got to see the doc within a half hour of my scheduled appointment time.

By the time I parked my car and made my way to the second-floor office, I was ten minutes late. I stepped up to the receptionist window and announced my arrival.

"Mr. Williams, you are late for your appointment. You can wait and see if the doctor can squeeze you in later this morning or you can reschedule," the woman behind the counter snarled. My shock quickly turned into annoyance.

"You have got to be kidding. All the times I have sat in this waiting room for thirty minutes or more beyond my scheduled appointment and now I'm a few minutes late and you give me attitude. I've been coming to Dr. Burton for thirty plus years and this is the way you treat me? Seriously?"

Other people in the waiting room turned their heads toward the little altercation that was starting to unfold. It certainly wasn't my intention to create a scene, but the receptionist was out of line.

"Mr. Williams, giving me a hard time is not going to help your situation. It was you that was late. We have a schedule to keep and we do our best to keep things moving along. It is not fair to the other patients who are here on time."

I had two choices at this point: I could sit down like a little sheep and wait until the "queen of the office" decided she could

5

squeeze me in or I could argue that this was completely unfair. I opted for choice two.

"Listen sweetheart, I don't know what kind of power trip you are on, but as a patient of Dr. Burton long before you arrived on the scene, I expect a little courtesy. Rarely, if ever, are you on schedule. Do I give you attitude when the doctor is running late? No, I don't because I understand that unforeseen circumstances sometimes make staying on schedule impossible. The same things happen on the patient end. Today, traffic was much heavier than it normally is, not to mention I got stuck at every red light between this office and my house. I did my best to get here on time, but despite my best intentions, I was late. Ten minutes…and now you have wasted more time by giving me a hard time about it." There was actually a smattering of applause from the other people waiting.

"Mr. Williams, I do not appreciate your attitude. I think you should leave this office at once or I will call for building security."

"Do what you need to do you pompous bitch," I responded louder than I intended to. "I deserve a little respect. Hell, I have moles that are older than you."

"How dare you?" Ms. Wetherby shrieked. "Get out of this office at once."

"Not until I see the doctor!"

Just then Dr. Burton appeared as nurses and patients peered from the rooms in the back.

"What may I ask is the problem out here?"

"Mr. Williams was late and is now creating a disturbance, not to mention calling me names that I do not care to repeat," Ms. Wetherby sputtered. The doctor turned to look at me seeking an explanation.

"Doc, traffic was ridiculous today and I arrived ten minutes late. Your receptionist decided to make a federal case out of it and told me I might need to reschedule or have a long wait until she could fit me

6

in. I found both of those choices objectionable." The doctor seemed to be weighing his options as he looked back at Ms. Wetherby. Finally, he spoke.

"Ms. Wetherby, why don't you take a break and calm down."

"I'm fine, Doctor Burton," she said. "Really...I don't need to do that."

"It wasn't a suggestion," Doctor Burton replied. Ms. Wetherby huffed to show her displeasure, which I could see annoyed Dr. Burton. "And in the future, Ms. Wetherby, please treat our long-time patients with a little more understanding and courtesy."

Ms. Wetherby was silent as she gathered her stuff, glaring at me the entire time. Just as she was turning to leave, I couldn't help myself.

"Enjoy your break, Ms. Wetherby," I said, eliciting a few chuckles from the other patients. Doctor Burton waited until Wetherby was out of the room.

"Come with me, Mr. Williams. I'll see you now before you start any other trouble, he said as he smiled at me.

Not surprisingly, my blood pressure was much higher than normal.

"I'll take it again before you leave. I'm sure your little altercation has something to do with the reading."

"Your receptionist needs a few lessons in learning how to treat your patients. Her attitude is not going to help your practice."

"You're not the first person to tell me that," Dr. Burton said. "She came with great references. I'm going to need to have a chat with her about her attitude. I've been putting it off, hoping that she would eventually settle into her new role, but it doesn't seem to be working. Anyway...let's get back to you. How have you been feeling since we switched your medication?"

"Things seem to be going fine," I answered. "I haven't had any acid reflux attacks since the change, although I must admit that I have been staying away from spicy foods."

I stepped on the scale and waited for the result. Doc Burton was pleased when it registered six pounds less than my last visit.

"It's an unfortunate fact that as we age, we can't eat the same way we did when we were younger," Doctor Burton said. "Between the medicine and watching what you eat, you shouldn't have any more problems with the reflux. Continue to watch your diet and keep that weight going in the right direction."

"Life was so much more fun when I was younger," I said. "I could eat what I wanted and do whatever I wanted. Now I need to make sure I don't overdo anything otherwise I always seem to pay the price either with a bad stomach, extra pounds, or aches and pains and injuries."

Doctor Burton laughed as he wrapped the blood pressure cuff on my arm once again. As expected, my blood pressure had returned to within a few points of where it normally is.

"Unless things change, why don't schedule an appointment for six months?" he suggested. "And keep in mind, you're not as young as you used to be."

"Gee, thanks doc for those words of encouragement," I replied. We both laughed and shook hands as I headed back out to reception. A different nurse was manning the station much to my relief, and I set up my appointment for my six-month checkup.

CHAPTER 2

Grace, my wife of thirty-four years, was tinkering in the kitchen as I walked into the house. She is the best thing that ever happened to me and I consider myself to be a very lucky man. We had both been married once before and both marriages had been disasters. I soon discovered that living with my first wife was much different than dating. When we had been dating, we had always been doing fun stuff and almost always ended in the sack every evening. What wasn't to like? The day-to-day grind presented different challenges which neither one of us were mature enough to handle. Little issues became big problems which grew even larger when neither one of us would ever back down. It quickly became apparent that it wasn't going to work out. We never made it to our third anniversary. It was a difficult thing for me to swallow. I watched one of my high school friends get married shortly after graduation. Less than a year later, they had already split. I could not understand that and swore it would never happen to me. And yet… it did.

Grace's marriage lasted a little longer than mine and the problems were different. She and her husband got along well and to their friends and family, everything seemed to be great. Unfortunately, her husband had a wandering eye and an insatiable sex drive, a combination that led to many flings, one-night stands, and affairs. Grace tried to ignore them in the beginning, figuring he would settle down and as long as he came back to her, things would be fine. Unfortunately, his trysts became more frequent and less discrete. Grace confronted him one night after arriving home very late. He informed her that this is who he was and she needed to learn to deal with it. One day, shortly after their confrontation, Grace arranged for all of her stuff to be moved out of their apartment while her husband was at work. She left a note for him explaining that she intended to file for divorce. Her husband promised to change, but Grace knew it would only be a matter of time before it all started again. She had suffered through enough, and filed for divorce.

I first noticed Grace in the hallways of the Bethlehem Steel office on Third Street. Some mornings I would see her coming into the main entrance while other days I would see her leaving. I was never close enough to strike up a conversation and wasn't sure what I would say even if the opportunity presented itself. One day luck turned in my favor. I had forgotten to bring my lunch that was still sitting on the kitchen counter at home. There was no time to turn around and go back home to retrieve my sandwich. I figured I would get something in the cafeteria.

Lunch time came and I headed down from the seventh floor to the cafeteria on the second floor. I walked in, grabbed a tray, and joined the line waiting to select my lunch. I opted for a tuna sandwich on wheat bread and Coke. I paid my tab and looked around for an open table. There were a few near the back, but a table closer to the front caught my attention. Grace was sitting there by herself. I paused for a moment and decided right there to go for it. What's the worst she could say? I headed in her direction.

"Mind if I join you?" I asked. She looked up and then glanced around the cafeteria. In my mind I was sure it was to see if there was a different table that she could direct me to. She looked at me, making a quick assessment and decided that I seemed harmless enough.

"Sure," she said. I took the seat on the opposite side of the table.

I'm Jason Williams. I work in accounting on the seventh floor."

"Nice to meet you, Jason," she answered. "I'm Grace and I'm a secretary on the fourth floor."

Now that introductions were finished, I was at a complete loss for further conversation. I could not tell her that I had noticed her coming and going without coming across as a stalker. While I froze, she saved me.

"How long have you worked at the Steel?" she asked. From that point on the conversation flowed. By the end of lunch, I had her phone number and I promised to call to arrange a date. Six months later, we were married in a small ceremony with only our closest friends and a few family members present.

Now thirty-four years and two kids later, we are both retired from the Steel and enjoying life. Sarah, our daughter is married to Mike and they have two kids. She still lives locally. Jackson, our son is married to Emily who is expecting her first child. Unfortunately, they live across the country in Portland, Oregon which means we do not get to see them nearly as much as we would like.

"So how did your doctor's appointment go?" Grace asked. I related my trouble with the receptionist. "I told you that you should have left earlier," she was quick to remind me. "You shouldn't have given the young girl at the desk a hard time. She was only doing her job." I wasn't in the mood for getting into a debate about this morning so I chose to remain silent.

She continued with her food prep at the counter as I picked up the morning paper and started reading where I left off after my morning coffee earlier today. After a few minutes I saw the mail truck stop in front of our house.

"I'm going to walk out and get the mail," I announced.

"Probably just more junk mail," Grace added.

I walked down the driveway and retrieved several envelopes from the box. I thumbed through as I walked back. Bills, ads, and junk mail accounted for all the envelopes except one. Handwritten and addressed to me, the return address had no name attached to it. My curiosity piqued, I tore the letter open and pulled out the contents. It was a final reminder that my fiftieth high school reunion was coming up this fall and I needed to respond by the end of next week if I planned to attend.

"You should go," Grace said after I told her about the letter. "The fiftieth reunion might be the last one. Some schools stop after fifty because the class sizes grow smaller and the surviving members of the class are older and find it too difficult to travel. You should really think about going. The last one you went to was what… twenty-five years ago?"

"I'll think it over," I said.

"Well think fast because you need to decide by next week."

CHAPTER 3

I rode my John Deere lawnmower back and forth across the yard as the afternoon sun sank lower in the sky. When I was younger, I dreaded cutting the lawn. Now it was something that helped fill my day. I still wasn't crazy about the trimming and edging, but it gave me a certain sense of satisfaction when I was finished and it looked just as good as the neighbors' yards and they all paid for a lawn service.

I still hadn't made up my mind whether or not to attend my reunion. I could hardly use distance as a reason not to attend since the site of the reunion was practically in my backyard. The Lehigh Valley Steel Club sat less than a mile from my house. Hell, I could even walk home if I got out of control. I laughed to myself at that thought. I hadn't gotten "out of control" in several years. That last hangover I suffered was a painful and unpleasant reminder to drink in moderation.

I began to wonder who would actually attend. We had a large class of slightly under five hundred students. The last accounting was that fifty-three members of our class were already dead and that number was from a few years ago. Our dwindling ranks was one reason to go. Without question, it would be the last time I saw some of those people. Of course, I hadn't seen many of those people for years, so did it really make a difference if I saw them one more time or not?

I never did a very good job of keeping in contact with my high school friends after graduation. A few of us went on to Temple University together. I kept in touch with them through our freshmen year, but then new friends that I met at Temple replaced my high school friends. Some of my other high school buddies went away to college like I did, and we only saw each other when we were home for holidays. That lasted for a few years before that stopped as well. Other former friends were moving on with their lives and got jobs and got married right out of high school. They were in a whole different place than the college life of frat parties and football games. High school became a distant memory.

13

I pulled the tractor into the shed in the backyard and cleaned it up a bit before closing the shed and heading back to the house for a well-deserved beer. As I took a swig of Voodoo Ranger IPA on the back patio, I realized I had to make a decision about the reunion. My response had to be in the mail by tomorrow to get there before the deadline.

Grace walked out to join me with a Dewars on the rocks with a twist, her go-to libation.

"The yard looks good," she said as she settled onto the chaise lounge. "So, are you going to your reunion?" she asked.

"If I go, do you want to go with me?" I asked.

"If I'm being honest, the answer is no. I really don't know your high school friends. I think you would have a better time without having to worry about keeping me entertained."

"I don't mind keeping you entertained."

"That's nice, but I would rather stay home. Go without me. I think you'll have fun catching up with your old crowd. Go see how everybody looks and find out what they have done with their lives. Besides, if it is terrible, you can be home in five minutes after dinner."

"I'll think about it." And I did. Before I went to bed, I found my high school yearbook and paged through it. People and places from my past peeked up at me from the pages. Past teachers and classmates. The prom and the football homecoming game and dance. The school play and the band concerts. A year of my life was crammed into those pages. It was so important to me at the time and now it was a distant memory becoming more distant with each passing day. What the hell... I would go. Who knows... maybe it would be fun?

I set the yearbook down on the end table and headed off to bed, my decision made. My fiftieth high school reunion... it didn't seem possible that so much time had elapsed since my high school years. It made me feel old as I crawled into bed. Grace snuggled up next to me as I closed my eyes and thought about my life fifty years ago.

Bright and early the next morning I filled out the response form, wrote out a check, filled out the envelope, stuck a stamp on it, and walked it out to the mailbox. Several times throughout the morning, I thought about going out to the mailbox to retrieve the envelope and trash it, but I didn't. The last time I considered scrapping the idea, the mail truck was already pulling away from our mailbox and along with it my reunion response. It was too late now. The letter was on its way. I would be added to the list of attendees for our fiftieth high school reunion. I can't be that old, can I?

CHAPTER 4

"I think it's great," Sarah said. "Better watch out, Mom. Maybe he'll run into an old girlfriend." We were sitting around the dinner table when Grace shared that I was planning on attending my reunion. Mike, Sarah's husband, didn't comment, but my daughter couldn't stop. "Fifty years… it is really unbelievable that you're that old."

Sarah, thirty-one, was our older child. She had graduated from Kutztown University with a degree in elementary education and married Mike Robertson shortly thereafter. They had Alison four years later and Bobby two years after that.

"What's a reunion?" Alison, my seven-year-old granddaughter asked.

"It is when really old people get together and talk about when they were young," Sarah answered.

"Why?" Alison asked.

"Because it reminds them of a time when their life was exciting and they knew how to have fun," Sarah answered and tried to suppress a chuckle.

"We're still plenty exciting," I said. "We keep plenty busy, don't we Grace?" I asked hoping my wife would come to my defense.

"We do have a very active social life," Grace added. "We have our monthly Bridge Club, we go to the gym in the winter, and we belong to the swim club in the summer. I belong to two different book clubs. Your father gets out to play golf once a week and plays pickleball a few times a week. He goes out with his buddies once a week for lunch. We go out to dinner occasionally, and regularly attend concerts, plays, and sporting events. Then there are the one or two trips a year abroad. You may find our lives boring, but for our age I think we are doing very well." Grace winked at me and smiled. I figured that would satisfy Sarah, but I was wrong.

"I'll admit that you have taken some great trips. What I can't figure out is what you do with all your time. All of the things you mentioned don't begin to cover the time you have each week. What do you do with the rest of your time? How do you fill your days?"

"You would be amazed to learn that we don't sit around and stare at the walls," I said. "There always seem to be little jobs and things to do around the house. We have time to fiddle around with our hobbies. Your mother still sews and I still dabble with my stained glass and my guitar. Believe it or not it, we manage to fill our days. We're never bored. I think it is a sweet deal. Look at your life. You get the kids ready for school, work all day, pick up the kids from the after-school program, make dinner, help the kids with their homework, watch a little television, and then go to bed only to start it all over the next day. You're busy; I'll give you that, but are you having fun?" Finally, Sarah did not have a comeback.

There were no other digs about my age or the reunion the rest of their visit. Sarah did not linger after dinner. She packed up the kids and was on her way less than thirty minutes after the table was cleared. Grace and I watched as they backed out of our driveway and turned toward their home.

"You know she was just pulling your chain, right?" Grace asked.

"I'm not so sure," I said. "I think she really believes we are old and boring."

"Well, we are old," Grace added.

"Age is just a number. What's important is how you feel."

"I don't disagree with you," Grace said. "Right now, I feel tired. I'm going to get ready for bed and read a bit. Are you coming?"

"I'll be in later. I'm going to see what's on television." Grace headed to the bedroom as I settled into my favorite recliner in the den. I flipped through channels and settled on an old Law and Order rerun. It wasn't long before I found my mind was no longer focused on the television. I hated to admit it, but I was bothered by Sarah's comments. Was I old and boring and just fooling myself thinking otherwise? Was life passing me by? Had I already lived the best years of my life? Was I on the irreversible downward slope to oblivion? I pondered what were the best years of my life. How would one go about defining the best years? Was it the period in your life when you had the most fun? Maybe it should be defined as the period that you were most productive. Maybe it should be defined as the period in your life when you were most successful. How does success differentiate from productivity? The more I tried to arrive at an answer, the more I realized how difficult it would be to pinpoint the best years in one's life. I finally gave up, turned off the television, headed off to the bedroom, and slipped under the sheets.

CHAPTER 5

I woke early as usual and poured myself a cup of coffee as I pulled up the local newspaper on my laptop. I scanned the national news before flipping to the obituaries. It was a good day; there were no names that I recognized. I was holding off on breakfast because I was meeting what remained of the Boys Club later this morning at Perkins for our weekly get-together.

The Boys Club used to be so much more. Initially it started out as a movie club when Jimmy was the first of the group to get a VCR. We would gather at his house most Friday nights with our wives and watch whatever videotapes we could lay our hands on at the video store. Once everyone had their own VCRs, the group morphed into a games club with the men only. Risk was the game of choice and we played it so many times that there simply were no new strategies to employ. We could have written the comprehensive manual for the game, so thorough was our understanding of the game. We often played games that ended well after midnight, even on a work night. Once Risk ran its course as we moved on to Rail Baron, another fine strategy game.

Board games were supplanted by pool when I bought a nice Brunswick table. We decided that Friday nights were better than playing during the week when we had to work the next day. Hours were spent learning the finer points of pool over a period of years. We mixed darts and Skee-ball into the evenings, but pool still reigned king of Friday nights. Eventually, two of the other Boys Club members got pool tables so we rotated around to the different tables.

Then at one point, poker was introduced into the mix. It started out as once a month, but soon took more and more of our Friday nights. It wasn't long before the pool tables started gathering dust as pots were won and lost on the poker table. This was far from high stakes poker; the largest winning night anybody ever had was thirty-four dollars. Losing twenty dollars was a really bad night and actually hard to do.

19

Over the years a couple of the original Boys Club moved on to other things that did not include Boys Club. Two new guys joined our group, the first changes in our group since we started.

Then a variety of schedule problems disrupted our weekly poker games. It went from being weekly to twice a month… if we were lucky. A number of miscellaneous personal issues seemed to arise on a weekly basis meaning there were never enough guys to play poker.

The Boys Club Lunch group grew out of the need to keep in touch with each other. Two of the Boys Club still worked so we were left with me and three other guys that could get together for lunch when babysitting grandkids or doctor appointments didn't interfere. Today was our next scheduled lunch. I kissed Grace goodbye and walked out to my car. Fifteen minutes later I pulled into Perkins.

The first person I saw was Jimmy. He was pulling into the parking lot at the same time I was. We had met at the Steel Company, actually attending orientation meetings on the same day. We have been friends ever since sharing common interests in Philly sports, music, and stereo equipment. Between the two of us we bought better and better stereo equipment until we couldn't afford the next step up. Jimmy had grown up in inner city Philadelphia while I grew up in Bethlehem, a much more suburban setting. Despite our different experiences as kids, we really got along great. Softball, bowling leagues, and Boys Club solidified our friendship.

George was already waiting for us as we got out of our cars. George was my neighbor. He spent his entire career as a physics teacher in the Bethlehem School District. When I first met George, he was married to a very unpleasant woman. He stayed with her a lot longer than I would have, but he did finally see the light and got divorced. Much to our surprise, he didn't waste any time and started dating a woman he met at his church. Six months later they were married. He is one of the charter members of Boys Club and an all-around good guy. He wasn't a skilled pool player and didn't have the best card sense, but he still holds the Boys Club record for Skee-ball, a feat of which he is very proud. Since none of us have a Skee-ball table any longer, George will hold that record forever.

The final member of the lunch group arrived a few minutes later. Don was a friend of a friend of a friend who we met playing in a softball league. Don worked his entire career in the Bethlehem Steel Beam Yards. Don did not go to college but was street smart. Growing up near a pool hall, his pool skills put the rest of ours to shame. His mechanical skills were his strength. Don was a born gambler and loved to play the ponies so poker was a natural for him. Our low stake poker games could not compare to what he bet on the horses. Trying to bluff Don out of a poker hand was an impossible task. It wasn't unusual for Don to be walking around with a roll of cash in his pocket upwards of five or six hundred dollars.

The four of us were led to our usual table in the back corner where we studied the menus and ordered our lunches As I sat back and started in on my second cup of coffee, I was ready to throw out a question for the group that I had haunted me since last night.

I relayed the conversation I had with my daughter which the guys found amusing. Their amusement gave me the perfect opening to ask my question.

"What do you guys consider as the best years of your life?" I asked. George wasted no time with his response.

"That's easy," George said. "Without question the best years of my life are right now."

"How can you be so sure?" I asked. "Look at where I'm at in my life right now. I am married to one of the most beautiful people I have ever met. Katie makes me feel so good every single day. I have never been with a woman that makes me feel the way she does."

"Hell, George… you're only married a few years," Don interrupted. "You are still in the honeymoon stage. No wonder you consider now the best years of your life." We all chuckled.

"Besides being in a great marriage, are there other reasons you believe you are in the best years of your life right now?" I asked.

"Where do I start?" George quipped. "I'm retired and can come and go as I please. My investments over the years have done well so I don't need to pinch pennies anymore. If I want to do something, I can do it... within reason. I have good friends and you guys aren't bad either." That brought laughter from the rest of us. "I didn't have many good friends growing up. After school, everybody in the neighborhood went to the playground to play basketball, football, or baseball. Playing sports wasn't my thing, but I tried and when I did, I could count on being selected last for a team. That always made me feel bad so I simply stopped going to the playground. Things got better in high school where at least I found a few people whose primary interest was not sports. Then in college, I met Jody. Things were great right up until the time I said "I do" and then after that, things went downhill."

"I could never see what you saw in her," Jimmy added. "She always seemed to be in a bitchy mood."

"You have no idea," George said. "I kept thinking things would get better only they didn't. To compound problems, Jody got pregnant and blamed me for bad timing because a child was going to have a negative impact on her career in real estate. I think the only reason we stayed together as long as we did, was because of Gregory. I'm sure it wasn't good for Greg to see his parents fighting all the time. There was very little love in our house. So...like I said when I started, the best years of my life are right now."

The waitress brought our food to the table and conversation was suspended temporarily as we all were busy eating. Once the feeding frenzy slowed down, Don was ready to weigh in with his answer.

"For me, my best years were definitely high school."

"High school?" George immediately questioned. "Where was the fun in having to go to class nine months a year not to mention homework and studying for tests?"

"Who said anything about studying?" Don answered bringing out a few chuckles from the Jimmy and me. "I didn't study much and if I didn't feel like going to school, I didn't go." Don said.

"Look at the good things in high school; the parties were great, the girls were easy, and the beer was plentiful. What more could you ask for?"

"Your parents let you get away with that stuff?" George asked.

"Who do you think supplied the beer?" Don said. "My dad and Uncle Sal ran a pool hall and bar and I helped clean up at closing time. On slow nights, I would go in there and watch the pool hustlers. On really slow nights I got to practice my shots on the old table in the back corner where very few people ever played. The regulars got to know me and started buying beer for me and offering me cigarettes. My dad gave me a beat-up Chevy for my sixteenth birthday if I promised to graduate from high school which I eventually did. I went everywhere in that car. I drove to school and took trips to the Jersey shore in the summer. I did a little drag racing on back country roads late at night, but mostly you could find me and my Chevy at the local lover's lane getting lucky with various girls."

"It's amazing you didn't end up in jail with company you kept," Jimmy said.

"Or dead," I added. Don laughed before continuing.

"That's just the way life was in my neighborhood. Nobody thought much about the consequences of what might happen. It was all about living for the moment and getting the most out of life."

"And that is what you consider the best years of your life?" I ask.

"Yeah, I guess so," Don answered. "Don't get me wrong, I have liked my life with Jeanie. I mean…come on…she gave me two great kids who now have seven kids of their own."

"I thought you had three kids," George said.

"I do. Like I said Jeanie gave me two great kids." That broke the group up before Don continued. "Other things got in the way though. I got laid off from a couple of different jobs which meant money was short from time to time. Health has been a factor, especially in the last fifteen years. Prostate cancer, having a mild heart attack, being diagnosed with diabetes, and most recently having open-heart surgery to repair a leaky valve all suck. Jeannie has been lucky enough to beat cancer twice. Although there were lots of good things that happened during those same times, I can't say they are the best years of my life."

Sensing we weren't ready to leave, the waitress appeared with refills for our coffee cups. The answers to my question that I had heard so far could not have been more different. George indicated that the present was best while Don chose a time more than fifty years ago. Maybe Jimmy could break the tie.

"I can understand why you guys picked the times that you did," Jimmy started. "Both of you picked the times that you were having the most fun which makes sense. I have been going back and forth between two different times in my life. One thing I can tell you for sure is that my answer is not the present. Don't get me wrong, I'm not unhappy or anything like that, but the present is definitely not the happiest period in my life. Between my emphysema and Beth and I having an up and down relationship throughout recent years, things could be better right now. My kids and grandkids do bring me a ton of happiness, but I find it hard to keep up with them. After a day babysitting my grandkids, I'm exhausted. Waking up every morning with various aches and pains is no fun either. I swear it takes me longer and longer to recover from a round of golf every time I play."

"I think we get it," I said. "So, what were the best years of your life?" I ask.

"It's close between my high school years and my college years," Jimmy began. "I had many friends in the neighborhood in high school. We did everything together. As nerdy as it sounds, I actually liked school. My grades were good and my friends, teachers, and parents all considered me smart and witty. There was such an innocence in those years. I remember listening to Phillies on my transistor radio as I lay in bed on hot summer nights. Occasionally my dad would take me down to Connie Mack Stadium to see the Phillies play in person. My parents were proud of me and I was proud to be their son."

"It sure sounds like those were the best years of your life. So, were they?" George asked. Jimmy hesitated before answering.

"Like I said, it is a tough call. My high school years were great, but my college years were great too. For the first time in my life, I was living on my own. I got to be my own boss. It was totally in my power if I went to class or not, what I ate for meals, when I studied, when I got out of bed and when I went to bed. For the first time in my life, I didn't feel like a kid anymore. The social life in college was great too. There were football games and frat parties, dances, and bonfires and a host of other things to keep me entertained. I met many new people during my college years, some of whom I still see. And of course, I met Beth. College was the first time I ever had a physical relationship with a girl...and I liked it. Not living at home made it easy for Beth and I to have fun whenever we wanted."

"So, what is your choice?" I asked.

"If I have to make a choice, I'll go with my college years," Jimmy said. "High school was fun, but college was really fun...if you get my drift."

Jimmy's choice did not break the tie, but instead made it a three-way tie. I may have been onto something last night when I decided it was going to be tough to pinpoint the best years in a person's life.

"You started this," Jimmy said. "Where do you stand?"

"It's close for me too between college and high school. My college experience was a little different than yours," I said to Jimmy. "I lived at home so I didn't have nearly the freedom that you had. My parents had expectations for me that I would need to meet. Unfortunately, I wasn't quite mature enough at the time to meet those expectations. My first year and a half of college were an academic struggle which was new to me. Of course, pledging a fraternity didn't do much to help my grades, but I did get to know a great group of guys.

There were a couple of unbelievable spring-break trips to Florida. Add in weekly fraternity parties, intramural sports ranging from football to badminton, and a few hot girlfriends along the way and you would think my college years would be the hands-down winner.

"You're saying it's not?" Don asked.

'I really think high school edges it out. In high school, things came easily to me. My grades were good with minimal studying. I was successful in athletics for the first time in my life. I played soccer in the fall, swam in the winter, and played on the volleyball team in the spring. In volleyball I was voted MVP one year and we finished fourth in the state in my senior year. Music also played a big role in my life in high school as I was in the band, the orchestra, and the glee club. I was in two circles between the music crowd and the sports crowd. I was invited to parties in both groups and made great friends in both circles. Tenth grade was a bit of a bummer as I liked a girl who liked someone else, but by eleventh grade I had my first girlfriend and physical experience. I was on top of the world. All things considered; I would have to say the best years of my life were in high school. I was successful in the classroom, on the athletic fields, and in the dating scene."

"What brought this wave of nostalgia on?" George asked.

"I received an invitation to my fiftieth high school reunion yesterday. I guess it got me thinking about that period in my life. Did you guys go to your fiftieth?" It turns out that none of the guys had gone to their fiftieth reunion. Jimmy swore he never got an invitation. Don said he had no interest in seeing a bunch of old people, and George said if he had been married to Katie before the reunion, he would have gone to show her off. Since he hadn't met her yet, he opted to decline the invitation. They were all surprised to hear that I planned to attend mine.

"Why are you going?" George asked.

"I guess the main reason is curiosity. Weren't any of you guys at least a little bit curious about what your classmates look like after all these years and what they did for the last fifty years?" I could see the three of them exchanging glances before they all answered in unison.

"No!" We all laughed. That concluded this week's lunch club as we headed to the cash register to pay our bills. We agreed to the same time, same place, next week as we headed to our cars.

CHAPTER 6

"How was lunch?" Grace asked as I walked in the front door.

"The usual," I said, "although we did have an interesting conversation."

"What sports topic was it this time?" Grace asked.

"It had nothing to do with sports."

"Don't tell me you four old geezers were ogling some hot new waitress."

"Very funny," I said. "We do have conversations about things other than sports and hot women." I paused before adding, "Not often, but we do talk about other things."

"So, what was today's riveting topic of conversation?"

"I posed the question to the group about what they saw as the best years in their life."

"Really?"

"Why is that so hard to believe?" I asked feeling a bit insulted that Grace didn't think we were capable of having intelligent conversations about anything other than sports and hot women.

"It just doesn't sound like a conversation that would hold your group's interest," Grace said. "This all goes back to your exchange with Sarah last night, doesn't it?"

"It does," I admitted. "It really bothers me to think that our daughter finds us old and boring."

"You need to let that go. She is looking at us through her eyes. She is in the prime of her life. It shouldn't be all that surprising that she finds our lives dull compared to hers. She'll see it differently when she is our age."

"By the time she gets it, we'll either be in an old age home or dead," I said.

"So, what were the best times in the guys' lives?"

"No one had the same answer. George picked the present time. Jimmy and Don ruled out the present based on health issues. Tom picked high school. Jimmy picked college. "

"George has no health issues?" Grace asked.

"He does, but still being a quasi-newly-wed may have influenced his answer."

"Unbelievable that at his age, he still considers sex to be such an important factor."

"Have you been living under a rock?" I asked. "Every guy on the planet does."

"How sad," Grace said.

"I guess that depends on your point of view. Just out of curiosity, where do you stand on the best years of your life question?"

"I don't know that I can answer that."

"You have no favorite time in your life?" I asked.

"Of course, I do, but the problem is I have many times in my life that I look back on in fondness."

"And none stand out above the others?"

"No because you are asking the impossible. There have been so many good times in my life. My childhood was ideal. High school was wonderful and so was college. Getting married to you, the birth of our children, the life we have built together, our retirement years…they all have been wonderful. How could I place one above the other? At the time each was happening they were the best years of my life. I don't know how anybody can capsulize their life and pick their best years."

"Apparently not everyone has had the fairy tale life you have been leading," I said.

"It hasn't all been roses. I've had my share of health problems. My first marriage ended in a shambles. It's funny, but I think I would have an easier time picking the worst years in my life."

"So, what would be the worst years in your life?" I asked.

"Without question the last few years with Dave as I watched our marriage dissolve. Those were tough years. I was devastated, but look what happened because of it."

"You mean us?"

"No, I mean my secret love affair. Of course, us!" Grace said. "You and the life we built together for our family."

"And our life right now isn't your favorite?"

"It is right now because that's the life I'm living. Ask me that forty years ago, it would be a different answer. Fifty years ago, a different answer still. Sixty years ago, yet another different answer. Asking me to pick a certain period in my life is impossible…like I said in the beginning."

The longer Grace spoke the more uneasy I grew. I realized that I had put myself into a box for which there would be no escape. Once Grace asked me for my answer to the same question, I was screwed. It didn't matter what my answer was if it wasn't the same answer as hers. She would be disappointed to say the least. I could always lie. That would be the safest route, but if the conversation ever came up with any of the Lunch Club guys, my lie would be exposed and I would be in even more trouble. The other option would be the truth and I knew that would hurt her which I certainly did not want to do. This was not going to end well for me.

"What was your answer this morning with the guys?" The moment of truth had arrived. I delayed.

"What do you think my answer was?"

"I know what I hope your answer was, but the fact that you are delaying tells me it's not."

"Delaying? What do you mean?" I asked trying to act incredulous.

"Jason, don't give me that act. I'm not buying it. I know you too well. Are you going to tell me your answer or do I need to call one of your friends?"

"Alright, alright. You won't have to call anybody. I told the guys that it was a very hard decision as there were many great times in my life…like you said earlier. When I factored everything into the equation, I said my favorite time was… Did I tell you lately how much I love you?" Grace laughed.

"Nice try. Is it safe to assume that the present time was not your answer?" Seeing no way out, I decided to tell the truth.

"Yes, you can safely assume that my answer was not the present, not that our life together hasn't been fantastic. You know I love you."

"Time to spill the beans, baby. No more stalling. What did you say?"

"Maybe I'm just feeling overly nostalgic because of all the reunion talk, but I picked my high school years." Grace sat quietly for a few moments before responding.

"Maybe Sarah was right," she said.

"What do you mean?"

"Maybe I should go to the reunion to make sure that you don't run off with some old flame. There has to be some reason why high school was the best time in your life. What's her name?"

"Whose name?" I asked.

"The old flame who I need to watch out for," she said.

"You can't be serious," I said.

31

"Last night I wasn't serious at all. Today, I'm not so sure. The best years of your life? What am I supposed to think?"

There was a bit of a chill around the house for the rest of the day. Grace seemed to be making it a point not to be in the same room of the house with me. I was amused to think that she might actually be jealous of someone that I knew fifty years ago. To my knowledge, I had never given Grace a reason to doubt my fidelity since we had been together. My dating history in high school was a mixed bag at best. In tenth grade, there was Pam. We had become good friends through our involvement in the band. I wanted our relationship to move to the next level, but all she talked about in our conversations was Mark. I waited for her interest in Mark to cool off. The problem was that it never did, and I never did ask her out, knowing that our friendship would be awkward after she said no.

Junior year there was Elena. I did go out with her a few times, but there was never any chemistry, especially on her end. I never went to the junior prom because I had absolutely nothing going on with anyone. That summer is when things really started to change. I had my first full summer job as a lifeguard at a local swim club. Being a lifeguard gave me a certain swagger that had been missing previously. I met Debbie who worked at the pool in the snack bar. We started going out and for the first time in my life the interest was mutual. We saw each other constantly all summer long. Summer came and went and there was a new wrinkle. She hung with an entirely different circle of friends than I did. Luckily, her friends accepted me and my friends accepted her. Our relationship continued and my self-confidence grew as I had a "steady". We made it through another year and we thought we were in love. I don't know; maybe we were.

Problems started after graduation when she started college three hours away. I was starting my own college career right in my hometown. We tried to see each other on weekends whenever we could, which wasn't that often. I met lots of new people in college and had many opportunities to broaden my dating portfolio. I'm sure she was faced with the same dilemma in her new school. Eventually the temptation to strike out in new directions was too great. We agreed it

32

made sense to start dating other people although we would continue seeing each other when possible. In the history of dating, I doubt that plan has ever worked for anyone, and it certainly didn't for us. By Christmas, we had both moved on. We never officially called it quits, but even when she came home for the summer it never got back anywhere close to where it had been. By the start of my sophomore year, we were not seeing each other at all.

I did run into her at the Denver airport of all places a few years later. We were both waiting for planes heading in opposite directions. We sat and had a coffee together and reminisced about our time together. I was surprised that my feelings for her were as strong as they were during our conversation. It was obvious that she still had a soft spot for me as well. We spent the better part of two hours talking until my plane was called for boarding. I reluctantly stood and started to say how great it was to see her which she cut short by pulling me in tight and kissing me. We stood there for several seconds locked in an embrace while memories swirled all around us.

"It was so great to run into you," I said. "Maybe we'll run into each other again." She looked up at me with the start of a few tears forming. I wanted to say more, but could not find the right words.

"I would really love that," she said before kissing me on the cheek. "I wish we could go back in time and start over. There are so many things I would do differently."

"We did have a good thing going, didn't we?" I asked as my flight was called for final boarding. "You better get going before you miss your plane."

"Just my luck," I said, "My flights are always late and this one has to be on time." Debbie laughed.

"Keep in touch," she said.

"I will." We hugged one more time and I turned and hurried to my gate. By the time I reached my seat on the plane, I realized we had not shared any contact information like current phone numbers or addresses. Just as well I thought as I settled back in my seat. At that point I was in a marriage that was on life support as it was, and any further contact with Debbie was only going to complicate my life more. Had things started up again with Debbie, I may have never met Grace.

For the entire four-hour flight home, I could not get Debbie out of my mind. We had so many good times together when we were dating. Now, I can't even remember where it went wrong. I wondered what would have happened if she hadn't gone away to college. I suspect my life would have been entirely different.

I drifted back into the present. As it turned out, I was very glad that I had not resurrected my relationship with Debbie. I doubt that it would have compared to a beautiful thirty-four- year marriage with an incredible woman. Grace was everything a man could want. I was a lucky man. Sarah couldn't have been more wrong suggesting that I might run away with an old flame. I was a lucky man right where I was. I wasn't going anywhere.

CHAPTER 7

"Wake up. You need to get a move on." The voice was familiar, but I couldn't place it. I rolled over, opened my eyes, and sat up. I looked around and although the room looked familiar, I had no idea where I was. I tried to engage my brain to figure out where I was and what was happening.

"Are you up yet?" the same female voice from earlier came from somewhere down the hallway. I began to panic. Did I end up getting so blitzed last night that I picked someone up and brought her back here? Holy shit…Grace was going to be pissed. Worse yet, I had no idea who it was. Am I having a dream? I closed my eyes, rubbed my head, and tried to clear my thoughts. I opened my eyes and I was still in the same place.

I stood up and realized I was wearing plaid pajamas. I never wear pajamas. Underwear and a t-shirt every night…never pajamas. I looked around the room. There was an old chest of drawers on the far wall. A simple desk and chair sat next to the bed. A beanbag chair completed the furnishing. Posters filled the empty wall space including a Phillies poster, a poster of the four Beatles, and a sunset poster that I recognized as Cannon Beach in Oregon because I had been there a few years ago. The Cannon Beach poster was really weird because I had the same poster in my room growing up. What I didn't see was any signs of my suit. What happened to the suit that I would have been wearing after my meetings yesterday?

"Get a move on Jay. Your breakfast is getting cold." The familiar voice called out again. This was getting stranger by the second. Nobody had called me Jay in years. How did this person know me by Jay? Did I pick up somebody I knew? This just kept getting worse. I slid open the closet door looking for my suit. There was a strange collection of shirts and pants, nothing close to business attire. I pulled open the chest of drawers and found underwear, t-shirts, and socks. I rifled through the shirts which was a collection of sports teams and rock groups. I went back to the closet and found a solid blue button-down shirt. I pulled on a pair of khaki pants and searched for a tie. Finding none, I set about looking for a nice pair of dress shoes. Other than sneakers, the only thing I found was a pair of penny loafers. I sure hoped I didn't have any important meetings today, because I certainly was not dressed appropriately.

"Are you done in the bathroom? I need to get in there." I stared at the person in my doorway in total shock; it was my sister, Connie or at least a much younger version of my sister.

"What's wrong with you today? Are you high or something?" Connie asked.

"Or something," I said. "The bathroom is all yours." Connie turned and disappeared down the hall. I looked around the room again. I knew why the room looked familiar; it's the same room where I had grown up. I poked my head out of the bedroom. I looked toward the stairs. I knew exactly where I was. I headed down to the kitchen expecting to snap out of my dream at any second.

"Finally," my mom said standing at the stove in her flowered apron with her hands on her hips. "Your breakfast was ready ten minutes ago. I go to all this trouble to make you a nice breakfast, at least you could be down here on time to eat it." I was stunned speechless. There in real flesh and blood was my living, breathing mother who I hadn't seen since her passing eleven years ago. "You have nothing to say?" Mom asked.

"I'm really sorry. I'll try to do better." I walked to the stove and gave my mom a huge hug.

"What prompted this?" she asked.

"I wanted to make sure you know how much I appreciated you and everything you did for me."

"Appreciated?" my mom said, puzzled. "You're not going to appreciate me in the future?" I realized my mistake.

"Of course, I am. I just want you to know that I know how special you have always been to me."

"This is getting deep," she responded. "Are you in trouble at school?"

School! I was going to be expected to go to school. What in the hell is going on here? I can't possibly go to school. I don't want to go back and repeat school. Wake up, wake up, wake up I kept thinking over and over. I was still standing in front of my very alive mother in my childhood home.

"So, are you in trouble?"

"No, not at all. Can't a guy tell his mother how much he loves her without getting second-guessed?"

"Sure, he can," Mom said. "I'm just not used to hearing it."

"Starting today, I'm going to make it a point to let you know how much you mean to me."

"Thank you, that would be very nice. Now sit down and eat your breakfast. Mark will be here in ten minutes." Mark, a name out of the past. Second half of junior year and all of senior year, Mark was my ride to school. He was in the same grade as me, but was close to a full year older than me. Not only did he have his license, he already had his own car. My dad contributed five dollars a week toward gas. Today that wouldn't even buy two gallons of gas. I should start buying stock in oil companies right now.

I gobbled down my scrambled eggs and bacon and washed it down with a glass of orange juice. What I really wanted was a cup of coffee.

"Do you have any coffee?" I asked Mom.

"Coffee…right. You are too young for coffee. It stunts your growth."

"You drink it," I countered.

"I'm still not growing like you. Now go brush your teeth. Mark will be here any minute." I raced upstairs. The bathroom was shared by the family. I found my blue toothbrush and did a quick brushing.

"Mark's here!" Mom called from downstairs. I rushed down the stairs, gave Mom a hug, and headed to the door. Just as I was stepping out of the door, Mom called out.

"No books today?" she called out. Funny thing… I knew exactly where they were… sitting on the corner of the dining room table where I deposited them every night when I got home. Most nights I did my homework at the dining room table and left them there for the next morning. I grabbed my books and headed out to the maroon Chevy Malibu idling in my driveway. I pulled open the door and slid in.

"Hey Mark. How have you been?"

"You mean since yesterday?"

"Sure," I said realizing I had to be more careful in the way I spoke to people.

"Are you going to the sports award banquet tonight?" he asked. Memories came flooding back in a rush. Coach Martz had been pestering me for days to attend. I had sent in the form, but never paid the money. The night came and went and I ended up not attending. The Coach called me down to his office at the pool the next morning before the first period started.

"Thanks for leaving me high and dry," he said. "I thought you were coming to the banquet."

"I needed to study for an English test," I said which was an outright lie. The amount of time I studied for the test would have left plenty of time to attend the banquet.

"You should have been there," he said. "This would have been much nicer if you could have received the recognition you deserved in front of everyone at the banquet." He handed me a plaque with a gold volleyball player jutting out from the front of it. Under the player the words Most Valuable Player were engraved on a little metal plate. On the line below was my name. I was stunned.

"Wow, thank you so much." I could see the disappointment in his face that I hadn't been there last night. "I'm really sorry. I should have been there."

"Well, it's too late now. You missed my speech about how important you were to the team. You get the idea." He reached his hand out and clasped mine in a firm handshake. "Congratulations. Now get out of here before you are late for class." I was practically emotional as I left his office. Volleyball was the only sport I ever excelled in despite trying others including soccer, swimming, and basketball. To think I won the MVP award and wasn't there to accept it. I missed my shining moment.

"I am going to the banquet," I answered Mark. I missed it once and it ranks as one of my biggest regrets from my high school years. Given this very unexpected second chance, I wasn't going to miss it tonight.

CHAPTER 8

I went through the day without a hitch. I knew exactly where I was supposed to be and when I was supposed to be there. I knew everyone's names. It was like I never left. I caught up with Trip, one of my best high school buddies during fifth period study hall. Since I was in the band, I was allowed to take my study hall in the bandroom.

"What happened to you at lunch?" Trip asked.

"I was at lunch," I said. "I didn't see you."

"No kidding," Trip said. "I was here. I thought we agreed to eat outside the bandroom today if it was nice?" Apparently, my memory of the past was not perfect. I had no recollection of agreeing to meet Trip at all. "So, who was she?"

"What do you mean?" I asked, fearing that I had forgotten something else.

"I figure you had your sights set on a hot sophomore and you had an opportunity to have lunch with her." I laughed.

"I wish," I said. "Nothing nearly as exciting I'm afraid. I simply forgot. Maybe I'm starting in with early Alzheimer's."

"What the heck is that?" Trip asked. I realized I had made another mistake. Alzheimer's wasn't well-known at all during this time period. I tried to cover my mistake.

"It's a nickname for one of my uncles who constantly forgets stuff. It's a family joke." I wasn't sure Trip bought my story, but he didn't push it. I had to be more careful when I spoke. There were many things I knew about that didn't exist yet.

"Are you ready for Mrs. Grisman's test?" Trip asked.

"What test?" I asked.

"What's with you today? Maybe you have the same thing your uncle has…Allshiner's or whatever you called it."

"I'm just pulling your chain," I said. "Of course, I studied." Luckily it came to me: *The Rime of the Ancient Mariner*... that was the test subject. We had been studying it for the best part of two weeks. "Water, water everywhere, nor any drop to drink."

"Why can't Coleridge just speak in plain English?" Trip asked.

"Because then it wouldn't be a famous poem that students need to study and analyze," I answered.

"I'm not sure how this is going to help either one of us in the future," Trip said. "I doubt I'm ever going to be in a situation when I'll use something I learned from the Ancient Mariner.

"He prayeth best, who loveth best, all creatures great and small," I quoted from the poem. "Call me crazy, but I think Coleridge was onto something."

"What's up with you today? You are acting weird."

"It's been a long day," I answered. Trip has no idea just how long my day has been given it started fifty years ago.

I remembered the material for the test surprisingly well and had no trouble answering the large majority of questions. Things that I had long forgotten were right there again. This was going to be interesting to see how this all played out.

On the way to my last period class, I ran into Mr. Martz, my volleyball coach. He had passed away a few years ago and now I had a chance to speak to him again.

"Coach, it's really good to see you," I blurted out.

"Well Jay, it's really good to see you too," he said and laughed. "Am I going to see you tonight at the banquet?"

"I'll be there," I answered. "I wouldn't miss it for the world." The coach stared at me suspiciously.

"Who told you?"

"Who told me what?" I asked trying to look as innocent as possible. Coach's gaze bore into me. I didn't flinch. "Who told me what?" I repeated.

"Nothing. I'll see you tonight. Wear a coat and tie. Now get to class." Without another word, he turned and headed the opposite way down the hall. I headed to Music Theory, the last class of the day.

Mrs. Ockley taught the class which was designed for students who were considering music as a major in college. I knew everybody in class as they were all members of either the band, orchestra, or glee club. This was not a class for people who were not into music.

I took the seat between Rob and Greg. Rob played sax and Greg played clarinet. Neither Rob or Greg noticed anything different about me and I managed not to put my foot in my mouth during class by mentioning Lady Gaga or Bruce Springsteen who were unknowns at this point in time.

Following class, the three of us hurried to our lockers just down the hallway from the music room. I gathered up the books I needed for homework, said my goodbyes, and headed to the bus platform. Bus 64 sat where it always sat and I was one of the first people on the bus. I moved to the back of the bus. None of the seniors were riding the bus because that wasn't cool. That meant the juniors had first dibs on the back seats.

As I settled into my seat, I realized how long it had been since I had ridden a school bus. One thing I noticed is school busses are not built for comfort. My knees were crunched into the seat in front of me. Every bump or hole in the road jarred my back. You had to hold on when the bus took corners, otherwise you would slide off the seat.

Twenty minutes later, the bus pulled up in front of my old elementary school, Clearview. I climbed off the bus and took a careful look at the school. The version in front of me looked just like it did when it opened. It hadn't looked like that for a long time after two expansions and some remodeling in the following years.

I turned and walked toward home, a block and a half away. I realized that I would soon be seeing my father for the first time in nine years and a younger version of himself before he was confined to a wheelchair. He worked as an accountant for the Bethlehem Steel ever since he moved back to the Lehigh Valley. He was the true definition of a family man. He doted on my mother and there wasn't anything he wouldn't do for her. On weekends, he loved to cut the grass and tinker with odd jobs around the house. Every summer we would take a week-long family vacation to the Jersey shore. I couldn't believe I was about to see him again. I walked faster even though I knew he wouldn't be home from work yet.

"How was your day?" my mom greeted me as I walked in the front door. It was the same greeting I had heard every day since I had been going to school. I started to give her my standard answer of same old, same old, but I stopped and realized that she deserved better than that. I actually took the time to give her a run-down of my entire day. She seemed genuinely surprised and grateful that I took the time. I had been back in this time and place for less than a day, and already I realized that I hadn't been as nice to my parents as I could have been. At the end of my long-winded description of the day, she reminded me to get my homework finished since I had the banquet tonight. Some things never change!

An hour later I was just wrapping up the last of my homework when I heard my dad arrive home. I rushed down the stairs to see him.

"Hi, Dad, I'm really glad to see you," I said. He looked at me trying to figure out why I was so excited to see him.

"What trouble are you in?" he asked.

"No trouble," I said. "It's been so long since I saw you…that's all."

"So long? Since last night? What's gotten into you?"

"Geez, can't a son be happy to see his father?" I asked.

"You sure there isn't anything going on?" he asked.

"Positive," I answered. "How was your day?"

"Seriously…what's wrong with you? Are you on drugs or something?"

"You and Mom always ask me about my day. I can't ask about yours?"

"Sure, you can, but you never have before. Why today?"

"I guess I realized I should appreciate you more," I said.

"I'm glad you finally realized that. Now, before this gets any weirder, I'm going to change my clothes before dinner." Dad climbed the stairs and disappeared into his bedroom. Judging by his reaction, I guess I hadn't been very interested in his day-to-day life in the past.

I was very careful at dinner with my sister and parents not to say anything out of character. I had made enough mistakes for one day. We carried on what I hoped was a normal conversation.

After dinner I changed into a solid light blue shirt and struggled to get the knot right on my red tie. I topped it off with a navy-blue blazer. I even put on my penny loafers. I knew that I was going to be on stage tonight. I knew I had to look nice. Tonight, I was going to correct one of the biggest mistakes of my high school years.

CHAPTER 9

Dad dropped me off at the American Legion Hall. The first person I saw when I walked in was Coach Martz.

"I'm glad you made it," Coach said. "I had a funny feeling you weren't going to show."

"I wasn't going to miss this aaa..." I almost said again which would have confused Coach. Luckily, I caught myself in time.

"We have a table for the team in the far corner. Head on over there. Some of the other guys are already here. And one other thing...thanks for getting dressed up."

"No problem," I answered, not knowing what else to say. I knew why it was important to him for me to look nice, but I couldn't let on. He was already suspicious that I knew about tonight's award. I headed over to the table and joined the rest of the guys.

As I walked through the room, I recognized many faces; faces that I hadn't seen in fifty years. There were the studs from the baseball team, the future tennis pros, the guys from track and field, and the girl jocks from the softball team, most of whom could probably hit a softball farther than I could.

Only John, the starting setter and three bench players were at the volleyball table. With me that meant more than half the team hadn't bothered to show up. Eventually, Mark, who stood 6'7" joined us. It was a disappointing showing for our team. Coach remained upbeat throughout dinner even though I was sure that he had to be disappointed with the turnout.

Dinner concluded quickly and the awards part of the evening was about to get underway. The program listed the teams in alphabetical order which meant that Coach would take the podium last. Coach Watson of the baseball team took the podium and summarized his team's accomplishments. He handed out an award for the most improved player and then begin to list the accomplishments of Steve

Brosky who received the Most Valuable Player plaque. When we got to volleyball, that was going to be me.

The evening rolled on as coaches from the other teams praised their teams and individual players. The table that had held all the awards began to empty as players claimed their hardware. One thing that was becoming apparent was that people were leaving after receiving their awards. There was a growing number of empty seats as the night moved to its conclusion.

I watched and listened as the tennis coach announced his winners. That left only the Track and Field team before volleyball. The crowd thinned even more. By the time they announced Coach Martz to present the volleyball team awards, there were fewer than twenty people still sitting in the audience and most of them were the coaches from the other teams.

"Next year I want to present first," Coach Martz said eliciting a laugh from the room. He went on to talk about our season in which we had won exactly half of our games. "It was a good year and almost the whole team will be back next year. I suspect we will challenge for the district title," Coach said. If he only knew how true those words would be. Next year we would go on to win the district championship and actually finish fourth in the state. Of course, I was the only one in attendance who knew that. Coach called John to podium to receive the most improved player award. I fidgeted in my seat as I knew my big moment was seconds away.

"My most valuable player award goes to…" Coach said. I heard my name and tried to look surprised as I walked to the podium. He handed me the plaque with my name inscribed under the MVP line. There was a smattering of applause as I accepted the award and shook Coach's hand. He leaned over and whispered in my ear, "I'm really glad you came tonight."

"Thanks, Coach. You'll never know how much this means to me." This was my shining moment. I knew that I would never again receive an individual award for excellence in my sport unless you counted my Most Improved Bowler award in the adult bowling league, an award that implied that I was a horrible bowler at the start of the season. I took my seat back at the table and accepted congratulations from the other players at my table. Five minutes later, it was over as Principal McIntyre thanked everyone for attending and closed the evening's festivities.

I was one of the last ones to leave the banquet hall. I cradled the MVP plaque in my right arm with a deep sense of satisfaction. I had corrected one of the biggest mistakes in my life although if I was honest with myself, I was a bit disappointed that more people were not in attendance to see me get that award. I guess I shouldn't feel that way; the important thing is that I was there to receive the award from Coach. It had to be so embarrassing for him fifty years ago when his MVP player was not at the banquet to accept the award.

Dad was waiting for me in the parking lot. I climbed in the car.

"So how was it?" he asked.

"It was great," I said as I held the plaque toward him. "I was named the MVP."

"Congratulations," my dad answered. "I'm so proud of you. Wait until your mother hears this." We drove home, both of us caught up in the moment.

Mom was equally excited when I showed her my award. "We'll get that hung in your room this weekend." I knew exactly where it would hang; the same place it hung all those years ago. That award stayed on the wall in my bedroom many years after I moved out to live on my own. Finally, one year, when my parents visited me, they brought the plaque with them explaining that they thought I might want it. They were right. It hung in a spare bedroom for a few years before I moved to a new house. Even in the new house, I found a spot for it down in the basement.

I turned in for the night and replayed the evening's events in my head. It would have been nicer if more people had been there, but I was glad that I had been there for Coach. He was a good guy and it was a good feeling knowing that I had not disappointed him.

I didn't know how long I was going to stay in this time period or if it was all just a long dream, but it was so satisfying to relive this moment from my past. I hoped I had more opportunities to change things that didn't go exactly my way half a century ago. Another thought crept into my mind before I could drift off to sleep; would there be any consequences in the future for the changes that I had managed to make in my past? In books and movies on this topic, there were always warnings about the dire consequences that might occur if you changed the past. I could not imagine how the changes to my past that I had made tonight would have any influence on me or my future or anyone else's future. I decided I wasn't going to worry about that tonight. I was tired and I had another day of school tomorrow. That's one thing that hadn't changed; I still wasn't looking forward to going to school the next day.

CHAPTER 10

I woke and instinctively looked for the time on my Apple watch. My wrist was empty. I was still living in 1969. I had to rely on desk clocks and wall clocks and old-fashioned wind-up wristwatches. I started to realize I could make a fortune by inventing all those things that weren't around yet. Laptop computers, PlayStation gaming consoles, cellphones, shoulder harnesses and airbags for cars, televisions with remote controls and streaming, and the whole concept of online shopping were just the tip of the iceberg. And talk about insider trading; I would know what stocks to buy just before they got hot. I could be a gazillionaire!

I glanced at the MVP award that sat on my desk. I was so glad that I had been there to accept it this time. I could check off one mistake from my past. There were so many others to still fix if I could.

Next on the list was the junior prom. The problem was that I hadn't been able to get a date and decided not to go at all despite the fact that lots of my classmates were going stag. In the days after the prom, I had regretted not going. Word filtered back the following week in school that the prom had been serious fun whether you went with a date or not. At the time, I was too embarrassed to go without one, figuring everyone would label me as a loser.

Correcting this mistake was going to be more difficult. The prom was a week from tonight and I had missed the deadline to pay for the evening by a full week. I headed off to school with a mission; I needed to find a way to get to the prom.

As soon as I arrived at school, I went in search of Patti who I knew was on the prom committee. I found her at her locker and wasted no time trying to correct another of my many mistakes.

"Hey, Patti. How are you?" I sidled up next to her.

"To what do I owe this unexpected pleasure?" she asked.

"I have a favor to ask."

"I hope this isn't about the prom," she said trying to guess my intentions.

"Why do you say that?" I asked, trying to play dumb.

"Because I already have a date," she answered. "I'm sorry."

"That's not my problem," I answered.

'Let me guess," she said, "You missed the deadline to buy a prom ticket."

"Exactly," I said. Trying to get some sympathy, I concocted a story on the spot. "I didn't want to bug my parents for money to pay for the ticket. My summer job doesn't start until this weekend, and I am flat broke. My parents asked me last night who I was taking to the prom and I had to tell them that I hadn't signed up for it. They handed me a twenty on the spot and insisted I go sign up for it today. They told me that they didn't want me to miss the prom because of money. I figured you might be the person to talk to and here I am."

"I really wish I could help you out, but I can't. I handed in the unsold tickets that I had left to Miss Sanderson. She is the faculty advisor for the prom."

"So, there were unsold tickets?" I asked.

"There were a few last week. I have no idea whether or not any are left. And even if there are, I'm not sure Sanderson will sell them. I think she had to turn in a final count to Principal McIntyre last week."

"What difference would one extra person possibly make? I asked.

"Don't you mean two people? Wouldn't you be bringing a date?"

"No, I would be coming alone. I hear that there are quite a few people coming without dates."

"I thought you were dating Jill?" she asked.

"I was. Now I'm not."

"Oh, I'm sorry to hear that," Patti answered as the bell rang for homeroom.

"I'm fine," I said." I guess my next step should be to talk to Miss Sanderson."

"You can try," Patti said, "but I wouldn't get my hopes up."

"I'll just need to turn on my charm," I answered. "Thanks for the info."

"Good luck," Patti answered.

I headed off to homeroom feeling better about my chances. Why wouldn't Miss Sanderson sell me a ticket if she still had unsold tickets? They had counted on a certain number to go and had not reached that number. It wasn't going to change the cost to the school. They still had to pay for the band and the rental for the hotel ballroom. My extra twenty bucks was only going to get them closer to breaking even for the event. During my fifth period study hall I would be going to see Miss Sanderson.

This time of year, school was always boring beyond all belief. Nothing serious was going to happen in the last two weeks of school. Finals were done and projects were in. There wasn't much that could happen that would have a big impact on your grade. Students knew it and teachers knew it. The only thing that could really screw things up was if you skipped class. All you had to do was show up for class. A few teachers still tried to teach while others resorted to movies and free reading time.

As easy as these days were, they were extremely boring. The clock hands crawled forward if they moved at all. Minute by minute for forty-five excruciating minutes I waited for each period to conclude. At the end of fourth period, I headed to the guidance wing where Miss Sanderson had her office. I took a deep breath and walked in to the guidance desk where Mrs. Ruth, the guidance secretary sat.

"Good morning and what can I do for you this fine morning? she asked.

"I would like to see Miss Sanderson if she is available," I answered.

"I will check. Who should I say is here to see her?"

"Jason Williams," I said. Mrs. Ruth disappeared down a hallway behind her desk. I waited, hopeful that my plan would work. Mrs. Ruth reappeared.

"Have a seat, Jason," Mrs. Ruth said. "She 'll see you in a few minutes." I sat and waited and went over what I planned to say. I wondered if I was going to be able to right my second fifty-year-old wrong in as many days. Mrs. Ruth brought me out of my daydream.

"You can go back now. Miss Sanderson is the third door on the left." I stood and walked back to the third door as directed. I knocked on the door and heard a voice from the other side tell me to enter. I opened the door.

"What can I do for you Jason?" Miss Sanderson asked. As I walked in, I noticed my file was sitting on her desk. She had obviously been checking up on me while I waited.

"I have a problem that I'm hoping you can help me with," I began. "I made a big mistake and I'm trying to correct it."

"Everyone makes mistakes and most times they can be easily fixed," Miss Sanderson spoke.

"I'm glad you feel that way because you are the person that can fix my mistake," I said.

"Oh my, this sounds serious. If you are disputing a grade with a teacher, you will need to discuss that with the teacher in question."

"My grades are fine. It has nothing to do with grades or my report card. My problem is a bit more personal in nature."

"Would you be more comfortable talking to one of the male counselors?" she asked.

"No, the problem I have only you can fix."

"I see. I guess you better tell me the problem," she said.

"I thought about making up a big story about my situation so you would be sympathetic toward me, but I decided that would be dishonest and that's not who I am."

"That's a very mature choice, Jason. Tell me the problem and let's see what we can do to fix it."

"I made a big mistake. I asked a girl...actually two different girls to the prom and I was shot down by both."

"That happens to many guys, "Miss Sanderson said. "It's nothing to be embarrassed about. We have many young men and women going to the prom without dates. You'll be fine."

"I'm not embarrassed about not having a date, but I am embarrassed about not having a ticket. When I was shot down, I acted out of anger and decided not to buy a ticket because I didn't want to be seen as a loser. I didn't realize that there were other people going to the prom without dates. Now I regret that I'm not going. I mean the junior prom isn't something that I'll ever have a chance to do again. That's what brings me here. Is there any way you can help me?"

"By help me, I assume you mean that you are asking me for a ticket," Miss Sanderson said.

"I'm not asking for a freebie. I'll pay for the ticket. I am just hoping for a chance to experience my one and only junior prom. I would hate to miss it...whether or not I have a date." I waited as she weighed her decision. I looked at the floor wondering whether or not she was going to grant my wish.

"I appreciate your honesty, Jason. Some young men would come in here and make up a story. You didn't do that. That should count for something. Unfortunately, the last day for ticket sales was last week. I can't sell you a ticket."

"I understand," I said, very disappointed. "I figured it wouldn't hurt to ask."

"Hold on, I'm not finished," she said. "I said that I couldn't sell you a ticket, but that doesn't mean I can't give you a ticket."

"Seriously? You would do that?" I asked.

"Yes, although my offer comes with a catch… actually two catches" I couldn't imagine what she could possibly want from me, but it didn't matter. I was going to be able to go to the junior prom.

"Anything," I answered. "What do I need to do?"

"First, I want you to go and have a great time."

"That's easy enough," I said. "What's the second thing?"

"Second, there are going to be some girls coming as singles too. I want you to make sure they have a good time by promising to dance with as many of the single girls as you can. They deserve to feel special." I could swear that Miss Sanderson had a tear in her eye when she said that. She was looking out for the girls who didn't get dates.

"I would be happy to do that, Miss Sanderson. I can't believe I'm going to the junior prom. Thank you so much."

"Go and have a good time and remember our deal," she said as she handed me the golden ticket.

"I will… I promise."

I walked back to study hall in the bandroom feeling great. I had just fixed another one of my high school mistakes. I wondered how the future might change because of another change in the past. I hoped I wasn't making ripples in the past so large that I wouldn't recognize the future. Somewhere down the road, I had to find my way back to Grace and my old life.

CHAPTER 11

I was on top of the world the rest of the day. I was going to the junior prom. I did wonder if either of the two girls who turned me down were going. That would be a bit awkward if I ran into either of them at the big dance. I decided it didn't matter. They didn't want to go with me, and as far as I was concerned, it was their loss. Of course, fifty years ago I didn't have that same attitude. I had been really bothered that two girls that I liked had turned me down. My confidence was shaken and I knew that it didn't come back for a long time after that. Knowing that my life turned out just fine in spite of being shot down, I didn't care. I would go to the prom and have a good time. I was curious whether Jean or Bonnie had accepted an invitation to the prom from anyone else. It would serve them right if neither was asked by anybody but me. After fifty years I was surprised at my bitter attitude toward them.

I dropped my news about the prom at the dinner table. My parents were happy for me.

My sister, on the other hand, was her wiseass self.

"What poor girl agreed to go to the prom with you?" she asked. "I mean how desperate was she?"

"Very funny," I snapped back. "For your information, I am going alone."

"Oh my god! How desperate are you to go to a big dance without a date? What a loser."

"There are a good number of people going without dates," I defended myself.

"Yeah, all the rest of the losers!" She broke out into hysterical laughter.

"That's enough of that young lady," Mom said, coming to my defense. Connie was still laughing as she retreated from the table.

"Don't pay any attention to her," Mom said. "I think it's great that you are going. I'm sure you will have a great time."

"Thanks," I answered.

"I thought the deadline for purchasing prom tickets had passed," Dad said. "How did you get a ticket?"

"I heard there were a few tickets that were unsold. I went to see Miss Sanderson, my guidance counselor and also the faculty person in charge of the prom. She said sales were closed, but she would be happy to give me a ticket for free."

"How nice of her," Mom said.

"She did insist that I dance with as many of the dateless girls as I could."

"That doesn't sound so bad," Dad said.

"I didn't think so. The guys that are taking dates will be dancing with the same girl all night. I'll be dancing with a different girl almost every dance."

"So, what are you going to do about a tux?" Dad asked.

"Good question. I hadn't thought about that. I'm sure by now there won't be many available."

"I'll talk to my buddy, Lenny, he owns Lenny's Formal Boutique. Maybe he can fix you up. I'll call him after we finish dinner. Maybe we can go tomorrow morning to get you fitted."

"Doesn't the pool open tomorrow? What time do you have to be at the pool?" mom asked.

I had forgotten all about my summer job which started on Memorial Day Weekend which officially began tomorrow. It would be my first full summer lifeguarding job. I had a ton of fun that summer including meeting Debbie, who turned out to be my first real girlfriend.

"I need to be there at 10:30 A.M."

"That doesn't give us much time to get you fitted. I'll see if Lenny can open early for us." Dad headed to the kitchen to make his call.

"I can't believe my little boy is going to his first prom," mom said. She was absolutely beaming.

"It is hard to believe," I answered.

"It wasn't that long ago that I was bouncing you on my knee and changing your diapers."

"Please don't say that in front of any of my friends," I pleaded.

"Why? I think it's cute. You were such a beautiful baby. You did know that you won a baby photo contest just before you turned two." I had heard this story more times than I could count over the years. My mother was so proud of the beautiful baby she had given birth to. I smiled, but made no comment. Dad returned a few minutes later.

"Good news. Lenny said he will open up for us at eight. That should be plenty of time to get you fitted and get you to your job on time." This whole prom thing was coming together better than I could have hoped.

Lenny met Dad and I at the door of his shop exactly at eight.

"For future reference, you may want to rent your tux earlier than a week before the big day," Lenny said.

"I definitely will. This year it was kind of unexpected. I just found out that I was going yesterday."

"Am I to assume that somebody you asked changed her mind?" Lenny asked.

"Actually, it was me that changed my mind," I answered. "A friend of mine at school convinced me that it would be fun to go with or without a date."

"You're going to the prom without a date?" Lenny asked, looking flabbergasted that I would even consider such a thing.

"Apparently there are many kids going without dates. Hopefully we can all have fun together."

"It sure was different when I went to school," Lenny said.

"If you didn't have a date, you didn't go to the prom. In my way of thinking, it would not have been fun to stand around and watch everyone else dance."

"That's the point. All of us without dates are going to dance with each other. We can still have a great time even if we don't have an official date. At least that's the idea."

"Well, good luck," Lenny said. "I hope it works out for you. Now let's get you measured up." Lenny started measuring my armlength and my inseam and all of the other appropriate measurements. He disappeared into the back room while Dad and I waited by the dressing rooms.

A few minutes later, Lenny or Mr. Kukavich to me, reappeared with two suit bags.

"I don't have much left, but we might be able to make one of these works." He pulled the first jacket out of the bag and asked me to slip it on. I could tell immediately that it was too small. Lenny tugged on the arms and pulled on the lapels looking for space that wasn't there. He helped me out of the jacket and handed me the second tux. It didn't feel like it fit any better than the first one. There was no way I could button it.

"Hmmm, this is no good," he muttered to no one in particular. "No good at all." He disappeared into the backroom once again muttering to himself as he went. A few minutes later he was back. "I will warn you now; it takes a special person to wear this tux. It is magnificent, but it is not for everybody." As he opened the suit bag, I got a glimpse of powder blue. He pulled the jacket out of the bag and it was powder blue...all powder blue.

"I don't know about this, Mr. Kukavich. It's really blue," I said, trying my best not to insult him.

"Try it on just for fit," he insisted. I did and it fit. In fact, it fit so well it was like it was tailored specifically for me. He handed me the matching pants which were also powder blue.

"Go in the dressing room and try the pants on," Mr. Kukavich said. I looked to my dad hoping he would bail me out. He didn't.

"You better get a move on," he said. "You don't want to be late for your first day on the job." I took the pants from Lenny and headed to the dressing room. I slipped my shorts off and pulled on the very blue pants. Other than being a little too long, they fit perfectly too. I looked in the mirror. I looked like an Easter egg. Lenny was right; it would take a special person to pull this off. I walked out of the dressing room and modeled the outfit for my dad and Mr. Kukavich.

"I know you don't want to hear this," my dad started, "but you actually look very stylish."

"I can shorten the pants a bit," Lenny said. "What do you think? You like?" I looked to my dad and then in the mirror again. I would definitely be making a statement if I showed up in this outfit. What the hell I thought to myself; I had been very conservative the first time through my high school years. Maybe this time I needed to loosen up. I looked in the mirror again.

"I'll take it," I said.

CHAPTER 12

On the drive to the swim club, I started to regret my decision to take the blue tux. One thing for sure; I would be noticed. Maybe that wasn't such a bad thing. My first time through high school I went largely unnoticed. If nothing else, it would be interesting to see how being noticed felt. By the time my dad pulled up to the gates of the swim club, I decided the blue tux would be fun. I thanked my dad for the ride and walked through the front gate.

I went and checked in with Mr. Hutchinson, the pool manager, my boss for the summer. He told me everyone would be meeting at the tables over by the snack bar in ten minutes. I headed in that direction after first dropping off my stuff in a locker. This was going to be interesting because fifty years ago I had a thing with the snack bar manager, Debbie. After that summer we dated off and on for two years before we decided our relationship just wasn't going to work. Debbie had been my first serious girlfriend. It would be interesting to see if there was any kind of spark the second time around. Truthfully, I wasn't sure I wanted to see a spark. I was a married man. I love Grace…or at least I would love Grace sometime in the future. This was going to be a tricky path to navigate.

I was the first guard to take a seat by the snack bar. I began to question everything. How could I be here and still remember my previous life? Should I try to change things? If I started to make big changes to my past, would my future still be the same? It was my past that led me to the life I led as an adult. I did not want to jeopardize my life with Grace. A voice behind me brought me out of daze.

"Is there anything I can get you?" My head snapped around, and there she was; Debbie.

"I didn't mean to startle you," she said.

"No problem. I was just lost in my thoughts," I answered.

"I'm Debbie. I'm going to be running the snack bar this summer."

"I know," I said without thinking once again.

"How would you know that?" she asked.

"I mean I just figured you were running the snack bar," I said. I'm Jason. I'll be a lifeguard this summer."

"I know," she answered and laughed.

"And how do you know that?" I asked and laughed.

"I just figured you wouldn't be here unless you were a lifeguard. It's nice to meet you, Jason. I guess we'll be seeing a lot more of each other this summer."

"I'm sure we will."

"Good," she said. "I'm looking forward to it," she added as she winked and headed back into the snack bar. Fifty years ago, I would have been too naïve to pick up on her signals. This time I knew exactly what she meant. Day one at the pool and she was already flirting with me. I had to be careful around her... at least until I could figure how I should proceed.

The other guards and Mr. Hutchinson assembled at the tables. Hutchinson laid out exactly what he expected from us for the summer. Be on time. When we were on the lifeguard stands, he expected us to be vigilant and not talking with our friends. He instructed us to be polite and respectful to adult members of the pool. He explained that if we needed any time off for family vacations, he needed at least two weeks-notice so he could arrange the schedule to have full coverage for the pool. He explained that we would rotate chair positions every fifteen minutes. Two fifteen -minute shifts would be on the adult pool and one would be on the kiddie pool. After every forty-five minutes, we would get fifteen minutes off. Sometimes we would be scheduled to work the early shift which meant we had to put the ring buoys and shepherd's crooks out and hose out the bathrooms and locker rooms. If we were scheduled to work the closing shift, we were

61

responsible for emptying the trash cans, putting any left-behind items in the lost and found, and putting away the lifesaving equipment. He told us to get ready for the first shift which started in fifteen minutes.

As I walked away from the snack bar, I could feel eyes on me. I turned my head toward the snack bar. Debbie gave me a wave from the window of the snack bar. I waved back and hurried over to the pool. I took my seat in the guard chair by the diving well. My first day as a lifeguard at Northwest Swim Club was about to start. I already knew I was in for a good summer.

The day went by much more quickly than I had expected. I enjoyed watching the kids have fun in the pool. I used my whistle sparingly; the main issue being kids running on the deck of the pool. During my breaks, I purposely stayed away from the snack bar. I didn't need to add any more fuel to the fire.

I was scheduled to work the full shift today which meant I got an hour for dinner. I had packed a sandwich and some chips before I left the house this morning and I retrieved them from my locker. The only place you were allowed to have food in the pool complex was by the snack bar, so I headed in that direction. I had no sooner sat down at one of the tables when Debbie popped out of the snack bar and took the seat across from me.

"So how is your first day going?" she asked.

"Fine," I answered. "I can't believe how fast it has gone. How was your day?"

"Busy, busy, busy," she responded. "I hope every day isn't going to be like this. I'm exhausted."

"I'm sure weekdays will be slower for you," I offered.

"I hope so."

We chatted for the next forty-five minutes between a few customers getting food. I found out that she was a year older than I was and went to my rival high school across town. Of course, I already knew that, and more. I remembered her parents' names and the names of her two sisters and a brother. I had to sit there and act interested. I knew that she was graduating from Liberty High School in a few weeks. I knew that she would be starting nursing school at St. Luke's Hospital at the end of the summer. She had always been easy to talk to and nothing was different now.

"You're a really good listener," she said as I got up to head back over to the pool.

"You're a really good talker," I said.

"Oh, I'm really sorry. I didn't mean to talk your head off," she apologized over and over.

"No, no," I interrupted. "I just meant I really enjoyed talking with you. I feel like I have known you my whole life." She had no idea how true that statement was.

"I really enjoy talking to you too." I could tell she wanted to say more, but I cut her short when I said I had to get back on duty.

By the time I finished for the day, the snack bar was closed and Debbie was gone. The rest of the night I went back and forth on how I should play this whole thing. If I didn't promote any kind of relationship, would it alter my future? That was the big question. I didn't want to do anything to jeopardize my future with Grace. In one sense being back here for a "redo" was kind of cool. On the other hand, it was terrifying knowing that I could possibly alter my future.

The next two days at the pool, followed a similar pattern. I would say hello to Debbie when I got to the pool and I would eat dinner at the tables by the snack bar where Debbie would join me between customers. By the end of day two, she asked me if I needed a ride home. Since I had ridden my bike, I declined.

Monday was Memorial Day and it turned out to be a cloudy day so the pool wasn't very crowded. I spent a few of my breaks talking to Debbie plus our dinner time conversation. Everything was going fine until she unexpectedly asked a question which caught me completely off guard.

"I know this is late notice and I know we haven't known each other that long, but I was wondering if you would like to go to my senior prom with me?" I was stunned; a senior was asking me, a junior, to go to her prom. Previously I had not gone to any proms in my junior year; now I had the chance to go to two.

"When is it?" Even when I asked the question, I wasn't sure what I hoped her answer would be. I was committed to my junior prom on Friday night. I could not disappoint Miss Sanderson.

"It's this coming Saturday night," she said. This really caught me off guard since I knew this had not happened fifty years ago. I wondered why she went off script. What had happened? Had I somehow already affected the future in my actions over the last few days?

"That's really nice of you to invite me, but I don't have a ticket," I answered, hoping that would be the end of it.

"That's not a problem. I have an extra ticket." She looked up at me. I could see the hope in her eyes.

"How do you happen to have an extra ticket?" I asked. She hesitated just enough for me to know she was uncomfortable answering that question.

"It's alright," I said. "It's none of my business."

"It's fine. I want to be honest with you. Until two weeks ago, I had a boyfriend. We had been together since October. Recently, things started going bad. It just got worse and worse until we both agreed to call it quits. He didn't want to go to the prom in the first place, so I'm sure he doesn't want his ticket. Besides, I paid for the tickets; I can do what I want with his ticket... and what I want is to give it to you."

"I don't know what to say," I said. "I feel honored that you want to go with me."

"You don't have to make excuses. You can just say no." I could see the hurt in her eyes. Here she was, a senior who thought she

64

was going to her high school prom and she ends up splitting with her boyfriend. She'll never have another chance to go to her senior prom. It will be a regret for the rest of her life. I can't let that happen. I always wanted to be somebody's knight in shining armor. Here was my chance.

"I'll go, I said. "How do you like powder blue?"

CHAPTER 13

When I arrived home from the pool, my parents were watching television in the family room. I wasn't sure how to tell them that I had been invited to a different prom as somebody's date.

"How did your day go?" Mom asked.

"Good," I answered. "More people today than yesterday."

"I'm not surprised," Dad chimed in. "It was a hot one today."

"Listen, I had something strange happen today," I said.

"What's up?" Dad asked.

"You know the girl I told you I met from the snack bar?"

"You mentioned her to us at breakfast this morning," Mom said.

"Right. Well... she asked me to her prom."

"I take it you turned her down since you are already committed to go to your prom," Dad said.

"No... actually I said yes because her senior prom is on Saturday night. Mine is on Friday night. I was wondering if you could check with Mr. Kukavich and see if I could keep the tux for an extra day."

"I don't know that I feel right about asking him. He was nice enough to let you have it for Friday night, not to mention that he is letting you have it for free. I don't want him to feel like I am taking advantage of him."

"I'll pay for it," I blurted out, "as soon as I get my first paycheck from the pool." My dad looked at my mom looking for help in making his decision.

"Well, I don't see any harm in asking Lenny if it is even a possibility," Mom finally said after a moment of deliberation.

"How are you going to get a ticket?" Dad asked.

"Debbie has an extra ticket." I went on to explain about her recent breakup with a boyfriend. "This is her senior prom. If she stays home, she won't get another chance to go."

"Alright, I'll check with Lenny, but no promises."

"Thanks, Dad. I really appreciate it."

"As of this past Friday, you weren't going to any proms and now apparently you are going to two. You are one lucky young man."

"Yeah, I guess I am," I said as I ran up the stairs to my bedroom.

Tuesday at lunch I told Rob and Trip that I had managed to get a ticket to the junior prom.

"Who are you taking?" Rob asked.

"I'm not taking anyone. Apparently there a bunch of people going without dates."

"Rob, Greg, and I are taking our dates to the Village Inn for dinner before the prom. Do you want to go with us?" Trip asked. I thought it over for a few seconds. I decided that would be too weird to be there with the three couples while I was alone.

"Thanks, but I'll pass on that. I'll see you at the dance though."

"Come on," Greg pushed. "It will be fun. Come to dinner with us."

"I can't afford another dinner," I said before quickly realizing that is going to require an explanation.

"What do you mean another dinner?" Rob asked.

"Believe it or not, I am attending Liberty's senior prom on Saturday." I could see the glances jumping back and forth between the three of them.

Wait a minute…let me see if I have this right," Trip started. "You are going to Liberty's senior prom… with a girl." The other guys laughed.

"Yes, with a girl."

"And she is a senior?" Trip continued probing for information.

"Correct, she is a senior," I answered.

"How about a name?" Rob asked.

"Debbie Gravely."

"And how do you know this Debbie person?" Rob asked.

"She works at the snack bar at the Northwest Swim Club where I am lifeguarding for the summer."

"How long have you known her?" Trip asked.

"I met her Saturday morning at the pool."

"You met her Saturday morning and you asked her to her senior prom?" Trip asked finding this all very hard to believe.

"I didn't ask her." I let that settle in for a few seconds before finishing my sentence. "She asked me." There was a stunned silence around the table for a few seconds.

"At the end of last week, you weren't going to any proms, and now you are going to two including Liberty's senior prom. How does that happen?" Greg asked. I couldn't resist from making a wiseass comment.

"Some guys have it…and some guys don't."

As I walked to my next class after lunch, I realized that I had a problem. The more I thought about it I realized I had more than one problem. First, I did not have Debbie's phone number to make arrangements for Saturday night. I would probably see her at the pool on Saturday, but I really didn't want to wait until then to find out whether or not she wanted to go to dinner. I hoped her phone number was in the book. I would check as soon as I got home. The other problem was I really hadn't looked at my lifeguard schedule for the upcoming weekend so I had no idea if I was expected to work Saturday night or not. I needed to check on that too.

As soon as I walked in the door after school, I grabbed the phonebook. There were three Gravely's listed. One lived in Allentown so I could rule that number out. I called one of the numbers for Bethlehem and a voice answered on the second ring.

"Could I please speak with Debbie?" I asked in my most polite voice.

"Could I ask who is calling," a voice I assumed to be her mother asked.

"This is Jason Williams from the swim club."

"Please hold. I'll get her to the phone." A few seconds later, Debbie was on the line.

"I'm so glad you called. I realized that I hadn't given you, my number."

"Luckily, you were in the phonebook," I said.

"You're not calling to cancel, are you?" she asked.

"No, no... not at all. I was actually calling to make arrangements for Saturday night. Would you like to go out to dinner beforehand?"

"That's sweet of you to ask, but you don't have to do that," she said.

"Actually, I would like to," I said.

"Are you sure?" she asked giving me another chance to back out.

"I'm sure. I'm not going to dinner before my junior prom so this works for both of us." I swore I could feel the temperature drop twenty degrees over the phone.

"Oh… I didn't realize you were going to your junior prom. Isn't that on Friday night?"

"Yes, it is."

"I have to admit that makes me feel strange knowing you are going to your prom with another girl on Friday night. Maybe we should just forget it."

"Wait, "I said. "It's not what you think. I wasn't planning on going to my junior prom at all. My previous girlfriend broke up with me a few months ago. I didn't find anybody I wanted to take. My friends convinced me to go without a date at the end of last week."

"You're going to your prom with no date?" Debbie asked. I could only imagine how much of a loser she thought I must be.

"From what I am told, there are quite a few people going without dates. We all just want to have fun. I guess you find this whole thing strange."

"No, not really. I just never considered going to a prom without a date. I haven't heard of anybody going to my prom without a date. Maybe some people are; I just don't know about them."

"If you want to change your mind about asking me, I understand," I offered. There was silence. I figured she was trying to find the words to let me down gently. I braced myself, fully expecting to be un-invited.

"No, I want you to come." I was surprised to say the least.

"So, what about dinner? I would love to take you somewhere nice."

"Where do you have in mind?" Debbie asked.

"Let me make a few calls to see where I can make a reservation. What time does the prom begin?"

"It starts at eight."

"Let me work on that and I'll get back to you," I said. I gave her my phone number and we talked a few more minutes before I said goodbye.

After hanging up, I raced up to my room and found the schedule Mr. Hutchinson handed out at the guard meeting. I was finished at five on Saturday. It should me just enough time to shower and be ready for dinner somewhere on Saturday night. Now I needed to find a place and find out if I had a tux to wear. Mom could help with some suggestions for a nice restaurant. I wouldn't know about the tux until Dad got home from work. Mom suggested Hotel Bethlehem and surprisingly, they had just had a cancellation for Saturday night at 6:30 which I claimed.

My thoughts turned to my real life as I lay in bed after a busy day. I wondered how Grace was. The truth was as much fun as this was, I missed her. A number of things had already happened that had not happened the first time around. I had taken Debbie to a prom fifty years ago, but it was my senior prom, not hers. I wondered how that was going to change things down the road. I couldn't help believing that the more changes I made now, the less likely I would ever get back to my first life. I decided I need to cool it moving forward. I would let things unfold as they had previously as much as I possibly could. I've been back here less than a week and I knew this was going to be difficult.

CHAPTER 14

Wednesday during another mind-numbing day of school, I made the decision to try and find Grace. Grace was two years older than me so she would have just finished her freshman year at Bryn Mahr College. I was certain her school year would have already ended, so the question was whether or not she returned home to her parent's house in Philipsburg, New Jersey. I remember driving by her childhood home on Rose Avenue a few years ago as we returned from a show in New York City. It was a modest two-story home on a street filled with a collection of singles and twins.

Getting to Philipsburg, New Jersey was going to be the trick. It would be a rather strange request to ask my parents if I could borrow the car to drive by the house of the girl who I was going to marry more than fifteen years down the road. Oh, and by the way, she doesn't know me yet. My parents would be making an appointment for me to see a shrink minutes after I made a request like that. It was too far to bike, especially on a school day. I needed a friend with a car, a friend like Trip. Trip had inherited a '63 Chevy Impala, when his father had passed away unexpectedly last year. I found Trip at lunch and hatched my plan.

"Feel like taking a road trip after school today? I'll pay for gas."

"Sounds like fun. Where are we going?" Trip asked.

"Philipsburg, New Jersey."

"And why do you want to go to New Jersey?"

"I'm looking for someone."

"Who?" Trip asked. I hated to lie to Trip, but I couldn't begin to explain that I was looking for my future wife. I made up a story on the spot.

"Back in second grade I had a crush on a girl named Grace. She moved away at the end of second grade. We kept in touch for a few years with letters. My parents thought it was cute. By junior high the letters stopped. I always wondered what happened to her. I thought it might be fun to try and find her."

"And I take it that she lives in Philipsburg, New Jersey?"

"Correct."

"What's the matter? Aren't you going to enough proms already? Trying to go for the trifecta?"

"Very funny. I'm just curious what she looks like after all this time."

"You could have asked for a photograph," Trip said as he shook his head.

"Never thought to do that. I haven't talked to her in years so it would be kind of weird to ask for a photo now. If you don't want to take me, that's fine."

"I don't see the point, but I'll take you. We'll need to leave right after dismissal so I'm not too late getting home."

"Thanks, Trip. I owe you."

"You do owe me...gas money."

The end of the day finally arrived. I made one stop at the payphone in the lobby. It was very strange using a payphone which I hadn't done in years. I explained to Mom that I was going with Trip while he ran some errands after school. I hung up the phone and sprinted to the student parking lot where Trip was already waiting for me.

"Do you have an address or are we just going to cruise around Philipsburg asking if anybody knows Grace?"

"Rose Avenue," I answered, hoping he wouldn't ask if I knew the street number. We hopped on Route 22 which would pass through Easton, across the Delaware River, and right into the heart of Philipsburg. Thirty minutes later we were crossing the river.

"Stop when you see a gas station. I need to use the rest room," I said. A few minutes later Trip pulled into an Esso station. I handed him a five and told him to get some gas. I hustled inside to find an attendant or mechanic.

"Can you give me directions to Rose Avenue?" I asked a mechanic who seemed to be quitting for the day. Luckily, he knew where it was and gave me the directions. It turned out Rose Avenue was only a few blocks away.

"Is there a phone book around?" I asked. He pointed to a counter by the cash register. I paged quickly to the Bs, looking for a Barnett on Rose Avenue. Luck was in my side. David Barnett, 274 Rose Avenue. I snapped the book shut and hurried out to the car where Trip was gassed up and ready to roll.

I gave Trip the turn-by-turn directions to 274 Rose Avenue which took less than five minutes to find. There it was; 274 Rose Avenue. Trip drove by slowly as I hoped to get a glimpse of Grace. No sign of her or anybody else at the house. Trip pulled into an open spot along the curb a few houses down the street.

"What's the plan?" he asked.

"I'm not sure," I said.

"We drove all this way. Aren't you at least going to knock on her door?" I looked at Trip and back at the 274 Rose Avenue. I opened the car door and walked slowly back toward her house. I had no idea what I was going to do. Just as I was about to turn back, I found my answer. On the front lawn, there was a Bryn Mahr College pennant stuck into the ground. I took a deep breath and walked to the front door. I could hear music coming from the back of the house through the screen door. I knocked on the screen door and waited. A person was walking to the front door. The house was too dark inside for me to know who it was. Then I heard a voice I knew very well.

74

"May I help you?" Grace asked and gave me the sweetest smile.

"I was walking by and I saw your Bryn Mahr College flag out front. Do you like it there?" Grace opened the screen door and stepped out on the front porch.

"I do. The campus is beautiful and the staff is wonderful. Bryn Mahr is such a great little town. It's everything I hoped college would be."

"What are you majoring in?" I asked although I already knew. I just wanted to extend the conversation. This was surreal standing here fifty years in the past talking to my future wife who didn't even know me at this point in time.

"General Studies," she answered.

"What do you hope to do when you graduate?" I asked.

"I don't know for sure. That's why I decided on General Studies," she answered.

"I'm sure you'll do great in whatever you decide," I said. "I can just tell."

"What are you majoring in?" she asked.

"I'm still in high school, but I hope to get into business. I'm thinking of applying to Bryn Mahr College," I said. Grace laughed.

"Well, don't get your hopes up. It's an all-girl school," she said. How could I have forgotten that? I looked like a fool. I tried to cover up the best I could.

"I had no idea. I had heard it was a good school, but I didn't know that it wasn't co-ed. I don't want to take up any more of your time since apparently, I won't be going to Bryn Mahr. Thanks for taking the time to talk to me."

"No problem. I'm sure you will find a good school. Good luck and nice meeting you," she said and began to turn away. She turned back. "By the way, I don't even know your name. I'm Grace," she said and extended her hand. I looked down at her hand. I felt like I might explode if I touched it. Slowly, I took her hand in mine.

"I'm Jason."

"It's nice to meet you, Jason. Maybe we'll run into each other again sometime." She had no idea how true that would be.

"That would be nice. I'd like that." I pulled my hand away. She turned and walked back into her house as I walked back to the Trip's car in a daze. This was too unreal. What had I done?

"How did it go?" Trip asked.

"Good… I guess. I mean we talked and she is very nice."

"She didn't invite you to another prom, did she?" I laughed.

"No, nothing like that," I answered. I decided not to tell Trip she was already in college. I didn't think he could handle that. I also didn't mention that we were going to get married…someday; I knew he definitely would not be able to handle that.

Later that night, I was thinking about my brief encounter with Grace. I wondered if she would remember my visit if I ever did get back now that I had changed the past. I could only imagine the fun she was having telling her friends all about this high school kid who stopped by and thought he could go to Bryn Mahr. I realized this was exactly the kind of event that could change the future. What if she remembered me when we met again? She might dismiss me as that nerd who stopped by her house without a clue. I really had to stop screwing around with the past before I screwed up the future.

CHAPTER 15

I managed to get through the rest of the week without making any additional changes to the past. Friday night all of that was going to change. I was going to my junior prom that I had not attended fifty years ago. I seriously thought about backing out, but Miss Sanderson, Lenny at the tux rental, and my dad had all gone out of their way for me so I could attend. I could not back out now. Just go, dance, have fun, and don't do anything stupid, and everything should be fine... at least that's what I told myself.

The prom didn't start until eight and since I wasn't going out to dinner first, there was no rush. Dad picked up the tux for me on his way home from work. He walked in the door with the suit bag draped over his arm.

"Open it up," my mom said. "I want to see this tux." I grabbed the tux from my dad's arm and pulled it away.

"You'll have to wait until I put it on," I said like it was going to be some great unveiling. Actually, it was just a stall tactic.

"Oooh... I can't wait," Mom said.

"No matter what you wear, you're still going to look like a geek," Connie said.

"That's not very nice," Mom said coming to my defense.

"It's the truth," Connie said. "It's better that he hears it from family."

"Just so you know," I started, "you're not really family. Somebody dropped you off on our doorstep. Tell her, Mom; it's about time she knows the truth."

"Alright, both of you stop this. Brothers and sisters are supposed to love one another." Neither Connie nor I said another word, but we glared at each other with a look that definitely wasn't love.

Following dinner, I headed upstairs to my room. I closed my bedroom door and looked at the suit bag that I had neatly laid out on the bed. I slowly pulled down the zipper on the bag and spread the bag open. Flashes of blue flooded my room. What had I done? The blue was much bluer than it looked in the store. Maybe it was the lighting in the room. Maybe it wouldn't look so "blue" in a different light. What if it looked worse? This is what happens when you tempt fate. I should have just left well enough alone and stayed home tonight. But no... I had to fix my "mistake". I fixed it alright; it went from a mistake to a catastrophe. I closed the zipper hoping that it would magically transform into a different color while I was in the shower.

I took a long shower as I debated my options. I could feign sickness. Miss Sanderson and my parents would be very disappointed. The second option was to have Dad drop me off and when he drove out of sight, I could find some place to hide. Miss Sanderson would still be disappointed and if my parents found out I lied about going to the prom, they would be angry. I could go to the prom and just wear my suitcoat and skip the whole tux thing. Dad would be disappointed with me considering all the trouble Lenny had gone through to make this possible. The truth was that I had no options. I had to go to the prom in the blue tux.

As I finished dressing, I had one last hope. Maybe when I appeared downstairs, my parents would find this tux so hideous that they would suggest I wear something else. I looked at my blue reflection in the mirror one last time and headed downstairs. Connie saw me first.

"You look like a smurf," she said and broke into hysterical laughter. My parents walked into the living room from the kitchen. Neither said anything for a few seconds.

"How bad is it?" I finally asked.

"It's not bad at all," Mom said as tears began to form in her eyes. "My little boy is all grown up. You look so handsome." She walked over and gave me a big hug.

"I still think you look like a smurf," Connie repeated in case I didn't hear her the first time.

"That's enough," Dad pointed to Connie. "Another word from you and you'll be spending the rest of the night in your room."

"Thanks for getting me in trouble," Connie said to me as she turned and stomped into the kitchen.

"Ignore her," Dad said. "My father once told me that it's not the clothes that make the man, but rather the man that makes the clothes. Remember that tonight if anybody gives you a hard time. Sure, most of the guys will be wearing black, but so what. They will all look the same. You'll be the one that stands apart. Know that all the girls in the room will notice you which won't be true for the large majority of the guys wearing black. Believe in yourself; that's all that matters." I was stunned. That might have been the most heartfelt advice my dad had ever given me. I reached out to shake his hand, but he pulled me into a bearhug.

"So, what do you say?" he asked. "Are you ready to get this party started?" I laughed and wondered if it was my dad should be credited for starting that phrase that would become very popular in the future.

"I am," I said. Mom followed me out to the car and kissed me just before I got in.

"Have a good time," she said.

"I will…thanks," I answered.

There was a line of cars in front of the Greek Orthodox Church dropping off the prom-goers. I watched as one black tux exited a car followed by another and another and another. To top it off, all had dates dressed in their fancy gowns.

"Drive around the block," I said. My dad seemed to understand and did so without asking why. "Pull over," I instructed my dad. "I'll walk from here."

"You sure?" Dad asked.

"I'm sure."

"Just remember what I told you; it's not the clothes that make the man."

"Got it," I said as I hopped out of the car. I watched as Dad pulled away from the curb. I started walking around the block to the entrance of the church. If anything, the line of cars was longer. I strutted down the sidewalk, confidence oozing from every pore or so I hoped everyone would think. I handed my ticket to Miss Sanderson at the front door.

"Looking good, Mr. Williams," she said. "You're going to be swooping the girls off their feet tonight." I laughed.

"You never know," I said and headed down the hall toward the large activity room that would serve as the ballroom. There were black and gold streamers and balloons covering everything. Gold tablecloths were matched with black napkins. There was a large fountain with a gold liquid flowing from all of its openings. The cups were black, of course. It was a world of black and gold...except for one very blue tux.

"Jason...over here," I heard a voice off to my right. I turned and there was Trip waving me over. Trip and Bonnie, Rob and Anna, and Greg and Vicki were all sitting around the table. "We saved you a seat," Trip said as I neared the table.

"Looking good," Bonnie commented as I said hi to everyone. I sat where I could see the dancefloor. I looked around the room and realized that although people may have come without a date, they were pairing up on the dancefloor. In the time I had been here all the songs had been faster numbers. The first slow song, saw the dancefloor swell as couples moved from their tables including all my friends. Suddenly I was alone at my table as the strains of *Love is Blue* filled the room. As the couples held each other tight and swayed to the music, my eyes bounced from table to table looking for all the singles that were supposed to be here. Three tables to my left stood a blond with a long

80

pale-yellow dress. I didn't know her name, but I think she had been in one of my classes in the first semester. I took a deep breath and walked in her direction.

"Hi. I'm Jason. Would you care to dance?" I asked.

"I would love to," she answered much to my relief. "By the way, my name is Linda." With introductions out of the way, I took her hand and led her onto the dancefloor. Left arm around her waist and my right hand taking hers, we began to dance. On one of my turns, I caught sight of Miss Sanderson who gave me a wink and a thumbs up. The band went right into another fast tune. Linda and I kept dancing. We made some small conversation, but it was awkward because it was difficult to hear each other with the volume of the band. A few songs later, the band announce they were taking a short break.

"Thanks for the dance," Linda said. "I'm going to find my friends. Maybe I'll see you later." She turned and was gone. I headed back to my table. I had danced at my junior prom. Scratch another regret off my list.

"Was that Linda Smith you were dancing with?" Greg asked when I got back to the table.

"I know her name is Linda, so I guess it was," I answered.

"Nice," he said. Vicki overheard his comment and punched him in the arm. "I just meant it was nice for him," he explained.

"I better not find you looking in her direction," Vicki said and laughed. I wasn't sure she was joking. I never realized how possessive Vicki was.

As the night rolled on, I did have fun. I only slow-danced with a few other girls. It seemed most of the singles had found partners for the evening. I guess I could have if I was looking, but I wasn't.

Toward the end of the evening, Linda found me and asked me to dance as I stood next to Trip. Just before I headed out onto the dancefloor he leaned over and whispered in my ear.

"You need to give me your secret." I laughed.

"I'll never tell," I answered as I took Linda's hand.

Linda and I danced the last half dozen songs together including the final two slow numbers. She seemed to hold on to me tighter than she had earlier. The song ended and she reached up and gave me a little peck on the cheek.

"Thanks, I really enjoyed meeting you."

"Likewise," I said. I figured the evening was coming to a close. I was wrong.

CHAPTER 16

"I don't know if you have any plans for later tonight, but one of my friends is having a party. I would love if you could come with me. I really don't want to be one person there without a date," Linda said. She waited for an answer as I began to panic. This was definitely not in the script plus I had been invited to the after-party at Vicki's house.

"That sounds like fun, but I don't have a car," I said confident that would end the conversation.

"That's even better," she said, "because I have my car." Uh-oh, a minor miscalculation. I never considered she might have driven herself here.

"I don't know what to say. I'm supposed to be stopping in at a party that one of my friends is having. With a junior license, you can't be on the road after midnight. There wouldn't be time to do both parties."

"That won't be a problem," she boasted and smiled. "I just turned eighteen and I have my senior license. We can go to both parties... as long as your friends wouldn't mind me crashing theirs. What do you say?" I didn't know what to say. What is it with me and older women. I was going to a prom with an older woman tomorrow night. I married an older woman in the future. And now here I am...getting involved with yet another older woman. I could see no way out and wasn't sure if I wanted to find a way out.

"I'm in," I said. "Let me tell my friends that I'll be late." I walked over to Vicki and explained what was happening. I could tell she wasn't thrilled with the idea, her jealous streak kicking in once again.

"That's fine," she answered. "Do me one favor... keep her away from Greg."

"He is crazy about you. You have nothing to worry about."

83

I found Linda near the door and we headed out to her car, a blue '64 Chevy Nova with a stick shift.

"Do want to drive?" Linda asked.

"I don't think that would be a good idea. I never drove a stick shift." She agreed and I climbed in the passenger seat as she fired up the ignition, shifted into gear, and headed out. It was a ten-minute drive to her friend's house in Stafore Estates. We drove past Martin Towers, the newest addition to the Bethlehem Steel. I watched that building being constructed from the windows of my junior high for three years. Now, my dad worked in that building. Little did anybody know that Martin Towers would be imploded fifty years in the future as the Steel folded and the building was too expensive to renovate. I studied the building as we zipped by it. It was a beautiful building and the tallest in Pennsylvania when it was built. Too bad it wasn't going to last.

We arrived in front of a nice four-bedroom colonial. A number of cars were already parked on the driveway. I removed my tie and my jacket and left them in Linda's car. Linda introduced me to Patti Jones, her friend who was hosting the party. She pointed to a door that led to a finished basement where strains of the Rolling Stones were blasting from below.

I recognized a few people, but really didn't know anybody. Linda tried to introduce me to a few people, but it was impossible with the loud music. Everybody was dancing. A few minutes later, someone switched off the lights throwing the basement into darkness except for a few blacklights scattered around. That almost seemed to be a signal. Couples found corners and chairs and the sofa to begin making out with each other. Linda and I continued to dance and tried not to stare at the passion all around us.

"You ready to get out of here? Linda asked less than thirty minutes after we had arrived.

"It's up to you," I said. "Won't you take grief for leaving so early?" I asked. Linda looked around the room.

"Do you honestly think anyone will notice?" she asked. I glanced around the room.

"Not a chance," was my reply. We quietly disappeared up the stairs and out of the house.

"Sorry about that," she said. "I knew eventually that it was going to turn out that way… I just didn't expect it would happen so fast."

"Not a problem," I responded. "To be truthful, I'm not sure we aren't going to run into the same thing at my friend's party."

"Do you want to skip it?" she asked.

"I need to make an appearance. Just a quick in and out to say we were there." I directed her to Vicki's house. I knocked on the door and Vicki's father answered the door.

"You two just made it on time," he said as he glanced at his watch. "Midnight and I'm locking this door. Nobody leaves until sunrise."

"Linda has her senior license, so midnight isn't the witching hour for us. We can't stay until sunrise," I explained.

"My house, my rules," Mr. Previk said.

"Could you at least let us go say hello? I promise we won't stay more than a few minutes."

"That's fine, but no more than a few minutes." I led Linda down to the basement where the music here was much softer. Five or six couples were spread across the room in much the same situation as we had just left. Vicki spied us and broke away from Greg.

"I'm glad you guys were able to make it," she said although I doubted that was true. "The food and drink are over there in the corner. Then find yourself someplace comfortable and enjoy yourself."

"We can't stay all night. For starters I have to work in the morning. Your father informed us that at midnight he is locking the door. Nobody in…nobody out. I just wanted to stop in and say hello to everyone.

"Hey everybody," Vicki called out. "Jason and his friend are here. Say hello." Hellos came from all corners of the room. "Now say goodbye to Jason. He' leaving." Goodbyes echoed from all corners. I thanked Vicki, grabbed a handful of pretzels on the way out and headed up the stairs before the gate to the castle got locked.

Mr. Previk was waiting at the door for us. He was looking at his watch.

"Be safe, you two," he said.

"We will. Thanks" Linda and I headed to the car. I figured the night was over, but Linda had one more surprise for me.

"I know an all-night diner in Allentown. You want to go?"

"Sure. I could use something to eat." We drove thirty minutes to get to the Sunset Diner on Fourth Street on the east side of Allentown. Much to my surprise, we weren't the only prom-goers in the diner. It seemed that three other couples had a similar idea. We took a booth near the back of the diner and talked for the next hour while enjoying two slices of the best blueberry pie I had ever eaten.

Linda was a very easy person to talk to and we talked about everything. It was approaching one in the morning before our conversation began to run out of steam. I used my lifeguarding job as an excuse to call it a night. I was already wondering how this evening was going to end. It turned out, it wasn't a problem. As we walked to Linda's car, I noticed a big guy leaning against the hood of her car.

"What are you doing here?" Linda challenged the guy.

"I'm looking for you," he answered. "So, this is the punk who you went to the prom with?" he asked. Before she could answer he turned his attention to me. He gave me a shove. "Who wears light blue pants," he said and laughed. I realized that it was the first time all night that somebody commented on my attire.

"Leave him alone, "Linda said stepping between us. "He's just a friend."

"Did you dance with my girl?" he asked trying to reach around Linda to give me another shove. This was not going well. Dying here in the parking lot would definitely mess up my future.

"Darren, if you want to have any chance with me ever, you need to stop this…right now. Jason is a friend. We just met tonight."

"Tonight? This guy moves fast."

"Why are you being such a jerk?" Linda asked. "You could have gone to the prom with me tonight, but you didn't think it was cool."

"Hey, I already graduated from high school last year, "he fired back. "Why would I want to go a junior prom?"

"You should have wanted to go because I wanted to go…that's why. I don't ask you for much. It's the least you could have done… for me… for me." That's when the tears began to flow. "Get out of here, Darren."

"Ah… gee… baby, I'm sorry."

"Get out of here…now. I don't want to talk to you tonight."

"Alright, alright… I'm going. I'll call you tomorrow. Ok?"

"Go…get out of here!" He gave me a look that left no doubt what he wanted to do to me. I stared right back at him, hoping he wouldn't do anything to jeopardize his chances of getting back with Linda. He fired up his '63 GTO and laid rubber leaving the parking lot.

"Are you alright?" I asked.

"I'll be fine. I'm really sorry that you had to see that."

"I'll call my dad for a ride if you would rather not take me home."

87

"Don't be silly. Hop in. I'll be glad to drive you home. I'm not going to leave you stranded in Allentown." The drive back to Bethlehem was quiet. She pulled up in front of my house and shut off the car.

"I just wanted to thank you for tonight," she said. "You are a great guy."

"Thank you," I responded. "Tonight turned out to be much more fun than I thought it would be and that is mainly because of you. At least most of the night was fun." She laughed.

"It certainly turned out to be a night that I'll remember," Linda replied.

"You can say that again," I responded.

"Again, I just want to apologize for Darren. I started dating him two years ago when I was a sophomore and he was a senior. Most times he is a really nice guy, but every so often he can be a real jerk…like tonight. I don't really see a future with Darren, especially after I graduate. I am really looking forward to going away for college. Darren has already dropped out of college after his first year and now is working at some bicycle manufacturing plant loading trucks. That isn't the future I am dreaming about. I should really end it with him now. Anyway… I really enjoyed getting to know you a little better tonight. You are going to make some girl really happy in the future." She leaned over and gave me a kiss.

"Now get out of here. You need to work tomorrow." She started up her car as I climbed out. "Maybe our paths will cross again. You never know."

"Maybe," I answered as she pulled away. The problem was that I did know. Our paths would likely never cross again. In a way that was too bad. She was a nice girl. I walked to the front door already thinking about tomorrow night. The thought of doing this all over again left me exhausted just thinking about it.

CHAPTER 17

It was nearing three in the morning by the time I crawled into bed. I had to be at work seven hours from now. That didn't leave much time for sleep. To compound the problem, I had a hard time falling asleep. I was really worried about how I might be changing the future. I wasn't worried about the awards banquet. I could not see how that was likely to change anything for anybody. Meeting up with Linda tonight; that was a different story. Things could have been set in motion tonight that would could lead to a different path for a number of people. Maybe Linda would break up with Darren. Maybe Darren would rearrange my face. Maybe this is the start of something for Linda and me. Then there is the prom later tonight with Debbie, a year earlier than the prom we attended before. What ramifications might that have? Would she and I even be together a year from now? Without Debbie, would there be somebody new in my life? While this might be fun and exciting now, I still wanted to end up with Grace for the long term. That possibility seemed further away than ever.

Mom shook me awake around 8:30 A.M.

"It's time for you to get up," she said. I pulled the pillow over my head and tried to block her out. "I'm making you a nice breakfast. Get up so you can tell me all about the prom." She nudged me again and I mumbled that I was getting up. I dragged myself to the shower and stood under the hot water trying to wake up.

I eventually made it to the kitchen table where Mom had a stack of pancakes and a few slices of bacon waiting for me.

"How was it?" she asked.

"It was fun," I answered not really wanting to get into the whole Linda thing.

"Who dropped you off last night?" she asked. "I didn't recognize the car." So much for keeping this under wraps.

"It was a friend of mine from one of my classes last term."

"Does she have a name?"

"Linda… Linda Smith."

"Wasn't she worried about driving past her curfew?"

"She has her senior license. She just turned eighteen."

"Where did the two of you go after the dance was over?" Mom asked.

"We started out at a party thrown by one of her friends. From there we went to Vicki Previk's party, but her father announced that after midnight nobody could leave until morning. Neither one of us wanted to stay that long so we left that party too. We ended up at the Sunset Diner over in Allentown, where we sat and talked and ate blueberry pie. We had a good time just getting a chance to talk." I didn't feel that mom needed to know about the love-fests going on at both parties or the whole run-in with Darren.

"That sounds nice," she said. "I'm glad you had a good time." I plowed through the pancakes. Mom was still hanging around the kitchen so I knew she had more on her mind.

"Now you get to do it all over again tonight," she said. "Are you excited?"

"Why would I be any more excited than I was last night?"

"I thought maybe because you had a date for this prom…that's all."

"I'm sure we'll have a good time. I'm a little nervous because I won't know that many people."

"I'm sure Debbie will introduce you to her friends. You don't have any trouble making friends. You'll be fine."

"I hope so," I said. Connie entered the kitchen and I knew she would give me a hard time. She did not disappoint me.

"Did anybody get blinded by your bright suit?" she asked and laughed.

"No, in fact I received a few compliments for your information."

"Was this a prom for the blind?" Connie asked.

"Connie… that's not very nice." Mom scolded.

"I bet you sat along the wall and didn't dance once," Connie challenged.

"Wrong again. I danced plenty and even got asked to dance a few times. Ha!"

"There must be some ugly desperate chicks in your school to want to dance with you," Connie said.

"Connie… that will be enough," Mom raised her voice a bit to make her point. Not wanting to hear anything more from my bratty sister, I excused myself from the table and went to gather what I needed for the pool. Fifteen minutes later I was walking out the door.

I checked at the snack bar for Debbie. She had the day off which made sense. Girls always seemed to have a lot more to do to get ready then guys did. There was a good size crowd at the pool and the day slipped by quickly. Before I knew it, I was on my way home to get ready for prom number two.

A quick shower and a change back into my magic blue threads and I was walking out the door. Mom and dad were waiting for me at the door. Dad has his camera in his hand.

"I never got a picture of you yesterday. Stand here with your mother." He pointed to a spot by the front door. I put my arm around my mother and smiled as Dad clicked off a few photos. Mom swapped places with Dad and she took a few pictures of her two favorite guys; her words.

"I figured you didn't have time to take care of this, so I did it for you," Mom said as she handed me a square box with a rose inside of it. "It's called a wristlet. It has a strap on the back of the flower. You put it around her wrist."

"Thanks, Mom. I'm glad you thought of that." I took the box and headed to the car. I was more nervous than I thought I would be as I drove across town to Debbie's house. I knew I would have a good time with Debbie, but I was worried that it might be awkward with her friends. I pulled up in front of her house and there were three couple plus Debbie all in their prom finery standing in her front yard.

"We're taking some pictures first," Debbie said, looking wonderful in her pale -yellow gown.

"Sure, not a problem. Here, this is for you." I handed her the box with the wristlet. "You look great," I added, feeling more awkward by the second as her friends checked me out.

"Thank you. This is really thoughtful of you," she said. "I'll wait until we get to the dance to put it on." She grabbed me by the hand and led me over to her friends where she made introductions. Her girlfriends were very nice. Their boyfriends looked like they were trying to figure out why Debbie had invited a junior from their rival school to the senior prom.

Photos were taken of individual couples plus group shots. Debbie's mom was snapping away, one photo after another. We hadn't been introduced yet, so I made the first move.

"Hi, I'm Jason," I said to her mom.

"I figured as much," she said and then moved away to take another picture. So much for making a good impression. It was obvious, at least to me, that Mrs. Gravely did not approve of her daughter's choice for a prom date.

"We need to get going if we 're going to make our dinner reservation on time," I said.

"I can't believe you are taking me to dinner. You really didn't have to do that, she answered.

"I want you to have the full experience," I said. She smiled and leaned over to give me a hug. She said goodbye to her parents and her friends and headed to my car. Her father was right on our tail. He walked over to me.

"Drive carefully and take good care of my daughter," he said.

"I will, sir."

"No drinking and no funny business… got it?" he asked.

"Yes sir," I answered. "I will be the perfect gentleman."

"Good. Now go and have a good time." I opened the car door for Debbie as much to impress her as to impress her father. I hurried around to the driver's side and slid in. I started up the car and pulled out, glad to be leaving the icy stares of her parents and friends.

"Don't mind my parents," she said. "It's not you, it's me. They don't trust me."

"I'll be on my best behavior," I answered.

"That would be disappointing," she responded and laughed. I forced a chuckle wondering if she was being serious. Luckily, we pulled up in front of the Hotel Bethlehem before anything else could be suggested.

Dinner was wonderful. The room was elegant. The service was great and the food was excellent. The evening was off to a good start. As I retrieved the car, I wondered how the evening would go. I wanted to take this slow since my first prom with Debbie was happening a year earlier than it had fifty years ago. Once again, I had no idea how these changes happening now would affect my future. Although this had been fun so far, I really didn't want to relive my entire life from this point forward.

Once we arrived at the dance, I barely had time to sit. Debbie was ready to dance for every song, whether it was slow or fast. One of the few breaks we took when was Debbie had to use the restroom. One of her friends from the photo session used the opportunity to pin me down.

"How do you know Debbie?" Joyce asked me.

"We're both working at Northwest Swim Club for the summer," I responded.

"You're a lifeguard?" she asked.

"I am," I said.

"That's cool," Joyce said. "Why haven't I seen you around school? she asked.

"Probably because I don't go here," I said. "I go to Freedom."

"That's too bad," she said. "What college are you going to in the fall?"

"None," I said stalling for time.

"You have a job lined up?" she continued to probe.

"No, I'll be a senior at Freedom." I figured it was going to come out sooner or later.

"Really? Did you stay back a year or something?" This girl was relentless.

"No, I'm only seventeen." Debbie appeared by side, ending the interrogation.

"What were you two talking about?" Debbie asked.

"I was just asking him how he met you. No big deal," Joyce answered.

"Keep your hands off him," Debbie said. "He's mine." She laughed, but I wasn't so sure that she wasn't serious.

"Don't worry," Joyce snapped back. "I don't want to get in trouble for fooling around with minors." I readied myself for the explosion. I thought for sure that Debbie was going to be angry. To my surprise, she kept her cool. She looked at Joyce and responded.

"I like playing with fire. You should try it sometime." With that, Debbie grabbed my hand and tugged me out on the dancefloor. I watched as Joyce went back to the table with her friends and reported her news that she couldn't wait to share. I figured the age thing would be offset at least a little bit with the fact that I was a lifeguard. I decided that I didn't care and put my efforts into dancing.

The night slipped by quickly and I genuinely had a good time despite the little brush-up with Joyce. As the dance was winding down to the last few songs, I began to realize that Debbie and I had not discussed what we were going to do after the prom. Obviously, none of my friends were having an after-party. I assumed that someone in her crowd probably was. The other problem was that I only had a junior license. A midnight deadline gave us exactly one hour after the prom ended.

We danced the last slow dance. Debbie held onto me tightly swaying to the strains of The Last Waltz sung by Connie Francis. As we walked out to the car, Debbie had very little to say. I wondered if I had inadvertently done something to offend her. Maybe she was mad that I told Joyce that I was only a junior.

"Where do you want to go?" I asked not knowing what else to do.

"I was hoping that you might have an idea," she said.

"Aren't any of your friends having a party?"

"My friends and their dates are all driving to the shore tonight and staying for the weekend. My parents vetoed that idea whether or not I had a date. I need to be home by midnight. I hope that doesn't bother you."

"Not at all. I only have my junior license." We both sat there quietly for a few seconds and then burst out laughing. I started up the car and pulled out of the parking lot.

"Where are we going?" she asked.

"To get the best blueberry you have ever eaten," I said.

We had just enough time to get to the Sunset Diner, order a couple slices of pie, and then get back to her house before midnight. I pulled up in front of her house with a new worry; the goodnight kiss.

"Kiss me here," she said as we sat in the car which ended any debate as to whether or not she wanted one. My dad will be watching from the window if you walk me to the door. She leaned over, closed her eyes, and waited. I was a bit slow, but recovered before she pulled away. I went in for a nice gentle kiss on the lips. She had a different idea. Her lips parted and her tongue found mine. It was the longest kiss of my life up until that point.

"I had a really good time," she said as the kiss ended.

"I did too," I said.

"I hope I will be seeing a lot more of you this summer," she said.

"Count on it." She leaned over and gave me another quick kiss just as the light by her front door flashed on and off.

"I told you he would be watching," she said. I got out of the car, went around and opened the door for her, and walked with her hand in hand to the front door.

"You have no idea how much this night has meant to me," she said.

"I think this will be the start of a beautiful relationship."

"I hope so," she answered as she closed the door behind her.

Driving home, I prayed that I hadn't done anything tonight to skew the future. At least I had no more proms to worry about for another year.

CHAPTER 18

After my double prom weekend, things settled into a more normal schedule as the calendar turned to June. I had eight and a half days of school left in my junior year, take two. My goal was to keep everything the same as it had been. The truth was I did not remember any specific things from that time period fifty years ago. It's funny how I had been certain that my high school years were some of the best days of my life, and yet here I was, bored and unable to remember much about my day-to-day life during that time so long ago.

I knew the weekend was likely to be more interesting. I was working both days which guaranteed that I would be seeing Debbie at the pool. I decided that I wasn't going to go out of my way to change things. My plan was to let things unfold naturally, although I wasn't quite sure what that looked like.

I purposely did not make a beeline over to the snack bar when I arrived at the pool Saturday morning nor did she come to find me. By the middle of the afternoon, my curiosity got the best of me and I sauntered over to the snack bar. There was a crowd of people there and Debbie appeared very busy. I caught her eye and waved. She waved back and went right back to serving customers.

I was off at six and strolled by the snack bar. There was a different girl working the window. Apparently, Debbie's shift had ended and she hadn't bothered to find me and say goodbye. I was disappointed. I was going to ask her to go to the movies with me.

I walked out of the swim club and unlocked my bike from the bike rack. There was a note taped to the handlebars. I knew without opening it who had written it. I peeled off the tape and unfolded the note. I wasn't sure what to expect. Could she be calling it off already? You're a nice guy, but... I didn't think that was likely since we had dated off and on for more than two years. I started reading.

Jason,

I wanted to thank you again for Saturday night. You made the night perfect. I don't know how it could have gone any better. It is a night I will cherish forever. I didn't want to bother you in the stand, so I wrote this note. I'm free tonight if you want to do anything... no pressure. Just a thought. Call me. See you soon.

Debbie

I was touched by her words. She was a nice girl, but then I already knew that. If our timing had been different fifty years ago, I could have easily ended up with her. It wasn't, and I didn't, and given where my life went, I have no regrets. As soon as I got home, I called her. We settled on going to the Big Scoop, the local ice cream shop, to get some Sundaes.

My parents were pleased that I was going out with Debbie again. My sister was her normal brat.

"Jay-Jay's got a girlfriend," Connie said. "Sitting in a tree, K-i-s-s-i-n-g."

"Could you get any more immature?" I asked. "Never mind... I already know the answer to that question."

Debbie was waiting out front of her house when I arrived. I pulled to the curb and she hopped in.

"I wish my parents had just an ounce of trust in me," she sighed.

"All parents are the same," I offered, trying to make her feel better.

"If that was true, I would be at the shore right now," she answered.

"If it will make you feel any better, I doubt my parents would have let me go anyway."

"That may be, but I'm about to graduate. Next year, there are a lot of kids my age going off to college. They will be free to run their own lives., coming and going as they please."

"Does that include you?" I asked. "Are you going off to college?" I asked already knowing the answer.

"I'll be staying in a dorm, but it's right here in Bethlehem at St. Luke's Nursing School."

"You'll have some freedom," I said.

"Some, but not enough. I can just imagine being out late one night and running into my parents in town. They would probably pull me out of school."

I pulled into the parking lot of the Big Scoop which appeared to be packed. We were no sooner in the front door when I heard a familiar voice calling me.

"Jason... back here." It was Trip. He was waving me back to his booth. I took Debbie by the hand and worked our way back to Trip's table. Trip, Bonnie, Greg, and Vicki slid closer together in the booth to make room for Debbie and me. I ordered my favorite dessert on the menu; the fudge flattop. Debbie took my recommendation and ordered one for herself.

Conversation swirled mostly about summer being right around the corner. There was some discussion about the party and everything was going fine until Vicki asked a question that put me in a very awkward position.

"Why didn't you and your date stay at my party after the prom?" she asked. This was bad. I looked toward Debbie hoping she hadn't heard. I could tell by her look that I wasn't that lucky.

"I wasn't able to stay all night. Your dad made it clear that once midnight rolled around, nobody was leaving the party until daybreak."

"You should have stayed. You would have had fun," Vicki said as she continued to push. Maybe she didn't realize that Debbie was not the girl with me on Friday night.

"Hey, excuse my manners," I said to Vicki. "I don't think I introduced you to Debbie. She and I had a great time at the Liberty prom last night." Vicki's eyes went wide. She immediately realized her mistake and knew she had put me in a difficult spot.

"It's so nice to meet you," Vicki said. Debbie nodded her head toward Vicki and then excused herself to the bathroom.

"I'm really sorry," Vicki said to me. "I wasn't thinking. Do you want me to talk to her?"

"No, I'll take care of it," I said.

Debbie came back to the table, and nibbled at her fudge flattop. She had little interest in engaging in any conversation. I knew I was going to need to address Friday night's prom. I didn't waste any time when we got back to my car.

"It's not what it sounds like," I said.

"I thought you told me that you didn't have a date," Debbie said.

"I didn't."

"So, you picked somebody up at the prom?" Debbie asked. There was no hint of amusement in her voice.

"Not exactly," I sputtered.

"What does that mean?" Debbie asked.

"We danced a few songs together. She asked me if I wanted to go with her to a party at one of her friend's houses. She didn't want to go to the party alone. We went, and it was a make-out fest so we left. I suggested going to Vicki's party… just as friends. You already heard that we didn't stay there either."

"Can I ask where you went after that?"

"We went to the Sunset Diner in Allentown and had some blueberry pie. We talked for a little while and then she took me home, but not before her boyfriend created a scene in the parking lot."

"Her boyfriend?"

"It's an on-again, off-again thing. He was supposed to go to the prom with her, but he backed out. That's why she was there without a date. We're just friends… nothing more."

"Have you talked to her since the prom?" Debbie asked.

"As a matter of fact, I have not. There is no reason for us to talk. We had a nice time together. We both got to experience our junior prom. That's all there was to it. I guess I didn't realize that you would be jealous."

"Isn't it obvious?" she asked. "My last relationship ended badly… as you know. I guess I thought we had gotten off to a good start."

"We have," I answered.

"I just couldn't take being led on… again."

"I am not leading you on. I promise."

"I feel like such a fool. You barely know me and already I'm coming off all possessive. You must think I'm some sort of nut. I'm really sorry."

"I don't think you're a nut. I'm looking forward to getting to know you. I really am."

"Being jealous for no reason wasn't the only mistake I made tonight," Debbie said.

"It wasn't? What was the other one?"

"Not finishing the fudge flattop. It was delicious." That broke the tension. We laughed and talked as I drove around town. Thirty minutes later, I pulled up in front of her house, we kissed goodnight, and I walked her to the door. The porch light flicked on and off. We both laughed. I gave her a little peck on the cheek and said goodnight.

Driving home I replayed the evening's events in my head. If there ever was an opportunity to nip it in the bud with Debbie, it was tonight. I could have ended it right there before it really got started. The problem was that I was afraid to do things differently than I had the first time I was here. Even knowing how my life played out in the past, there are so many variables as I am going through it all again. It will be difficult for me to follow the exact path I took when I was here fifty years ago. I had to be very careful.

CHAPTER 19

I called Debbie a few times during the week, but did not see her. During the day, I was in school putting in the time to fulfill the requirements for my junior year. Not much meaningful learning was taking place for me or anybody else during this time. The teachers went through the motions to fulfill their obligations to receive their paychecks.

I spent as much time in the bandroom as I could. Depending on who was there, we would sometimes pull out our instruments and have a little jam session. Sometimes we would just sit around and talk about our plans for the summer. Sometimes we would sit outside the back door of the bandroom and catch a few rays.

In class we were often stuck watching old black and white films on the old reel-to-reel projectors. At least the school was air-conditioned which made it tolerable. During those movies which I paid no attention to, I wondered how or when I would be returning to my former life, the one fifty years in the future. Was this all a dream? It didn't feel like a dream; too much time had elapsed. Was I destined to be stuck here in the past and relive my life again? I had already been able to fix some of my regrets from my past life, and I'm sure there were many other things that could have turned out better if I thought about it. The problem was that there were other parts of my life that I wouldn't change for the world. Number one on that list was Grace. There was no guarantee that I would end up with Grace if I stayed in this life. In fact, the odds would be astronomical against that happening. So many things had happened to us at just the right moments for us to end up together. The chances of all those events unfolding at the precise moments in time again were a million to one...or worse.

Friday night arrived without answers to any of my questions. I took Debbie miniature golfing at a place on Lehigh Street in Allentown. I followed that up with a movie on Saturday night; Mackenna's Gold starring Omar Sharif, Telly Savalas, and Gregory

Peck. Both nights, I avoided the temptation of going to any quiet, dark place afterwards. I wasn't ready to take that step. Debbie and I were already way ahead of schedule. We hadn't even gone out on a date the first time around, let alone a prom. I promised myself to take it slow, but it was already getting difficult to do.

Finally, the last day of school had come and gone. My first day of official summer vacation I was lifeguarding as I would be for most days of the summer. On one of my breaks, I wandered over to the snack bar to see Debbie. She was taking a break as well so we had a chance to sit at one of the picnic tables and talk.

"This is so great," she began, "we'll get to see each other every day." I knew I had to respond, but I wasn't sure what to say. I didn't want to shut her down, but I also didn't want to seem too eager.

"That's true," I answered, choosing a non-committal answer.

"Try not to sound so excited," she said, picking up on my hesitation instantly.

"That's not how I meant it," I said. "I mean summer's here… what could be better?"

"Hey, if I'm misreading the signals, tell me. I'll back off. I thought we were mutually interested in each other. I know I am interested in you, but maybe I should just speak for myself." Here was another moment in time when I could have shut this whole thing down. It would have been so easy. I knew what was holding me back from bailing out of this budding relationship; it was the possibility that I would alter what happened to me in the future. Everything decision I was making had one goal in mind; get back to my former life.

"No, you are not misreading the signals," I said. "I like you too. I just don't want to scare you off by moving too fast."

"I can guarantee you are not moving too fast," she said and winked.

"Good to know," I answered.

"By the way, one of my friends is having a graduation party on Saturday night. You're invited," she said.

"Can I bring a date?" I asked. She reached over and slugged me in the arm.

"Very funny. If you come, who knows…maybe you'll get lucky," she said as she got up from the table and walked back into the snack bar. I had no response to that. She made it very clear that she was ready to take this relationship to the next level. I wondered what the next level was to her. I wondered if I was ready for the next level… whatever it was.

The rest of the day I could not get Debbie's comment out of my head. Was she serious or just making a joke? I tried to remember if anything like that happened fifty years ago. For the life of me I could not remember the specifics of the "first time" with Debbie. One thing for certain, fifty years ago I had no idea of what I was doing, but now I wasn't a virgin any more. I knew exactly what I was doing. I almost felt that I would be taking advantage of Debbie if I did anything. I had half a century of experience in that area now. My plan to go slowly was falling apart.

Debbie came to find me at the end of her shift on Thursday.

"Are you in for Saturday night?" she asked.

"Of course, I'm in. How could I pass up an opportunity like that?"

"Great… I'll give you the details for the party tomorrow when I see you," she said. With that she squeezed my shoulder, turned, and walked away leaving me with my thoughts.

Friday turned out to be a washout. It had drizzled all morning and the forecast for the afternoon was for heavier rain. Mr. Hutchinson called around eleven informing me that the pool was closed for the day. Shortly after I hung up, the phone rang again. I expected it would be Debbie, but I was wrong.

"I'm having some of the guys over this afternoon for some penny poker," Trip said. "You in?"

"Sure," I said relieved that I didn't need to make up an excuse not to see Debbie all day. Fifteen minutes later the phone rang again. This time it was Debbie.

"So, what do you want to do on our day off?" she asked. She was not going to be happy with my answer.

"Trip invited me over this afternoon for a poker game," I said.

"Oh," was the only response on the other end of the phone.

"Maybe we can get together after dinner tonight," I offered up as a consolation prize.

"Maybe... we'll see." Her response told me everything I needed to know. She was unhappy with me as I knew she would be. I chose not to get into with her.

"I'll call you when I get back from Trip's house. In the meantime, you can figure out if you want to go out tonight or not." I should not have added that last part. Too late now. I pressed on. "What's the plan for tomorrow night?" I asked.

"I'm not sure I'm going," she said.

"What happened?" I asked already knowing the answer.

"I not sure I feel like it." So much for getting lucky tomorrow night. My chances just went way down. I wasn't sure that was a bad thing.

"I'll call later," I said. "We can figure out what we are or are not doing then." There was no response. "Are you still there?" I asked wondering if she had hung up on me.

"I'm here," she answered. "Is there anything else?" she asked. I wasn't in the mood for games.

"No, nothing at all," I said. "Take care." The only response was the click on the other end of the line when she hung up. Funny, I didn't remember Debbie being this possessive in the past.

The afternoon at Trip's house was fun. Besides Trip, Rob and Greg, two of Trip's cousins who were visiting from New York state were there for the game. Nobody made or lost a fortune that afternoon. With penny stakes it was difficult to make or lose more than two dollars. It was a great way to while away a gray, rainy afternoon.

The best part of the afternoon was news from one of Trip's cousins. He told the group that there was supposed to be a major rock concert at a place called Wallkill, New York. Supposedly most the big rock acts were going to be there, possibly even the Stones and the Beatles. I realized he was talking about what would become the biggest rock festival in history; Woodstock. I knew it would not be held in Wallkill because the town decided to pull out of the arrangement they had with the organizers. I also knew that neither the Beatles or the Stones would be at the festival although many other legendary performers would be. Woodstock would define a generation. I had missed it the first time. If I was still here in the middle of August, I needed to find a way to be at Woodstock.

I can't honestly say that Woodstock was a regret. I hadn't even heard of the festival until the news reported that the New York Thruway was blocked for miles because of the concert. I doubted that my parents would have let me attend even if I had known about it. There were big problems standing in my way if I was to get there this time around. First, I had no transportation of my own. My parents were not going to let me take the family car for four or five days. Second problem was that it was very doubtful that my parents would let me go this time even if I could find a ride. They would assume that with all the hippies attending there would be drugs…and they would be right. I knew the dates and the location. Now I just needed to come up with a plan that would get me to Max Yasgur's dairy farm in Bethel, New York in the middle of August.

I got home in time for dinner after the poker game. Mom was setting the table when I walked in.

"A young lady called for you three times in the last hour. She wouldn't leave her name," Mom said.

"It was probably Debbie. We're supposed to go to a party tomorrow night. I'll give her a call." The house phone was in the kitchen. There was no such thing as a private call when I was growing up. Cellphones sure made things a lot simpler… and more private. I called and got her father.

"We're just sitting down to dinner. You'll have to call back," he said.

"No problem. Please tell her that Jason called."

"I will" he said. "In the future I would appreciate it if you would not call around our dinnertime."

"My apologies, sir. Enjoy your dinner." There was no goodbye, just a click as he hung up the phone. I wondered if he was this hostile to all of Debbie's callers or if he was extra chippy with me. I didn't remember him having a particular dislike for me when I dated his daughter previously. I also realized that I hadn't suggested that Debbie call me back and I was not fond of the idea of making a return call. I decided I would wait for her call.

After dinner, the family settled in the den to watch television. Another improvement that didn't exist growing up was a remote control for the television. Somebody had to get up and physically turn the channel dial to change channels. What a pain! Kids in the future are so spoiled with all the modern conveniences they have at their disposal.

By the time the clock reached eight, I was doubtful that Debbie was going to call. By the time it reached nine, I knew she wasn't going to call. Tomorrow at the pool should be an interesting day. Obviously, she was not going to be happy with me. The party was looking doubtful. The thought of me getting lucky was out of the question.

CHAPTER 20

Saturday morning was gray and misty. I wasn't sure the pool would open if the day didn't improve. I hadn't heard anything by the time I had to leave. Due to the questionable weather, Dad gave me a lift.

"Call me if you need a ride home," he said as I opened the car door.

"Will do. Thanks for the ride." I walked through the gates of the swim club and headed to the locker room. I dropped off my stuff and went to find Mr. Hutchinson to see what the plan was for today.

"We're going with a skeleton crew today because of the weather. I'm looking for volunteers that would like the day off. You interested?" he asked.

"Not really," I said.

"I'll check with the other guards. If none of them volunteer, I may have to use seniority to see who goes home." That meant it would come down to three of us who were new this year. As it turned out, it didn't matter because Don and Tony, two of the senior guards volunteered to take the day off.

I did the usual opening chores and when I finished, I took a walk by the snack bar. Debbie was just closing the door and appeared to be locking it.

"No work today?" I asked. She glanced over her shoulder and turned back to the door. I knew already this wasn't going to go well.

"The snack bar is closed today," she said.

"Hutchinson sent two guards home too," I said.

"Good for you. I guess you get to stay." There was no sense avoiding the issue any longer.

"Listen…about last night…" I started.

"It would have been nice to hear from you," she said.

"I did call, but your father said you were sitting down to dinner."

"You could have called back," she said as she headed to the exit.

"I wasn't sure what time your dinner would be over and I didn't want your father to dislike me any more than he already does," I said.

"You don't get it, do you? He doesn't dislike you… he doesn't trust me. The thought of me having a boyfriend scares him."

"I was hoping you were going to call me back," I responded.

"I had already called three times earlier in the day. You weren't there."

"You knew where I was."

"All afternoon?"

"Yes, all afternoon. Where else did you think I would be?"

"I don't know. You tell me."

"I was at Trip's house all afternoon. That's the truth."

"Uh-huh," she responded. She had reached the gate and it was obvious she was not going to stop.

"Hold up a minute," I said. "Where is all this hostility coming from? To my knowledge I haven't done anything to you that should have you upset with me. If I have, you need to tell me what it is." She paused as she opened her car door, but she did not look back. "Seriously… tell me what I've done. I'll try to fix it." She slowly turned to face me.

"I'm sorry. It's not you. I just don't want to get burned again. Add in my dad's lack of trust and this whole dating scene is one big mess for me."

"I can see that. I know we haven't been going out long, but you can trust me. I'm not going to burn you. I like you and would really enjoy getting to know you better."

"You're not just saying that to make me feel better?"

"I would never lead you on like that." I could see the anger fade from her eyes. She looked down at the ground, somewhat embarrassed I imagined for her attitude. "So, are we still on for the party tonight?" I asked.

"We are, assuming you still want to go with me."

"Of course, I want to go with you. You're the only person I'll know at the party." She laughed.

"Pick me up at seven?" she asked.

"You have a date."

"Jason, I really appreciate you being patient with me." She leaned over and gave me a hug and a kiss on the cheek.

"Hey loverboy," a voice called from the front desk, "I'm not paying you to make-out in the parking lot." Hutchinson was standing with his hands on his hips staring at us.

"See you tonight," I said as I hustled back inside the pool grounds.

It never rained, but the sun never appeared either. A cool gray day kept attendance way down. When I wasn't on the guard stand, I was hunkered down in the office reading The *Andromeda Strain* by Michael Crichton to stave off the boredom. I had forgotten how boring days like this could be at the pool. At least on a warm sunny day, there was lots of action to watch over. It made the time pass quickly. Not so on a day like this.

At four when Hutchinson asked for a volunteer to go home, my hand shot up without hesitation. I called my dad for a lift and stood by the front desk waiting his arrival. Standing there I had time to think about this time travel adventure I was experiencing. Being able to see and talk to my parents again years after their deaths was a gift that I needed to appreciate more than I had so far. I know growing up I had not always given them the love and gratitude I should have for all the things they had done for me throughout my life. You rush through your life and before you know it, the people that are most important to you are gone. You wish that you would have told them that you love them one more time, but in an ordinary life…it's too late. They're gone and you live with yet one more regret. Unless you get to travel back in time for a redo, there isn't a thing you can do about it.

I promised myself as I watched my dad's car pull into the parking lot, that I was going to rewrite the way I treated my parents. No more rushing through "life" without taking the time to talk to them and do things with them that would have meant the world to them years ago. Here was yet another chance to change something that I regretted. I would not waste this opportunity.

I started my new approach at the dinner table. We had real conversations about our respective days. I suggested going to the shore for a day as a family. I suggested going out to eat as a family. I could tell quickly that my parents were pleased with my new interest in family affairs. My sister, on the other hand, gave me some grief after dinner.

"What's with all the kissing-up at dinner tonight?" asked Connie.

"I wasn't kissing-up. I was just trying to be nice to let Mom and Dad know that they are appreciated," I answered.

"Give me a break," Connie said. "You expect me to buy that?"

"Buy it or don't, it's how I feel. When you get older, you'll understand what I'm talking about."

"What's wrong with you? Are you on drugs?"

"You may not get it now, but trust me…someday you will." I gently guided my sister out of my bedroom and closed the door. I changed into a nice pair of khaki shorts and an Ocean City t-shirt. Debbie had assured me the attire was casual. I didn't want to look like a dork. It was neither a good option to be overdressed nor underdressed for a party. I was going for cool casual. Looking in the mirror, I think I nailed it.

I had arranged to use the car tonight and went to get the keys off the hook in the kitchen.

"Remember to be home by midnight," Dad said.

"Absolutely," I said. "Thanks for allowing me to borrow the car tonight. I really appreciate it." The look on my father's face was a cross between confusion and disbelief. He stuttered, not knowing exactly how to respond to me.

"Uh…yeah…sure. I know I can trust you. Have a good time."

"I will. Thanks." I could see the puzzled looks darting back and forth between my parents. My sister was on the far side of the room rolling her eyes at me. My parents are/were great people. It's weird talking about them. I'm not sure if I should refer to them in past tense or present tense. I could see by their reaction tonight that I clearly had not shown enough appreciation to them the first time around.

Ten minutes later, feeling very pleased with myself, I knocked on Debbie's door. Her father opened the door.

"You again?" he asked. I wasn't sure if he was truly annoyed or just trying to be funny. I went with the latter choice.

"What can I say? I like your daughter."

"I expect that you will have her home by midnight," Mr. Gravely snorted at me.

"Not a problem, sir. I have to be in by midnight myself."

113

"Good…that's good," he said. Debbie appeared behind him.

"Dad, you're being nice, right?" she asked.

"Sweet as cherry pie, honey," he said and gave a half-hearted laugh. I did not want to get involved with whatever was going on between the two of them right now. "I was just telling Jack what time I would appreciate him having you home."

"Jason, Dad… not Jack." Debbie corrected him.

"My mistake, sweetheart. Of course, it is Jason. My apologies Jason," he said as he glanced at me.

"It's fine," I answered. "I have an aunt who calls me Jackie all the time. I'm used to it."

"Well go…you two get out of here. Have a good time at the party," Mr. Gravely said. Debbie walked out of the door, took me by the hand and walked to my car.

"What was that all about?" I asked as I was pulling away from the house.

"I had enough of the way he talked to me and my friends. I told him that it wasn't fair. Surprisingly, he seemed to get it… at least for tonight." I was silently amused that we had both had conversations with our parents tonight. Maybe there was something in the air tonight. I should write a song to that effect. I could beat the Phil Collin's version by twelve years.

CHAPTER 21

The party was at Karen Salabsky's house in the northeast section of town. It was a modest 3- bedroom Cape Cod style house with three bedrooms and a basement like all the other houses on the street. We walked to the door, knocked and waited…and waited…and waited. This was a perfect situation where a cell phone would come in handy. Too bad they weren't around yet.

I suggested we walk around the back of the house since it was obvious from the number of cars parked out front, that there was a party around here…somewhere. As soon as we turned the corner at the back of the house, you could hear music floating up from the basement. The Bilco doors were flung open at the top of the stairs leading to the basement.

"I guess this is the entrance," Debbie said.

"Looks that way." Debbie led the way, entering the door at the bottom of the steps. The music was deafening as Led Zeppelin's first album exploded through the speakers. A few strands of Christmas lights were hung across the basement providing the only light. There were people everywhere.

"Hey, you made it," a girl who I assumed was the hostess of the party said to Debbie.

"You remember Jason?" Debbie asked pointing to me.

"Sure, your prom date. Nice to see you again, Jason."

"Likewise," I said.

"There's beer in the washing machine," Karen said pointing to the corner where an old washer and dryer sat.

"Pretzels in the dryer?" I asked as a joke. Karen looked at me like I had just grown a third eye.

"Don't mind him. He's always making bad jokes," Debbie said coming to my rescue.

"Whatever," Karen said. "Only rule is that the beer stays in the basement. My parents aren't home, but we do have nosy neighbors who I'm sure would love to report underage drinking back to my parents."

"Got it," Debbie answered before I could put my foot in my mouth with another dumb joke.

Debbie led me through the maze of people, introducing me as we went. We reached the washer. Debbie lifted the top of the washer and pulled out two Pabst Blue Ribbon beers.

"Here you go," she said, "I assume you have had beer before." I had but only when my dad or uncle would let me finish a near empty can. I never really cared for the taste and even fifty years later I never acquired a taste for it. I reached out and took the beer from Debbie. I popped the top like I had been doing it all my life which I had…but they were soda cans. I tapped Debbie's can and took a big swallow… and immediately began to choke as it went down the wrong pipe. I sprayed beer all over my shirt and Debbie as well.

"Nice move, Sherlock," she said as she jumped away from me. A number of people nearby turned in my direction and watched the spectacle. They all began to laugh.

"All right, show's over," Debbie said as she pulled me away. I hadn't been here five minutes and I had already made a fool of myself trying to act like a bigshot. We stopped in front of another door and she tried to open it. It was locked. She banged on the door.

"Let's not take all day," she shouted. "Other people are waiting." Another few minutes passed before Debbie banged on the door again. Finally, the door swung open.

"Alright, keep your pants on," a girl I didn't know said. She exited towing a big guy behind her who didn't look happy about our interruption. I realized that there were other uses for this bathroom tonight.

Debbie ignored them and pushed her way into the bathroom and pulled me in behind her. She closed the door, but not before Karen caught a glimpse of us.

"Take your shirt off," she said. I looked at her and hesitated. Was this it? Was she tired of waiting for me to make a move?

"Seriously... I see you every day at the pool with your shirt off. Do you really want to go home smelling like a brewery?" she asked. Phew... I breathed a big sigh of relief.

"No, that would get me grounded for sure since I'm driving."

"Exactly, now get your shirt off," she ordered. I pulled the shirt over my head and handed it to her. She turned on the sink and rubbed a little soap anywhere I had sprayed beer. Then she began to vigorously rub the shirt creating a nice lather and followed that up with a good rinsing. She had wrung the shirt and rubbed it with a hand towel to semi-dry it. She hung it off the edge of the sink before beginning to unbutton her blouse.

"Want me to leave?" I asked.

"With no shirt...people might have questions, but it's up to you." She slid her blouse off her shoulders and stood there in a flimsy white bra. She looked up at me waiting for my response. "Like what you see?" she asked and smiled. I hesitated...briefly.

"I like it very much," I answered throwing caution to the wind. We had played around plenty fifty years ago; I couldn't see how this could change much. She reached up and pulled me in close. Her lips found mine. I didn't resist. I was saved by someone banging on the door before things went too far.

"Hold your horses," Debbie yelled through the door. She turned to me and said, "We can pick this up again later."

"Sounds good," I lied. Things were moving too fast. We pulled on our damp tops and threw open the door. A very surprised guy I didn't know apologized for the interruption. I assured him that it was no problem. Our beers were no longer sitting on top of the dryer where we had left them.

"I'm getting another beer," Debbie said. "Can I trust that you won't spit it all over me if I give you another one?"

"I promise," I said although I didn't really want another beer. That beer lasted me the rest of the night. I took little baby sips. Debbie, in the meantime, had another three beers between dancing and trying to talk with her friends over the music. It seemed to me that I was just there for decoration. Whatever…it didn't matter. I knew how this all turned out.

"I'm ready to leave," Debbie announced a little before eleven.

"You sure?" I asked. "I don't have to be home for an hour."

"Who said we were going home?" she asked. "We have unfinished business." She took my hand and led me out of the basement.

"Where are we going?" I asked.

"Do you know where Atwood Lane is?" All kinds of memories flashed through my head. I knew Atwood for sure; it was one of my favorite parking spots. I had been there many, many times although not in the last fifty years. Debbie was the girl I spent the most time with there…by far. I could not remember if she had introduced me to this spot or I had introduced it to her. I just remembered that I reached the various bases at one time or another on a regular basis. Now here I was; going back once again to try my luck on the basepath. The difference tonight was that I didn't want any luck.

"It's over by Bethlehem Catholic High School somewhere, right?"

"You've been there before?" Debbie asked, her curiosity piqued.

118

"Heard some of the guys talking about it, that's all," I said. I let her give me directions. It wasn't long before we were pulled in under a tree on a quiet street with no houses in sight. A few other cars were already here, obviously having the same idea.

Debbie wasted no time and began to kiss me like I hadn't been kissed in a long time. There was passion and urgency. Grace and I used to kiss like that, but the physical aspect of our relationship had faded with time. I felt more than a little guilty; I was a married man…sort of. Did it count since technically I wasn't married right at this moment? Fifty years ago, I hadn't even met Grace yet. I only saw her on this trip because I knew where to find her. I don't think she was impressed especially when I told her I was going to apply to an all-girl's school.

Debbie continued her passionate kissing, barely taking time to breathe. Was I that good or was she that needy? Back then I'm sure I would have convinced myself that I was that good. I responded to Debbie's amorous advances. I mean I am a man. Even a man my age has needs. How old am I at this point in time? My mind has had nearly seventy years of experience. What about my body? This definitely isn't my seventy-year -old body. I would already be out of breath.

Fate must have been watching over me. Just as clothing was about to become optional, a cop car came cruising down the street shining a spotlight into the cars parked on the street. The police car rolled to a stop next to my car. I rolled down my window.

"Everything alright in there, Miss?" he asked.

"Fine, officer," Debbie said.

"You sure?" he asked again.

"Positive," Debbie responded.

"We were just about to leave," I blurted out. I could feel Debbie's eyes boring holes into my skull.

"That's probably a good idea," the officer said. "I'll check back in ten minutes." He moved on to the next car in the line.

"Why did you say that?" Debbie asked.

"I didn't want any trouble," I said. "What if he checked to see if we had been drinking?" Debbie had no answer. I started the car and waited for the windows to defog before pulling out.

Debbie was quiet as I drove her home. I knew she was upset with me on a few different levels, and I didn't really want to get into it with her so I remained quiet as well. I pulled up in front of her house. She opened her door and was out of the car before I even had shifted the car into park.

"No need to walk me to the door," she said.

"See you tomorrow at the pool," I called after her. She did not respond nor turn back toward me. She simply opened the front door, stepped inside and disappeared into the house. A few seconds later the front light went out and my night was over. I wondered if my relationship which had barely begun was over already too. I feared that I was really screwing up the future.

All the way home, I wondered what was going to happen to me. How would this night affect my future? Would I end up going down a completely different path with my life? Most importantly, would it lead back to Grace? I tried to make sense of what was happening. Why was I thrust back in time? Why was I back here at this specific time in my life? Was there some big thing I was supposed to accomplish? Was there some big wrong that I was supposed to fix? I had no answers to any of my questions.

Although I had enjoyed reliving and changing a few things in my life, I didn't want to restart from this point. There were too many things that I would miss; Grace being at the top of the list. Not everything was perfect in my old life, but I wanted to be back with Grace more than anything. I had to find a way back...and soon before being here became irreversible.

CHAPTER 22

Sunday morning, I went to the church with the family. I sat in the pew at St. Peter's Lutheran Church on Ridge Avenue in Allentown. I knew something that nobody else in attendance knew; this church would close twenty years down the road due to a dwindling congregation.

During his sermon, Pastor Kopperman urged people to slow down and enjoy the important things in life; mainly your family and friends. He would be so disappointed to see what the future would bring. The world I had come from moved at a frenetic pace. People were more detached than ever, faces buried in front of their cell phones, laptops, and game systems. Both parents in a family, assuming they hadn't divorced, often worked leaving the children to fend for themselves after school giving rise to the term "latchkey children". This was not the world Pastor Kopperman envisioned.

After church, our family walked the block down Railroad Street to my uncle's house. The street was barely wide enough for two cars to pass moving in opposite directions. My aunt and uncle lived in the right half of a skinny brick twin. A small strip of grass and a sidewalk ran down the side of the house. The backyard had a small patio covered with a thick grapevine and a small plot of grass behind that. The back gate opened into a sunken alley. In my younger days whenever I heard a train whistle, I would rush out the back gate and run down the alley which led to train tracks. I would watch and count the number of cars in the train. I still remember the record was two hundred seven cars.

My aunt always served cookies and milk for my sister and me while the adults enjoyed coffee. My mom's mother, Grammy, lived with my aunt and uncle. She joined us at the kitchen table before she headed off to the German church service later in the morning. I listened to her talk in her combination of German and English. If history stayed true, I knew she would no longer be with us five months from now. Before she left for church, I gave her a big hug and whispered into her ear.

"I love you Grammy." She hugged me even tighter.

"Yah, you are such a good boy," she whispered back to me. I watched her as she walked away. I don't ever remember me telling her that I loved her like I had today. It was a little thing, but it made me feel good. One more thing I was glad I was able to change.

As we returned home, I was sad that Grammy would be gone so soon. My other grandmother, who we called Nana, had passed away last October. I hadn't had the chance to tell her that I loved her. That was one regret I would not be able to fix. I rode my bike to the pool still feeling down. The time I was living in now is so simple compared to the future. There is an innocence that I miss.

I reached the pool and wondered what kind of reception I was going to get from Debbie. I purposely stayed away from the snack bar the whole afternoon. The fallout from last night was something I did not want to deal with today. I figured Debbie was still upset with me since she didn't come looking for me.

I was off at six and was feeling much better by that time. I decided I would say hello to Debbie before I left. I walked over and poked my head in the door of the snack bar. Carol stood at the window helping customers. She glanced over at me.

"Debbie is off today. I assume that is who you came to see," she said.

"Oh… I didn't know," I uttered as I closed the door and made my way to the front gate. I headed to the bike rack. A familiar face was sitting on the rack next to my orange Schwinn ten-speed.

"I was off today," Debbie said as I approached.

"Did you do something fun?" I asked.

"My Aunt Tilda came for a visit so I had to hang around the house most of the afternoon," she said. "Kind of a waste of a day."

"You shouldn't think that way. Your aunt won't be here forever."

"I know that. She already left," Debbie said.

"No, I mean as in alive," I said. Debbie looked up with a confused look on her face.

"You going all philosophical on me or what?" she asked.

"Not at all. I just think we should appreciate our elders when we have the chance."

"Whatever," Debbie said. "That's not what I came to talk about." Oh boy, here we go.

"I assume you want to talk about last night," I said.

"Don't you?"

"I guess," I answered.

"Look, if it's not important to you…skip it." She started to get up.

"Of course, it's important to me," I said trying to calm her down.

"You don't seem that interested in me," she said. "I practically threw myself at you…twice and you weren't interested."

"First off, neither situation was ideal. Other people were waiting for the bathroom and I felt weird that everyone figured we were fooling around in there."

"So, what if they did?" she asked not giving me any slack at all.

"Sorry, but it made me feel weird. All I wanted to do was get out of there."

"What about later in the car?" she asked.

"That bothered me too," I said. "I was worried that somebody would see us and then when the cop showed up…forget it… I was done."

123

"Haven't you ever been parking before?" she asked. I didn't know how to answer that question. I had been parking numerous times, many of them with her. If I answered yes, then she would think the problem was with her. I didn't want her to think I didn't find her appealing.

"Oh my god…you have never been parking before," she said when I failed to answer after a few seconds.

"Are you still a virgin?" she asked which really put me in a spot. If I said yes, I was a nerd. If I said no, she would want to know the details.

"I'm not answering that question on the grounds that it might incriminate me." I hoped that might satisfy her curiosity. It did not.

"That would explain everything," she said and smiled at me. "That's what I get for dating a younger man." I didn't like the assumption she was making.

"I didn't say I was a virgin," I answered.

"You didn't say you weren't either. It's not a problem if you don't want to tell me, but I personally think the answer is obvious."

Now I was annoyed and embarrassed. I had fifty more years of experience than she did. The problem was that she would never believe that. Besides, if she did believe me, she would want me to prove it and I wasn't ready to go there. I wasn't sure if I would ever be ready to go there because of Grace. How could I bed another woman knowing Grace was waiting for me…somewhere…. sometime?

"I'm sorry I'm a disappointment," I finally said.

"You are not a disappointment. I like you and I'm sorry if I was rushing things a little too fast for your comfort. We can take it as slow as you need to go. The truth is that I don't want to lose you."

"Thank you," I answered. "I don't want to lose you either." She leaned over and wrapped her arms around me and held me tight.

"How did you get here?" I asked after the hug was over.

"I rode my bike," she answered and pointed to a blue bike a few spots down the rack.

"In that case, I'll ride home with you," I said.

"I'd like that."

We pedaled together talking about last night's party all the way to her house. Her father was sitting on the front patio reading the Sunday paper. I waved to her father and I got the smallest little wave back. Debbie walked her bike into the garage where she planted a big kiss on me.

"I'm glad we had this talk," she said.

"Me too," I answered not really sure if that was the truth. She gave me another quick kiss before we exited the garage.

"See you tomorrow," I said as I climbed on my bike and hustled home, already late for dinner.

CHAPTER 23

Our little talk on Sunday seemed to do the trick. Debbie backed off a bit which was fine with me. We still saw each other almost every day at the pool. We also went out Tuesday, Friday, and Saturday nights. I didn't make any suggestions to go to Atwood Lane and neither did she. We were just having fun and not moving to the next step which is exactly the way I wanted it.

Some evenings, I spent at home talking to Mom and Dad. I realized how special this was to have the opportunity to talk to them again. It had been a long time since my last conversation with either one of them and I missed them immensely. It felt so good to take the time to talk to them and to help out around the house which I only did when I had to previously.

I was a kinder, gentler version of myself this time around. I was considerate of neighbors that had been gone for many years. I was more considerate to people who I didn't even know. On our Saturday night date, Debbie and I had gone to the movies to see Easy Rider. Afterwards we stopped at the Big Scoop Ice Cream shop. We ordered sundaes and sat at a table near the front of the store. Toward the back I recognized one of my classmates who I had known from elementary school days, Mike Bowman. As we had gotten older, we drifted apart. By high school, it was nothing more than a quick hello as we passed in the hallways.

"I'll be right back," I said as I stood and headed back to see Mike.

"Mike, how have you been?" I asked. He looked up, surprised that I had made an effort to talk to him.

"Alright, I guess," he answered.

"Can you believe we're going to be seniors?" I asked.

"Yeah, I can't wait until I'm done with school," he responded.

"Hey, why don't you join us instead of sitting here by yourself?" I asked. He looked over toward Debbie.

"Are you sure she wouldn't mind?" he asked.

"I'm positive. Come on over. I want to hear what your plans are for the summer." He gathered up his ice cream and soda and followed me over to my table.

"Debbie, this is one of my old friends from elementary school, Mike Bowman."

"Hi Mike," Debbie said. Her look told me that she wasn't thrilled with this development, but I pressed on.

Mike and I swapped stories from our grade school days like when Lori Jensen was out at recess the period before us. She was running and stumbled and ended up putting her hand and arm through one of our classroom windows. Needless to say, that lesson was over as they cleaned up the broken glass and the blood that had dripped on everything from Lori's arm. We talked about some of our favorite teachers from Clearview Elementary like Mrs. Damsel, who was really cool. We talked about kids from the neighborhood that we used to hang out with. We talked about Jimmy Turner who had his foot crushed by a school bus when he got pushed into its path in eighth grade.

An hour had passed before the attendant at the Big Scoop chased us out so they could close.

"It was really good to catch up with you, Mike," I said. "I hope I run into you again."

"Likewise, man. It was good to talk to you and meet Debbie. You take care," he said and reached out his hand. I took his hand and shook it like I meant it.

"Good talking to you too, Mike," I said. "You take care." I watched as he turned and walked to his car in the parking lot. This was another case when I knew something that nobody else in the world knew; Mike would be dead in eighteen months. Mike would join the

Army right after graduation and would be killed in Vietnam six months later. Dead man walking took on a whole new context at that moment.

"So, what was that all about?" Debbie asked as we drove back to her house.

"I felt sorry for him sitting there all by himself," I answered.

"I wasn't good enough company for you?" she asked.

"You are fine company. It just looked like he could use a friend." Debbie seemed to mull that over for a few seconds before responding.

"You really are a nice guy."

"I haven't always been," I said. "I guess I'm trying to be more considerate of people this time around." The words were out of my mouth before I could stop myself.

"This time around?" Debbie had caught my slip.

"Yeah, like this time around from this point forward." I decided to stay quiet and not make it any worse. Debbie didn't push it so I could only hope that she bought my explanation. It had been my first slip-up in a few weeks. I was getting too comfortable in my "replay" life. I still had to be careful.

I walked Debbie to her door. We sat on the rockers on her front patio. I was expecting the porch lights to start flicking on and off any second, but they did not. I wondered if Mr. Gravely was starting accept me or simply had fallen asleep standing guard.

"That was really nice of you tonight," she said. "I don't know if I would have done the same thing if it had been somebody I knew."

"Thanks," I answered not knowing what else to say. The truth was that if that same thing had happened fifty years ago, I probably would not have invited Mike to sit with us. Like the old expression; "Hindsight is twenty-twenty." It is easy to do the right thing if you know what the future holds."

128

"I mean it. I am really impressed with your thoughtfulness," Debbie said.

"Don't be," I said. "I wasn't always like that. It's been a recent change. I guess I have come to realize that you never know what's down the road so it's a good idea to be considerate to people while you can be. There will come a time when it's too late to do that, and then you will regret that you weren't nicer when you had the chance."

"What are you, a Buddhist or something? You're spouting off some deep stuff."

"Sorry, I'm not trying to be all preachy. It's just the way I have been feeling of late."

"No need to be sorry," Debbie said. "I like it. I don't want you to change. If anything, I want to start treating people more like you do. See that," she said reaching over and punching me in the shoulder, "you are starting to have a positive effect on me." Like it was timed, the porch lights flicked off and on. Mr. Gravely was back on duty.

I was only too happy to end this conversation. I stood and gave Debbie a hug and peck on the lips. She pulled me in tighter and gave me a long, tongue-laced kiss. The porch lights flicked on and off several times in a row. It was time to go.

Driving home, I thought about whether having the knowledge of what was going to happen to my friends and family in the future was a blessing or a curse. Would I or should I try to interfere? Should I encourage Mike to do something else other than join the Army when he graduates? Would it make a difference? Who's to say he wouldn't end up in a car crash if he didn't join the Army? Then I'm right back to the question that has haunted me since I have arrived back here: do the decisions I make here and now change the future? I was no closer to an answer, but I was becoming ever more fearful of never having the chance to return to my previous life and Grace.

Chapter 24

This coming weekend was the Fourth of July. Fifty years ago, my lifeguarding career almost ended during that holiday. I wondered as I sat in the stand watching the pool if I should try and change what happened. It could possibly save me a lot of trouble. All week leading up to the Fourth I debated what I should do. Here I am, possibly tampering with the past and having no idea of what it would mean to the future.

The Fourth dawned a beautiful day. By nine it was obvious that today was going to be a scorcher which meant the holiday crowd at the pool would be even larger than normal. I was a bit disappointed that I was scheduled to work the whole day because my parents were throwing a picnic at the house. My aunts, uncles, cousins, and neighbors would all be there. There would be cornhole games going constantly. Of course, in those days it was called beanbags. My Uncle Carl's invention, hoops, would be played all day as well. Tire rims looking like giant quoits would be tossed onto steel pipes that stuck up three feet from the ground. I still have the original set of hoops in my garage from fifty years ago. The charcoal grill would be going all day with dogs and burgers being cooked up. Ice-filled coolers would be crammed with beer and soda. I was sorry I wasn't going to have the chance to be there.

Mr. Hutchinson called a guard meeting shortly before the noon opening.

"Everybody needs to stay sharp today," he started. "The place is going to be packed and we don't want any accidents today. We may have to go to an extra guard on the main pool if it gets crazy. I'll let you know. Also, it's going to be hot today. Keep water bottles handy so you don't get dehydrated. Any questions?" We all looked at each other. Nobody said a word. "Alright, get ready. We open in five minutes."

A crowd was already lined up at the front gate. It was going to be a busy day. I jogged over to the snack bar to say hello to Debbie who I hadn't seen yet today. She was busy getting everything in order for what promised to be a crazy day.

"Happy Fourth," I said.

"Judging by the number of people out front already, I think today is going to be nuts," she responded.

"Don't forget, some of us are hanging out at the close of the day to watch the fireworks here" I reminded her.

"If I can still stand, I'll be there."

"Should be fun. I'll check in on you during my breaks." With that I trotted over to the baby pool where I had my first shift. Ten minutes after we opened, the grassy area between the main pool and the baby pool was filled with towels and beach chairs. Another twenty minutes and there wasn't a grassy spot left anywhere around the pools. Busy was an understatement.

The one good thing about a day like this is that it went fast. There was very little down time. By one, Hutchinson added the third guard on the main pool which meant fewer breaks. By two, the temperature was already in the mid-nineties which meant more people were in the pool. Sitting in the guard chair, I looked out over a solid mass of people. It was difficult to see the bottom of the pool. Hutchison started calling for fifteen -minute adult swims every hour which served three purposes: First it cleared the pool of all the kids forcing them to take a break. Second, it gave the adults a chance to have a more peaceful swim without splashing, screaming kids in their faces. Third; it gave the guards including me a chance to catch our breath. I felt sorry for Debbie because I knew that every adult swim meant the kids would descend on the snack bar like a horde of locusts.

I had dinner from five to six so I took the opportunity to peddle home to enjoy what I could of the picnic. I grabbed a burger, a dog, and some of my Aunt Cile's potato salad. In all the years since, I have never had any potato salad that rivaled hers. It was a treat to be able to taste that again. I joined the adults who were sitting in their lawn chairs in a big circle in the shade. As I finished gulping down my dinner, I paused and looked around the circle. There were so many people I hadn't seen in years gathered around me; my other two uncles and aunts and various cousins were all here. This is what family is all about…right here…right now. I missed those days. Those big family/neighborhood picnics don't happen anymore. Reluctantly I stood and said my goodbyes before hopping on my bike and getting back to the madness at the pool.

Most days the crowd at the pool after dinner time would have diminished considerably by six. Today was not most days. I was surprised how full the parking lot was as I locked my bike in the rack. I had a few minutes before I was back on duty. I decided to check in with Debbie to see how she was managing. Business was brisk and she wasn't smiling. I decided not to mention that I had been home for dinner. She looked up and saw me. I gave her a big smile and waved. I got a quick smileless nod in return. I took my cue and left.

Finally, by seven, the pool started to empty. A few minutes before nine, John McHern, the assistant manager, came on the PA system and announced that the pool complex was closing in ten minutes and everybody had to be out by nine. I think every guard there breathed a sigh of relief knowing that we had gotten through the busiest day of the year without any serious incidents.

As I was beginning my cleanup duties around the pool when Debbie came to see me.

"I just finished closing up. I'm beat. Would you mind terribly if I skipped tonight?"

"Are you sure? It's going to be fun."

"I know, but I'm sweaty and smelly and tired. I don't think I would be very good company. Plus, I would need a ride home." I realized that would be a problem. I had ridden my bike. If I had thought this through, I would have asked my dad if I could take the car back after dinner. But I didn't and so now I have no way to get Debbie home after the party. Maybe history does repeat itself. All day I could not remember if Debbie had been with me to this same party fifty years ago. Apparently, she had not and now I know why. She didn't have a ride home.

"I'm really sorry. I rode my bike."

"That's fine," she answered. "It's better this way. I just want to get home and take a nice long cool shower, put my feet up, and relax. You can tell me all about the party tomorrow."

"I understand. We'll do something tomorrow night. We'll have our own celebration a day late."

"That sounds nice," she said. "I need to run. My dad is picking me up out front." She gave me a hug and a quick kiss and was gone. I was left with my thoughts about the upcoming party which was about to start in twenty minutes when the fireworks at Bethlehem Stadium would commence. I had decisions to make.

John McHern locked the front gate after bringing in supplies which included bags of chips and pretzels, a watermelon, a sheet cake, and a case of beer. The party was ready to start. We decided to climb on top of the pumphouse to get a better view of the fireworks which had just sent up its initial display. Besides myself and John, there were three other guards, Susie, Margo, and Bob. Susie and Bob had brought dates bringing our total to seven for our party.

The view was better than I thought it would be. The sound was on a delay because of the distance to the stadium. We sat and oohed and aahed and ate and drank. It wasn't long before the first piece of cake flew through the air and hit Bob right in the face. I'm not certain, but I think it was John who was the culprit. One thing led to another and as the fireworks were coming to their grand finale, a major food fight ensued on the top of the pumphouse. Everybody was splattered with cake and watermelon and splashed with beer. It only stopped because there was no more food to throw. The group climbed down from the pumphouse and stripped to our bathing suits and jumped into the pool to rinse off.

That led to the second crazy part of the evening. John, Bob, and I started doing some interesting stuff off the diving boards including

133

riding a bicycle from lost and found off the diving boards. Another favorite was the horse and rider move. The first person would take a big high jump off the board and spread his legs. The second person, following close behind would dive low between the first person's legs. Timing was critical. If it was off, both people would crash midair and fall into the water. After mastering the move on the low board, Bob and I even managed to do it off the high board without killing ourselves. The culmination of the evening's fun was riding a tricycle off the diving boards. We just had to make sure that we weren't still sitting on the tricycle when it hit the water. That could prove to be very painful and possibly ruin any hopes for children in the future. The girls were laughing hysterically as we continued with our antics off the diving boards. The grand finale was riding the tricycle off the high board. John did it and dared Bob and I to follow suit. Bob agreed to try it which showed some real guts. I agreed to do it, secure with the knowledge that I had successfully done the same thing fifty years ago. Bob had a close call, barely clearing the tricycle before he hit the water. I retrieved the tricycle and hoisted it up the ladder of the high dive. I positioned myself on the seat and pedaled furiously to reach the end of the board while the others cheered me on from below. As soon as the back wheels of the tricycle left the board, I leapt and dove, landing safely beyond the falling tricycle.

It was going on eleven before we decided to call a halt to the party. John said since he was opening the pool tomorrow, we could wait to clean off the top of the pumphouse until tomorrow morning. I knew from experience his suggestion was a bad idea.

"What if it rains?" I asked.

"What if it does?" John said.

"Don't you think it will be a mess?" I asked knowing full well that it would rain. History told me that there would be a bad thunderstorm later this evening which nobody knew except me. The torrential rain and wind would wash all the cake and watermelon and other assorted stuff off the roof and it would slide down the wall closest to the pool leaving a pink sheen on the wall and sidewalk. Because of the storm, Hutchinson would come in on his day off and see the mess we left behind. Needless to say, he would not be happy with us and it would definitely be the last after-hours party at the swim club this summer.

"Hutchinson is off tomorrow," John replied. "We can clean it up tomorrow morning. He'll never know."

"According to the weather forecast I heard, there is supposed to be a bad thunderstorm tonight." I lied. "What if Hutchinson comes back to check on the filters?" I could see the others started to understand the potential risk of leaving it until tomorrow. John looked around at the others. He could read the same thing in their faces.

"Alright, if it makes you guys feel better, we'll clean it up tonight." Everybody agreed that was a good idea. There was so much stuff on the roof that John finally just took the hose and sprayed it off. The rest of us gathered up beer cans, watermelon rinds, and other assorted food bits and stuffed it all in trash bags which we deposited in the big dumpster just outside the gate.

It took over a half an hour before we were all outside and watched John lock the gate. I climbed on my bike and rode home. It was just before midnight when I walked into the house.

"It must have been a good party," Dad said as I entered.

"It was fun. We watched the fireworks, ate some snacks, and then stayed for a swim."

"How did Debbie get home?" he asked.

"She wasn't there. She was too tired after working the snack bar all day."

"Who was at the party?" I gave him the list of people and once he heard that the assistant manager was there, he seemed to relax. What he didn't know was that it was John who started the food fight, brought the beer, and started the whole thing with the tricycles off the diving boards. Not exactly the most responsible assistant manager a place could have.

135

Somewhere around 3 A.M., thunder woke me from my sleep right on cue. As promised, the storm was a doozy. I eventually fell back asleep knowing at least Hutchinson wouldn't walk into the pool and find the mess we left. Check- one more item fixed.

CHAPTER 25

The next morning Hutchinson was at the pool when I arrived. He was quieter than usual; probably because he had to come in on his day off to check the filters. I didn't give it much thought until I ran into John. He didn't have much to say either. Something was wrong; I could sense it.

Thirty minutes before opening, Hutchinson announced a guard meeting in his office. There was no way it could be about the party because we had cleaned everything up before we left. I fixed our mistake from the past... or so I thought.

"First off, let me just say I'm disappointed," Hutchinson started. All of us were taking peeks back and forth as Hutchinson continued. "I put my trust in all of you when I gave permission for the staff to watch the fireworks from the pool after closing time. Your actions reflect on me and the swim club. Our members expect the staff to set a good example. You're lucky I was able to defuse the situation with the person who called me last night. He wanted to call the police and have you all arrested. I assured him I would deal with the situation and getting the police involved was not necessary."

"It's my responsibility," John interrupted the manager.

"No interruptions, please," Hutchinson barked. "I'll be dealing with you in a few minutes. If I could, I would fire everybody that was here last night. Obviously, I can't do that and keep the pool open. Underage drinking is no laughing matter. If one of you had gotten into an accident last night, it would be my head on the chopping block. Add in the crazy stunts off the diving boards that could have resulted in serious injury, and I'm at a loss for words. It is your job, to keep people safe, to stop people from doing things that could cause injury to themselves or others. Then I come to find out that you threw any semblance of common sense away last night. How can the members expect you to keep them safe when you don't practice safe habits yourself? Needless to say, after-hour parties in the future are banned. Consider yourselves on probation for the rest of the summer. One more problem or complaint and you will not get another chance. Now get out of here and get this place ready to open. John, you stay; we're not finished."

We all scattered and made ourselves busy. Hutchinson was on the warpath. I imagined John was getting ripped up one side and down the other. Five minutes later, John stormed out of the manager's office and slammed the door behind him. I caught up with him in the locker room.

"Everything alright?" I asked.

"No, Hutchinson told me he was demoting me. He told me he could not have an assistant manager who he didn't trust. I told him that I thought he was overreacting over one bad decision I had made. He began to list all of my bad decisions; supplying beer to minors, not only allowing but participating in all the crazy stuff off the diving boards, lying about it when he first called me into his office earlier, not taking responsibility for this whole mess. Didn't you hear me say that I took full responsibility?"

"I did hear you say that," I answered. "Do you want me to tell Hutchinson I heard you say that?" I asked.

"Don't bother. It doesn't matter anymore. I quit and told him to stuff it where the sun don't shine." With that he grabbed the stuff in his locker and stomped out of the pool complex. I was in shock. This was much worse than what happened fifty years ago. How could that be? I fixed it.

I had a few minutes before my first shift. I walked over to say hi to Debbie. She was stocking shelves and filling napkin holders. She would not look at me as she kept busy. This day was getting stranger by the minute.

"What's up?" I asked, trying to make sense of what was going on. She started to tear up.

"I'm so sorry," she said. I was confused. Why was she sorry? Did she hear us getting yelled at by Hutchinson? Even if she had, what would it matter to her? She wasn't even there.

"Why are you sorry?" I asked. "I'm confused. "

"You don't know, do you?" she asked.

"Know what? I have no idea what you are talking about."

"Williams, you have ten seconds to get to where you belong," Hutchinson snarled as he entered the snack bar. I looked at Debbie trying to make sense of what she just apologized for and still have no idea what that might be. I had no choice, but to hightail it out of there. This was not a day to give Hutchinson a reason to fire me.

I sat through my first three guard stations thinking of nothing else but what Debbie had said. I could not come up with a plausible scenario that would explain why she needed to apologize to me. My first break, I headed back to the snack bar. I was surprised to see that Hutchinson was still at the snack bar. I beat a hasty retreat. My conversation with Debbie would need to wait until later.

All day I could not get Debbie's apology out of my mind. What was going on? None of this happened fifty years ago. How is this possible. I fixed it. Hutchinson was never supposed to find out about the party… but he did. I realized that I had my answer about the effect of changing the past. Changes that I made would have an effect on what happened after in the future…and apparently, despite good intentions, not always for the better.

I checked the snack bar before I left for the day at six. Debbie was already gone. She hadn't even said goodbye to me. Something was up. Riding home, I reflected on my day. It had not been a good one and somehow, I didn't think I knew the worst of it yet.

CHAPTER 26

I didn't say a word to my parents about the trouble at the pool. I didn't need another lecture. As soon as dinner was over, I gave Debbie a call. Her father answered the phone.

"Who is this?" he asked.

"Hi, this is Jason," I responded.

"Stay away from my daughter. I don't need you filling her head with bad ideas."

"I have no idea what you are talking about," I replied.

"You heard me. Stay away from my daughter. I don't want to have to tell you again." There was a click on the other end of the line. He had hung up on me. I knew he wasn't crazy about me, but I had no idea what I had done to upset him this much.

I decided to go see Trip. Maybe he could help me figure out where I had gone wrong. I rode my bike over to his house and found him on the back patio. Bonnie was snuggled next to him.

"What's going on," Trip asked. "How are things going with Debbie?"

"Funny that you ask," I replied.

"Uh-oh, this doesn't sound good," Bonnie said.

I went on to explain that things had been going just fine until today.

"We had a good talk a few nights ago and everything was good. There was a party at the pool after closing. Debbie had been too tired to come. She went home. I went to the party myself. Things did get a bit out of control at the party. Somehow Hutchinson, the manager, found out about it. He was pissed and even fired the assistant manager, John."

"So how does Debbie fit into this?" Trip asked.

"That's what I'm trying to figure out. I got to the pool today and she couldn't even look at me. She started crying and told me that she was sorry. Problem is that I have no idea what she is sorry about."

"Did you ask her to explain?" Bonnie asked.

"Hutchinson chased me out of the snack bar before I could get an answer. Debbie left before I had a chance to talk to her. After dinner, I called her house. Her father, who hated me already, answered and informed me that I was to stay away from his daughter. He slammed the phone down before I had a chance to ask him what I had done to upset him. I could understand it better if she had been at the party last night and found out that there was beer there, but she wasn't there. She had no idea what went on at the party and neither did her father."

"Could Debbie have talked to one of the other guards before you got to the pool today? Maybe she knew what went on at the party."

"Even if she did, it wasn't like I was cheating on her. And that still doesn't explain why her father is so angry with me."

"There's a piece you are missing," Trip said. "There has to be because otherwise this whole thing makes no sense."

"I agree, but what is it that we're not seeing?" I asked throwing my hands in the air in frustration.

"Is it possible that someone else saw what was going on at the pool and reported it back to Debbie?" Bonnie asked.

"Somebody saw something because they called Hutchinson at his home to complain. According to Hutchinson, whoever it was wanted to call the police and he talked them out of that idea assuring the person he would deal with the matter himself."

"So, whoever it was that went to see Hutchinson somehow has a connection to Debbie or her father," Trip suggested. The three of us stayed silent for a few seconds mulling that idea over in our heads.

"I think you may be onto somethings, Trip," I answered. "It's the only thing that makes even a little sense. Maybe Debbie was apologizing because she knew that somebody her father knew reported you guys to Hutchinson and she knew you would get into trouble."

"Once our mystery person told Debbie's father, he figured you were there and that is all he needed," Bonnie said.

"I don't know what it is with her father," I said. "It is obvious that he doesn't trust her much at all. Then she starts to hang around with me who he considers a bad influence. I don't know why, but he didn't like me very much from the beginning. I must admit, it makes sense."

"Hey, we're your friends," Trip said.

"I really appreciate the two of you helping me unravel this mess. At least I'll be able to get some sleep tonight. Thanks."

"Anytime, my friend." I gave each of them a hug and rode back home trying to figure out a way I could change Mr. Gravely's opinion of me. I knew it wasn't going to be easy, but I had to try. None of this happened fifty years ago; nothing even close. This was definitely going to have implications on my future. This was so different, that it is very unlikely I will end up on the path that will take me back to Grace. That is completely unacceptable. I have to fix this. I have to get my life back on its previous track. The thought of my world without Grace... I would not be able to deal with that.

Even though I now had a plausible explanation of what was going on, I still needed confirmation from Debbie. I needed to know exactly what I was dealing with before I could make a plan to repair it. I had to find a way to get Mr. Gravely to see that I was a decent guy and not some degenerate who was going to corrupt his daughter's morals. Of course, there was always the possibility that the conclusion that we reached tonight was wrong. I had no other answers.

I awoke and the first thing on my mind was Debbie and how to fix it with her father. One thing for sure, I had to talk to Debbie. It was my day off today. I didn't need to go to the pool, but that was my best chance to talk to her. If I was lucky, maybe Hutchinson wasn't in this morning. Considering he had fired the assistant manager yesterday, I

142

realized he almost had to be there. I would take my chances. Maybe he wouldn't realize that I had off today. Maybe he wouldn't care. If worse came to worse, maybe I could volunteer to pick up a few hours of time because John wasn't employed anymore. I headed to the pool, more nervous than I had been about anything in a long time. What I was about to find out would reshape my whole future.

CHAPTER 27

I saw Hutchinson disappear into the filter room as I entered the pool area. I wasted no time and hurried to the snack bar. Debbie was there restocking inventory.

"We need to talk," I said without wasting time. She turned and looked at me.

"This isn't a good time," she answered and went back to work.

"This can't wait," I said. "I am thoroughly confused and I need some answers." She turned, hands on hips, and huffed.

"What do you want to know?" she asked, sounding annoyed.

"How did your father know about the pool party? Why would he even care? You weren't there."

"He knew about the party because he was there," she said.

"What do you mean that he was there?"

"He drove to the pool and watched from the fence. He saw the beer and all the crazy stuff you guys were doing."

"Why would he come to the pool?"

"He was looking for me."

"Why would he be looking for you? You were home...weren't you?" I started to get a bad feeling about where this conversation was going.

"I wasn't at home," she said.

"But you said you were too tired to go to the party. If you weren't at home, where were you?"

"I was out." Those three words hung in the air as I tried to make sense of what they meant.

"You were out? With who?" I asked.

"It doesn't matter," she answered. And then suddenly I understood. She let her father think that she was out with me at the pool party, but she was with somebody else. I was forbidden to see her because she lied to her father.

"Wow," I muttered over and over. "I thought we had a good thing going. Obviously, I was wrong. So, who was it?"

"Nobody you know."

"Tell me anyway."

"We dated my sophomore year. He was a freshman in college. My father caught us in a delicate situation if you get my drift, more than once. By the end of my sophomore year, I was forbidden to see him. The thing was we snuck around and I continued to see him. My father found out and was furious. It didn't stop until Mark got tired of me. Anyway, he was home from college for the summer and he called me."

"Hmmph," I mumbled. "Now I understand why your father doesn't trust you. And now I know that I can't either."

"It was a mistake and I'm sorry."

"You can say that again. Damn... and I was really starting to like you." I stepped out of the snack bar and ran right into Hutchinson.

"What are you doing here?" he asked. "I thought it is your day off."

"It is, but I thought maybe you needed someone to fill John's hours."

"That is very thoughtful of you, but I hired a new assistant last night." He pointed to the guy standing next to him. "This is George Little, the pool's new assistant manager." We shook hands and I headed for the exit without giving Debbie a backward glance. I reached the bike rack and heard someone calling me. It was Debbie.

"Wait a minute. I don't want you to leave being upset with me."

"I guess you can't get everything you want," I answered turning back to fiddle with my bike lock.

"I made a mistake. I don't want to lose you."

"You should have thought about that before you hooked up with Mark. Does your father even know that you saw Mark again?" Her silence gave me my answer. "I didn't think so. You let me take the blame for being a bad influence on you. Nice… real nice."

"Come on, you know I like you," she said.

"Did you and Mark fool around?" I asked. Again, her silence told me the answer. "That's just great. I guess because I wanted to go slow, you needed to find someone else to take care of your needs. You're a piece of work. Say hi to Mark for me next time he shows up for a little bootie call." I pulled my bike out of the rack and climbed aboard. I was done with her. It was time to go in a different direction…despite future implications.

"Please, don't be like this," she begged.

"What does it matter?" I asked. "Your father has forbidden me to see you. So, even if I wanted to, I can't."

"I'll fix it with my dad. I'll explain everything to him and let him know that I wasn't at the pool party."

"It isn't going to matter. He saw me with the beer. By the way, John McHern got fired because of your deceit. You might want to apologize to him too. Look, I have to go. I have plans to see someone today." I had no plans to see anybody, but I wanted to hurt her.

"You're not wasting any time," she said, her attitude changing on the fly.

"Why should I? I'm not seeing anyone."

"Give me a second chance…please." She pleaded. I appeared to think it over before answering.

146

"Yeah, I'll think about a second chance when you tell your father what really happened the other night. In the meantime, I need to give some serious thought about whether or not I can ever trust you again. To be completely truthful, I'm not even sure if I want to see you anymore. So, if there is nothing else, I'm going to head out and enjoy my day off."

Tears began to form in her eyes, and I almost cracked... but I didn't. She didn't deserve my understanding...at least not right now. I pedaled out of the parking lot and did not look back.

I didn't feel like going home so I pedaled around town with no particular destination in mind. The longer I rode, the angrier I became. She was out with an old boyfriend; that was just dandy! My future had just taken a major hit. Nothing like this happened fifty years ago. I would have been crushed the first time around. At one time, I had thought that Debbie was the one. This time around, I knew that was not going to be the case. My biggest concern was what this change would do to my chances of a life with Grace. I seemed to be moving further and further away from that possibility. I needed to figure out a way back to my former life and I needed to do it now.

CHAPTER 28

I rode down to Monocacy Park. Being a weekday, there were not many people around. The creek was running higher than normal due to the big storm two nights ago. I took the road that led back to the stone pavilions that stood next to the small waterfall. A small bridge connected the two sides of the creek right in front of the pavilions.

I climbed the stairs to the east pavilion and leaned against the railing. I watched as the water cascaded over a series of concrete steps before continuing on its journey downstream. It was a beautiful spot, one of my favorites in the whole town. I had been coming to this spot for many years; first as a fishing spot and later as a nice place to take a walk with a date. Now here I was again.

I was mesmerized by the falling water as I contemplated how I was ever going to get back to my real life. I tried to remember what I had done the night before I woke up in the past. Did I do anything out of the ordinary that might have triggered my time travel? I could not think of anything that was unusual or different about that day. I had been having discussions with my friends and Grace about what the best years in our lives which had been triggered by the invitation to my fiftieth high school reunion. Maybe my return was as simple as spending the entire day thinking about my life with Grace. Maybe I would wake up tomorrow and be back where I belonged. Somehow, I didn't think it would be that simple.

I initially thought that being able to fix some of my regrets from my youth was a good thing. Now I wasn't so sure. By tinkering with the past, I may have skewed the future. This is strange talking about my former life. I wonder if this has ever happened to anyone else? I have so many questions and can't seem to find a single answer. This isn't the kind of thing you can talk to people about; they will think I am crazy. Maybe I am. Maybe this is all a dream... a very long dream.

My thoughts turn to Debbie. What a mess! Certainly, nothing like this had happened fifty years ago. We dated for a couple of years. Over time, we drifted apart and eventually moved on to other people.

There was no major fight. There was no sneaking around with someone else… at least I didn't think there was. I considered a new possibility; maybe Debbie had been sneaking around behind my back previously only I never found out about it. Maybe the same thing had happened, but I was oblivious. I didn't think so. Another thing that was different; her father was not openly hostile to me. What had caused that this time around? One thing I knew for certain; it was impossible to stick to the script from my past. Maybe in the long run it didn't make any difference. Maybe it was all preordained to happen. Maybe I would end up in the same place in the future no matter what happened in the past. I latched onto that idea because it gave me hope for a future with Grace.

"What are the chances?" a voice from behind me brought me out of my trance. I turned to see Linda, the girl I danced with at the prom.

"This is a surprise," I said. "What are you doing here?"

"I come here when I want to be alone," she answered.

"You want me to leave?" I asked. "I don't want to be intruding on your private time."

"No, actually I'm glad you're here. I could use a friend." With that, the tears began. "I'm sorry."

"No need to be sorry," I replied. "What's going on that has you so upset?"

"You remember Darren, the guy that gave you a hard time at the diner after the prom?"

"I remember him."

"Well after that night at the diner, we started seeing each other again. The other night I see him sitting in his car in a lip-lock with some blond."

"What did you do?"

"Believe it or not, I walked right up to his car and banged on his window. The two of them practically jumped out of their pants. He flung open the car door and got out before remembering his zipper was still open. He started telling me that it wasn't what it looked like as he stands there pulling up his zipper. Meanwhile I can see the blond in his car buttoning her blouse as he continues to try and convince me that nothing was going on. What a jerk!"

"This is ironic," I said. "I just found out this morning that a girl I had been dating had a fling with her ex-boyfriend. To make it even worse, her father thought she was out with me and now has forbidden me to see her anymore…not that I really want to anyway."

"That is ironic, and then we both end up here at the same time. Maybe fate is trying to tell us something."

"I think it already told us one thing; that we're not very good at selecting trustworthy partners." That brought a laugh from Linda. She pointed to a bag she had in her hand.

"I brought some lunch. Want to join me?"

"I would like that."

Linda emptied the bag on the table. There was a sandwich, a small bag of chips, an apple, and a can of Coke. We sat and talked as we shared her lunch. She had a summer job working at BonTon in the Westgate Mall behind the cosmetic counter. We continued to talk as we ate lunch. She explained how her parents had her repeat first grade when they moved here halfway through the year which explained how she was a year older than I was and still in the same grade. I told her about the pool and the whole fiasco on the Fourth.

"Would you like to go for a walk? she asked.

"Sure," I answered as I looked for a spot to lock my bike. I chose a railing at the back of the pavilion.

"Have you ever walked the trail above the falls?" she asked.

"Not in a long time," I answered honestly. She grabbed my hand and pulled me in the direction of the upper trail. I knew from experience that very few people ever walked in this area.

It was shaping up to be a beautiful day. The sun was climbing in the sky. The temperature was rising. A gentle breeze gently stirred the leaves on the trees. Neither of us spoke as we walked along the trail. The further we went, the more the woods encroached on the creek. Soon we were in almost constant shade from the trees above.

We hadn't seen a single person since we started, not that I was surprised. It was like we were all alone in the world, two lost souls looking for love in all the wrong places. I think that was a song lyric from somewhere in my past.

"Do you like to swim?" Linda broke the silence.

"Love it," I said.

"I know a good spot a little further up the trail. You game?"

"I don't have my bathing suit," I said naively.

"Neither do I," Linda answered and laughed. "It doesn't matter to me if it doesn't matter to you." I recovered in time so as not to look like a total innocent.

"Sounds good to me," I said. "Lead on." She stepped up the pace as she led me along the trail. I was going up the creek and definitely did not have a paddle.

Five minutes later we came to a wide bend in the creek. The water was deeper in this area. Linda wasted no time starting to disrobe. I was a little self-conscious but soon found myself pulling off my clothes. I watched Linda to see exactly how far she was going to disrobe. Her t-shirt fell to the ground revealing a perky set of breasts. She slid her shorts down, but much to my relief, left her panties on. She ditched her sandals and waded into the water.

"Come on, pokey. Don't be shy," she said as she slid into the water. I pulled off my shirt and shorts and kicked off my sneakers. I

151

stepped into the water It was chillier than the pool water, that was for sure. I waded to the deeper section and sunk to chest level.

"Isn't this a beautiful spot?" Linda asked.

"It is and the company isn't bad either," I said warming to the opportunity before me as the sky peeked between the leaves.

"I couldn't agree more." She waded over toward me and wrapped her arms around my neck. She pulled me close and kissed me. The cold water was helping to keep things under control for which I was glad. After a few minutes, she pulled back and looked at me.

"You are such a nice guy. Most guys would have been all hands and would have ruined the moment," she said. I had no idea what I was supposed to say here. All my years had not prepared me for this very unexpected moment. "I hope I haven't shocked you," she said.

"Not at all," I lied. "This is really nice. A beautiful spot with a beautiful girl. It doesn't get any better." With that she wrapped her arms around me again and kissed me even harder than the first time.

"I can't tell you how much your words mean to me," she said.

"I think we both needed this," I answered.

"I think you are absolutely right," she answered back.

We stayed in the water for another ten minutes and then climbed out and found a grassy spot in the sun to dry off. We lay there together, both hurting in our separate ways. After the sun had warmed us, we got dressed and headed back down the trail hand in hand. There was not much conversation on the return trip, both of us feeling a little awkward I suspect after sharing an intimate moment.

"Well, this day has certainly been a welcome diversion," I said as we reached the pavilion.

"I wish it could be like this every day," she answered. I wasn't sure what her comment was implying. I knew I could really enjoy getting to know her better, but I didn't know if she was interested in jumping right back into another relationship. For that matter, I wasn't sure if I should be either. Would this new wrinkle move me further away from Grace or bring me closer or matter at all? I decided to throw caution to the wind since I had no way of knowing if this would change anything.

"Can I call you?" I asked. She hesitated before answering which I didn't take as a good sign.

"Call me as in to talk or call me as in to ask me out on a date?" she asked. She looked at me waiting for an answer. I weighed the options. I wasn't really interested in calling to talk. What would be the point? My decision was easier than I thought it would be.

"I would be calling to ask you out on a date," I said watching closely for her reaction.

"I would like that," she answered. "I would like that a great deal. I need a nice guy in my life."

"Any chance you are free to go to the movies tonight?" I asked. She laughed.

"My, my, you don't waste any time," she said.

"I don't want to take the chance that some other nice guy will come along and sweep you off your feet before I have a chance."

"Call me later. I have some plans with my parents, but let me see if I can change them. I don't want to take the chance either that some hot girl will come along and steal you." It was my turn to laugh.

I walked her to her car and we kissed again. I watched her drive down the road back to the park entrance. I could hardly believe what just happened. This kind of stuff definitely did not happen to me the first time I was here. I wondered where this was going to lead. I wondered if Debbie and I were finished for good. I guess I did know the answer to that question already; we were done for the foreseeable future. I was moving on to a new horizon. What would the long-term consequences be? I had no way of knowing, so I might as well enjoy the ride... at least that's what I told myself in this particular moment.

Chapter 29

"Match point," I called across the net. Rob and I were one point away from closing out the match against Greg and Trip. I took aim at Trip across the net from me. I tossed the ball high and went for the ace. The ball sailed wide and I readied myself for my second serve. Once again, I tossed the ball high, but this time just tapped it lightly to get it inbounds. The volley was on. After several volleys back and forth Rob put it away at the net. Final score was 6-4, 3-6, 6-3.

The four of us collapsed onto the bench at the side of the court. Despite the early hour, the day was already warm. We sat emptying our water bottles as we cooled off.

"What did you do last night?" Trip asked. "I called, but your dad said you were out." I laughed. "What's so funny?"

"You're not going to believe this," I said and laughed again.

"This must be good," Greg jumped into the conversation.

"Yeah, spill the beans," Rob added.

"Remember I told you about the whole party fiasco?" I asked. They all shook their heads to the affirmative. "I got to the bottom of the story. It turns out the person who reported us to the manager was Debbie's father. He came by the pool and saw what was going on."

"Wait a minute," Trip said. "I thought Debbie didn't go to the party."

"She didn't, but her father didn't know that."

"Wasn't she at home?" Rob asked.

"This is where the story gets interesting. It turns out that she went out with her old boyfriend but neglected to tell her father. Her father still thought she was with me at the pool party."

"Holy moly," Trip said. "She cheated on you?"

"Yes, she did and now her father thinks I'm scum of the earth and I'm forbidden to see his daughter."

"Do you even want to see her after what she did?" asked Greg.

"Not right now... maybe never. She has apologized over and over and says she wants to be with me. But now there is a wrinkle."

"Uh-oh...a wrinkle," said Trip. "I hate wrinkles."

"Yesterday I went to the pool to talk to Debbie. That's when I found about her ex-boyfriend and her father. After our talk I rode around town since it was my day off. I ended up down at Monocacy Park. I'm standing in one of the pavilions by the waterfall and I hear a voice behind me. I turn around and it is Linda."

"Linda from the prom?" Trip asked.

"Correct... Linda from the prom. She invites me to share lunch with her. We sit and talk and I come to find out that her on and off boyfriend cheated on her again. I share my story with her about my cheating girlfriend. We sort of bond over our troubles. We go for a walk in the upper part of the creek. We end up skinny-dipping."

"What!" my three friends shout out in unison.

"I know...right? It is unbelievable, isn't it?"

"You are the freakin' luckiest person I know," Rob said.

"You are one lucky son of a gun," Greg added.

"Let me guess," Trip said, "you were out with Linda last night."

"Correct."

"You break up with one girl and on the same day you end up skinny-dipping with a different girl. I need to know your secret," Trip said.

"Clean living, good luck, and charm... I guess," I answered.

"Time to go," Rob said. "It's getting deep."

"I guess you're not getting back together with Debbie anytime soon?" Trip asked as we walked to his car.

"I don't think so. I think I'm going to see what happens with Linda. We had a really good time yesterday. At least her father doesn't hate me."

"Have you even met Linda's father?" Trip asked.

"No."

"That explains it. Just give it time."

"Very funny. And here I thought you were my friend."

"Bonnie won't believe this," Trip said.

"I'm not sure I believe it either."

"You're working today, right?" Trip asked.

"Eleven to seven."

"Are you going to say anything to Debbie to make your breakup official?"

"I sort of did yesterday. I told her I had plans with somebody else."

"I thought you told me it was a surprise when you ran into Linda at the park?"

"It was. I just said that to Debbie to annoy her. I figured she deserved it."

"This story just keeps getting better and better. You tell Debbie that you're going to see someone and presto… the stars all fall into alignment and you meet someone completely unexpectedly. Wow- seriously… I need some of your luck."

Trip dropped me off at home a few minutes later. I rushed in, took a shower, grabbed an apple, and headed to the pool for my shift. I wasn't sure how to play this with Debbie. I was still concerned about how far off I was now straying from my past. I wasn't sure what I could do about it or whether I wanted to do anything about it. There would certainly be less drama in my life going out with Linda. Even if I wanted to still see Debbie, I could see no way around her father. By the time I arrived at the front gate of the pool, I had decided: I was going to ride with Linda and see where it might go.

I purposely avoided the snack bar. I didn't want there to be a scene. It was an average day for the pool in July; a good crowd but certainly nothing like the Fourth had been. I moved from station to station guarding the pool. At break time I retreated to the pool office and stayed there to cool off and to avoid Debbie.

As seven approached, I realized that there was a good chance that Debbie would be leaving about the same time as me. When my shift was done, I hurried to the locker room and decided to take a shower to kill some time. After I dried off and dressed, I peeked out of the locker room just in time to see Debbie climbing into her father's car and drive away. I walked to the bike rack, pleased that I had managed to avoid Debbie all day.

As soon as I got home, I gave Linda a call and asked if she was busy. She wasn't and soon after I finished dinner, a horn blew out on the street. It was Linda.

"Who's waiting for you?" Dad asked.

"It's Linda, the girl I met at the junior prom," I answered.

"Oh," was my father's only comment as he glanced at my mother who also looked a bit puzzled.

"I'll explain it all when I get home," I said as I rushed out the front door.

"What do you want to do?" I asked Linda as I slid into the front seat.

"Patti invited us over. She and her boyfriend are going to listen to some new music. Her boyfriend bought some albums including the new Doors album and the new Credence Clearwater Revival album. Do

157

you like either one of those bands?" Like them? I loved the *Soft Parade* and *Green River*. I had listened to both of them more times than I could count in the last fifty years.

"It sounds like fun," I answered. "The Doors are one of my favorite groups."

Fifteen minutes later, I was sitting in Patti's basement as the strains of *Tell All the People* by the Doors swirled around me with Linda snuggled up next to me. I was liking this new arrangement... liking it maybe too much. I thought of Grace for just a fleeting moment before I pushed that thought out of my mind. What the hell was I doing? I wasn't sure, but for now I was going to enjoy this... especially since I had no idea if I ever would return to my former life.

CHAPTER 30

I was surprised to see Mom waiting for me when I walked through the front door after Linda had dropped me off.

"I hate to pry, but what is going on?" she asked. "I thought you were seeing Debbie."

"I was," I said as I tried to figure out exactly how to exclude certain parts of what led up to our breakup. "There are several problems. First, her father doesn't seem to like me."

"Have you given him a reason not to like you?" Mom asked.

"Honestly. I don't think so. Debbie kept telling me that her father didn't trust her and it had nothing to do with me, but I don't think that's the case."

"Let me remind you," Mom started, "you aren't dating her father."

"I know that, but it makes it difficult for Debbie and me. But there are other reasons too. I found out that she went out with her old boyfriend who is back from college for the summer."

"How long ago was that?" Mom asked.

"On the Fourth. She told me she was too tired to go to the pool party with me, but then turned around and went out with her ex."

"I'm surprised. I didn't think Debbie was the kind of girl who would do that."

"I didn't either. She has apologized over and over and told me it was a big mistake. The problem is that I have lost trust in her. Even if we did get back together, I'm not sure I could ever fully trust her again."

"I can see that," Mom said. "Tell me about this new girl. How do you know her?"

"She is going to be a senior, the same as me. She was in a few of my classes over the last few years. She was the girl that I danced with at the junior prom."

"How is it that she is a year older than you?" Mom asked.

"From what she told me, her parents thought it would be a good idea for her to repeat first grade after moving in the middle of the school year. There was a lot of chaos that year with them getting ready to move and changing to a new district and a new school. It's not like she flunked or anything like that."

"What are your plans with Linda?" Mom asked.

"I have no idea. What I do know is that whenever we are together, we have fun." We both want to continue seeing each other. Whether this turns into something serious or not… I really don't know. What's with all the questions?" I inquired.

"Your father and I are concerned about you. You've been different these last few months."

"Different? You mean because I have been more appreciative of what you and dad do for me? You and dad deserve it."

"Who are you? Don't get me wrong, I'm not complaining," Mom said.

"I'm fine, Mom."

"I want you to know that you can come to your father or me with anything. We're here to help."

"Thanks, Mom."

Why don't you invite Linda to come to dinner one night so we can meet her?" Mom suggested.

"Thanks, I'll do that. Let me check to find out what her schedule is, and I'll let you know."

"Wonderful. Now, I'm off to bed. I'll see you in the morning."

"Goodnight, Mom," I watched as she walked up the stairs to her bedroom. I wished I had appreciated her more the first time I was here. She is a great lady, and it is obvious that she and dad want nothing but the best for me. I tried to imagine how I would have likely reacted all those years ago if she had been waiting up to talk to me. I probably would have felt like I was being interrogated because she didn't trust my judgement. Now I realize, she and dad were genuinely concerned about my well-being. Once I realized that it was her love for me that led her to ask questions, I didn't mind at all. There is an old Pennsylvania Dutch saying I used to hear my Nana say; "You grow old too fast and smart too late." There was wisdom in those words. I could understand that phrase better than most given my unique perspective.

I crawled into bed and for a change, didn't torture myself thinking about where this was all going to end up. I had come to accept that where this went wasn't really under my control. I thought I would be able to rewrite my past just the way I wanted it to be. Given the last few days, it was obvious that it didn't work that way. While it was true that there were things that I could control like going to the awards banquet and the prom; it was equally true that I could not control how people reacted to the things I did. The biggest problem was that I still had no idea what had triggered my move to the past and I certainly had no idea how to leap forward into the future. Even if I did manage to move back to my future, what guarantee did I have that it would be the same? The bottom line was that I had no idea how long I would be living in this alternate universe. I fell asleep with many questions and very few answers.

I think it was the grandfather clock downstairs chiming four times that woke me. I was in the middle of a strange dream. Linda was my wife. We had three kids who were grown and out of the house. I had been a lawyer and Linda worked as a cosmetic company's executive. It all seemed so real which troubled me because I wasn't living the life that I had been leading when I was transported back in time. There was no sign of Grace. Apparently, we had never met and fallen in love in this alternate universe. I wondered how many alternate lives a person could lead. Maybe all of us had alternate versions of our lives running concurrently depending on the choices we did and did not make. Wow… this was getting deep. It reminded me of those books I enjoyed reading in grade school with all the alternate endings. One decision changed outcomes down the road. There could be numerous endings depending on your choices along the way. If any part of this was true, my chances for finding my way back to Grace had become significantly less. I would not be getting back to sleep now. My mind was on overdrive.

CHAPTER 31

My mind was still focused on all my thoughts from last night about alternate universes. I was still rattled about that possibility which is why I let my guard down later this morning. I had been very careful to avoid Debbie since our breakup. I didn't want to get involved in a scene here at the pool and that is exactly what would happen if she knew I was going out with Linda. I dropped off my stuff in a locker and headed to the manager's office to see what he wanted me to do. I was assigned to sweep off the deck around the baby pool which was close to the snack bar. I was mindlessly sweeping when I heard a voice behind me.

"Hello stranger," Debbie said. I wasn't paying attention and had not seen her emerge from the snack bar.

"Hi," I answered.

"If I didn't know better, I would say you are trying to avoid me," she said. Here it comes; exactly what I had been trying to avoid all week.

"What makes you say that?" I asked.

"Gee, I don't know. Maybe the fact you haven't even come over to the snack bar to at least say hello. Maybe the fact you haven't called me. You're not over this, are you?" I could see that she was not happy.

"No, I guess I'm not over this," I answered while continuing to sweep around the pool.

"What's it going to take? I apologized. I told you that I didn't want to stop seeing you."

"It's not that simple," I replied.

"It can be if you just accept my apology. It can go back to like it was before all this mess," she said.

163

"So, you cheat on me with an old boyfriend and I'm just supposed to act like it never happened? Trust is an important part of any relationship and now I don't know if I can trust you or not. Besides, it's a moot point; I'm seeing someone else." Debbie actually took a step back when I said that. I could see that she had not been expecting this.

"You didn't waste any time, did you?"

"I didn't go out looking for someone else, it just sort of happened… more dumb luck than anything."

"You expect me to believe that?" she said, her anger apparent.

"I don't really care if you believe me or not," I answered, not intending for my answer to sound as harsh as it did.

"I guess that you didn't have the same feelings for me as I had for you."

"I'm curious. Were those the same feelings you had for me when you went out with Mark?"

"It was a mistake… I told you."

"Your feelings for me weren't strong enough to stop you from going out with Mark, were they?"

"Can't you get it through your head that I made a mistake?" she said, on the verge of begging me for forgiveness.

"Look, I don't want to fight with you. I enjoyed our time together and maybe sometime down the road we'll get back together. Right now, I would like to see where things might go with Linda. I'm sorry."

"Like I said; your feelings for me could not have been that strong," Debbie replied.

"I'm not the one who cheated," I replied with attitude. "I need to get back to work. I see Hutchinson looking this way. I'll see you later."

"Don't bother," she seethed as she turned and strode back to the snack bar.

That could have gone better, but I can't say that I was surprised. I knew Debbie wasn't going to be happy whenever we had this conversation. At least everything was out in the open. She knows where she stands. Luckily, with her being stuck in the snack bar most of the time, there will be very little chance of me running into her as long as I stay away from that part of the pool complex. I'll have to start bringing snacks from home. I finished sweeping the pool deck and got ready to start my first shift in the guard stand.

I spent most of the time in the stand thinking about how my recent decisions were going to play out. I think I could still get back together with Debbie. That was the track closest to what happened fifty years ago. I just didn't know if that guaranteed me a return to my old life. There were so many other variables that could affect where I end up assuming that I could even make it back to 2019. My head was spinning as I wrestled with this ever-more complicated problem. The more I tried to unravel this problem, the more twists and turns I found in my way.

At the end of my shift, I walked out of the pool gates and had a nice surprise. Linda was sitting on the hood of her '64 Chevy Nova next to the bike rack.

"What are you doing here?" I asked.

"I missed you," she said as she jumped off the hood and wrapped her arms around me. She gave me a kiss right there in the parking lot. I looked up just in time to see Debbie staring at us from the passenger window of her father's car. I had a feeling that any chance of reuniting with Debbie had just gone up in smoke. The fact that she shot me the bird as her father pulled out was a good indicator.

"Are you busy tonight?" Linda asked me.

"What do you have in mind?" I asked.

"I thought maybe we could so over to the Sunset Diner and get a couple of pieces of that blueberry pie."

"That sounds like a plan. Let me throw my bike in your trunk and you can take me home so I can change first. Besides, my parents would love to meet you."

"Really? You told your parents about us?" she said somewhat surprised.

"Sure. They were curious who the mystery woman was picking me up in front of their house."

I tried to assure Linda that there was nothing to be nervous about as we approached my house. She pulled into the driveway where I unloaded my bike and rolled it into the garage. We walked in the side door of the house that led directly to the kitchen. Mom was standing in front of the stove and Dad was sitting at the table with the evening newspaper.

"Hey, I want to introduce you to my friend, Linda," I said. Mom turned around and dad looked up from his paper.

"It's nice to meet you, Linda. We have heard so much about you," Mom said.

"It's nice to meet you too," Linda responded.

"Mom, Linda and I are going to go to the Sunset Diner if you don't mind," I said.

"What about dinner?" Mom asked.

"We'll get some there," I answered.

"Don't be ridiculous," Mom said. "We have plenty. The two of you can eat here. We're having meatloaf, one of your favorites." It was true; Mom's meatloaf was fabulous. I looked toward Linda. I had no idea if she even liked meatloaf. I didn't have to worry because Linda solved the problem for me.

"I would love to stay for dinner," she answered. Mom and Linda both turned toward me and smiled. Dad, who had been quiet during this whole exchange, finally spoke.

"When do we eat?" Everybody looked at him and laughed.

Dinner went as well as it could have. Mom and Dad genuinely seemed to like Linda, who seemed to enjoy herself too. Connie stayed unusually quiet for which I was very glad. When the main course was finished, Linda surprised me.

"Why don't you all come with us?" she said. "The blueberry pie is to die for." I think Mom was actually considering it before Dad saved me.

"You two run along. You don't need us tagging along. Linda, it was very nice to meet you. Hopefully, we'll be seeing more of you this summer."

"I would like that," Linda said. With that, we made our exit.

"That was really nice that you agreed to stay for dinner. I hope you didn't mind getting grilled," I said.

"I had a great time. Your parents are so nice. They are the kind of people who make a person feel so welcome. It's like I've known them my whole life."

"I have," I responded.

"You have what?" Linda asked.

"Known them my whole life," I said. Linda laughed at my corny joke which was truer than she realized.

"Is your sister always that quiet?" Linda asked.

"No, quite the opposite. She must have gotten in trouble before dinner."

Fifteen minutes later, we were sitting at the diner enjoying our blueberry pie. It had been a good day. Debbie who?

CHAPTER 32

July continued to roll along under the unrelenting summer sun. Other than a few quick thunderstorms, rain didn't appear to be in the forecast. Sitting on the guard stand for hours every day baking in temperatures that frequently topped ninety, I was starting to look like a chocolate berry according to my grandmother. I knew later in my life, that continued exposure to the sun with no protection could lead to some serious health concerns down the road including skin cancer. Any serious sunscreen products didn't hit the mainstream until the nineties. This was 1969. Sunscreen for lifeguards like me meant zinc oxide smeared on noses before taking the stand. Even though I knew better, there wasn't much I could do about it. The products that would protect my skin simply did not exist. I could have made a fortune except that people didn't fully realize the dangers of prolonged tanning so there would have been no market for the product.

My summer days fell into a routine. On the days I worked, I would eat a late breakfast, shower, and head to the pool to work my shift. Most days after work, I would head home for a quick dinner with my parents and then get together with Linda. Sometimes I would go to her house. Her mother seemed to approve of me and her father was out of the picture due to a nasty divorce. Linda's younger sister and brother always vied for my attention when I was there. Sometimes we would stay at my house. My parents clearly approved of my choice which made things easy. Sometimes we would go out to the movies or get together with other friends.

Sundays would include the 8 A.M. church service with my family and then a short walk down Railroad Street to visit with my Aunt Cile, Uncle Carl, and Grammy for cookies and milk. To call Railroad Street a street was really a misnomer. It was so narrow that two cars coming from opposite directions made for a tight squeeze, with one or the other of the vehicles having to climb up on the sidewalk to be able to pass each other unscathed. I knew that in the years down the road, they would finally make Railroad Street a one-way street which was long overdue. Sitting in church these past Sundays, I had a new appreciation for the church that had stood on this site since a few years after the Civil War. Growing up, I just assumed it would always be here. Unfortunately, I knew that would not be the case. St. Peter's Lutheran Church would eventually fall victim to a declining congregation and would be sold to another church ending our family's decades long involvement with St. Peters. Driving home from Railroad Street, there were often stops at Egypt Star Bakery. Fresh poppyseed rolls and assorted pastries bought on Sunday wouldn't make it past Tuesday. Amazingly, the bakery was still operating fifty years in the future.

On my days off, I tried to see Trip, Rob, and Greg. In the mornings before it got hot, we would meet at the Freedom High School tennis courts and do battle. The closer it came to August, the more our conversations between sets turned to the upcoming school year. Schedules were due any day now, but of more interest than that was the beginning of band camp which started in the middle of August. All of us were members of the band and enjoyed drilling for the upcoming halftime shows we would be performing at football games. It was a chance to see many friends that we hadn't seen all summer.

The timing of band camp was perfect because it started the day after the concert at Woodstock would end. History told me that Woodstock ran from Friday, August 15th to Monday morning, August 18th. I was hopeful that Linda might be able to drive us there although I had not brought it up as of yet. I wasn't sure her mother would approve any more than I was sure my parents would approve. I had some serious planning to do before August 15th.

I finally brought Woodstock up at a picnic that Anna was hosting at her parents' house. Rob was there along with Greg and Vicki as well as Trip and Bonnie.

"Have you guys heard about the Woodstock music festival they are having in New York?" I asked the group.

"I heard something about it," Trip answered. "I heard the Beatles and the Stones might both be performing."

"Where is Woodstock?" Bonnie asked.

"The concert is actually going to be in Bethel which is about an hour and a half northeast of Scranton," I replied.

"Then why are they calling it Woodstock?" Bonnie asked.

"It has something to do with the guys that are sponsoring it. Their company is called Woodstock Ventures."

"Who is supposed to be there?" Greg asked.

"Credence Clearwater Revival, the Who, Hendrix, among others," I said. "Rumors are running crazy."

"Are you thinking of going?" Greg asked.

"I would love to," I said without hesitation. "What a great end to the summer. Besides, this will be a concert that will be remembered for a long time."

"You really think it's going to be that big?" Rob asked.

"I do. I just have a feeling this will be one of those times that you will regret forever if you aren't there." Linda had been quiet during this whole exchange. I was trying to gauge her reaction, but she wasn't giving any clues about her feelings.

"My father would never let me go to something like that," Vicki said. "Do you think your parents would let you go?" Vicki asked me.

"That's a good question," I said. "I guess it would depend on who else was going and how I was getting there." The heavens opened up when Linda finally spoke!

"I could drive," she said.

"Do you think your mother would approve?" I asked.

"I guess that would depend on how much she trusts the person I would be going with," she said which brought out some laughs.

"I wouldn't trust Jason if I was your mother," Trip said which brought more laughs.

170

"Here I thought you were my friend," I said.

"Hey, I trust you," Trip shot back. "I'm just not sure Linda's mother should." More laughter.

"I think we should all go," I said. "It would be a blast."

"Have fun," Vicki said. "No chance for me. My dad would never approve."

"If you're not going, then I'm not going," Greg added.

"I doubt my parents would agree," Anna said.

"Truthfully, I don't think my parents would allow me to go either," Rob said.

"I'm in," Trip said. "My mom would be glad to get rid of me for a few days."

"I can ask," Bonnie added. "I'm guessing my chances are fifty-fifty at best."

The conversation drifted onto other things. There were hot dogs and burgers to devour and beanbags to play. We had a great time. The most important part of the night to me was the fact that the Woodstock seed had been planted. Now, if I could just get it to grow!

"Were you serious about driving to the concert?" I asked as we drove home from the picnic.

"Sure… if my mom allows me to go. The music will be great, but spending three days and two nights with you would be even better."

"We would probably need to leave Thursday night to beat the crowds," I said knowing full well that traffic was going to be a nightmare.

"Even better," Linda said. "Three nights with you. Where would we stay?"

"We would be camping," I answered.

"Camping? As in tent and sleeping bags?"

"It will be fun," I said.

"What do we do about tickets?" Linda asked.

"We can get them there," I said, knowing that by Friday they had given up collecting tickets and made it a free concert. Knowing all this stuff in advance sure made planning easier. I also knew that rain gear was a must as there would be some really heavy rains during the weekend. I was getting excited; this might actually happen. I can't say Woodstock was a regret from my past because I knew very little about it prior to the story breaking in the national news as it was happening. I wasn't sure my parents would have allowed me to attend even if I had known. This time around I was going to do anything I could to get there. I needed to convince my parents that they could trust me.

CHAPTER 33

For the next few days, I wrestled with how to best bring it up with my parents. Without their approval there was no way I could go. There were other important factors that played into this whole thing too. Getting approval from Linda's mom was critical; she was our transportation. If Trip and Bonnie were able to go that would only enhance my chances. My biggest question was whether I should paint this as three days of rock and roll or three days of camping in New York. My parents were not big fans of rock and roll. They believed all rock musicians were druggies, which probably isn't too far from the truth. Just because I liked their music didn't mean I was going to start doing drugs. I would have to decide on the best approach, but I was leaning toward a camping trip.

July 20th was going to be a special day. I already knew what was going to happen, but it was still exciting. Today was the day of the first moonwalk. History told me that the Eagle, the lunar module, landed on the moon a little after 6 P.M. The moonwalk was still almost five hours away when I raised the subject at dinner.

"So, who is going to watch the first steps on the moon?" I asked.

"I think it could be a disaster," my dad said. "What happens if they can't get back to the mothership? They'll be stranded there until they die."

"How horrible," my mother lamented.

"That won't happen. Those guys in NASA know what they're doing."

"What if moon monsters attack them?" Connie asked.

"There are no such things as moon monsters," I replied.

"How do you know? Have you ever been to the moon?" she asked.

"No, I haven't, but I bet you any money there are no moon monsters ready to strike," I said shaking my head at my sister's naiveté.

"I'll probably tune in to see what happens," my dad said.

"I'll watch it with you," I said, excited to share this moment in history with my dad.

My dad was already in front of the television when I joined him later that evening. Mom had already gone to bed, stating that she would watch it on the morning news if it actually happened. My sister was asleep on the recliner. A few minutes later, the broadcast began. It was unbelievable to see the surface of the moon. I nudged Connie to wake her, but she muttered something and rolled away from me.

"Let her sleep," Dad said.

"This is unbelievable, isn't it?" I asked.

"It sure is," he answered. "I read *From Earth to the Moon* by Jules Verne when I was a boy. I never imagined that it might really happen." We sat and watched as the hatch opened and Neil Armstrong started down the ladder to the surface. I waited for his words which would become one of the most well-known phrases in American history. "One small step for man, one giant leap for mankind."

I glanced over at my dad. He was transfixed.

"My god, they actually did it," he whispered quietly.

"They sure did," I replied. We sat there for another twenty minutes before heading off to bed. It was a special moment between my dad and I that I got to relive again. I couldn't have been happier.

The calendar turned to August. The summer was disappearing. I remember I used to start getting depressed after July Fourth, feeling that the summer was half over. By August, I was already dreading the start of another school year. I knew I had to ask Hutchinson permission to have August 15th-17th off or nothing else mattered. Much to my surprise, he gave me those three days with no questions. I was one step closer to Woodstock.

Life at the pool had been simpler since I stopped dating Debbie. I still wondered if I made the right decision. The truth of the matter was that Debbie, by cheating on me, had made the decision for me. As it turned out, Debbie started dating Mark again steadily after we broke up. Whether or not that would have happened if I wasn't out of the picture is debatable. A cordial hello was the extent of my involvement with her when I did see her around the pool. On a few different occasions I thought I detected a hint of regret in her eyes, but maybe that was just me reading too much into the situation.

Thursday night I invited Trip and Bonnie to go to the Big Scoop with Linda and me for some ice cream and some planning. We needed to make some decisions.

"Is it better if we tell our parents we're going on a camping trip rather than a hippie music festival? I asked the group.

"Too late," Trip said. "I already told my mom it is a music festival."

"She was good with that?" I asked.

"She was. Like I told you before, she is only too happy to get me out of the house for a few days so she can have some peace and quiet. However, there is a catch."

"This sounds like trouble," I replied.

"She'll only let me go if I take Corinne along." Corinne was Trip's thirteen-year-old sister. Nobody around the table said a word as we all tried to process what impact having Corinne along would have on us. Hanky-panky was going to be severely limited if not completely impossible. On the positive side of things, having her along might help convince my parents that this isn't one big lovefest.

Once we had gotten over the shock of Trip's announcement, we got onto logistics. We talked about the necessities; food, raingear, tents and sleeping bags. We agreed to split the cost of the food and the gas. Trip suggested that we just buy food at the concert. I vetoed that idea because I knew that food would be in short supply because of the

175

overflow crowd that would show up for the weekend. My excuse was that the price of food there would be very high and it would be cheaper to bring our own.

After Trip and Bonnie left, Linda and I found ourselves sitting at our favorite pavilion along the Monocacy Creek.

"I think we should ask your mother tomorrow night whether or not you can go," I suggested. Linda mulled my suggestion over before replying.

"I thought it would be better if you talked to your parents first," she said. "If you can't go, then it doesn't really matter."

"I understand that, but if your mother and Trip's mother have already said yes, it makes it that much harder for my parents to say no. Besides, you're my ride." I knew that was a mistake to say that before the sound of my voice died away.

"So, you just like me because I have a car?" she asked. I could tell she wasn't happy with my last comment.

"No, don't be ridiculous. I'm crazy about you. The car is just a bonus. Linda seemed to debate the truthfulness of my answer.

"Good comeback," she said and smiled. "Now, kiss me." And I did many times over the next thirty minutes.

Linda was very quiet on the drive back to my house.

"Are you sure you're not upset with me?" I asked.

"Why? Should I be?" This did not sound like a girl who was fine with everything.

"Talk to me. Are you still angry with me over the car comment?"

"Maybe... I'm not sure. It would definitely bother me if my car was part of your attraction to me."

"I'm not sure what I can say to convince you that isn't true. If we get to Woodstock...great. If we don't... I'm fine with that too as long as I can still be with you. Trust me… it isn't the car, it's you. You are one of the most beautiful people I have ever known… and I have known countless people in my life. Car or no car; it really doesn't matter. I want to be with you." She had tears in her eyes as she leaned over and gave me a long, passionate kiss.

"That's one of the nicest things anybody has ever said to me."

"It's only just the start," I replied drawing on past song lyrics once more.

CHAPTER 34

One of the things about working at Northwest Swim Club was the radio was always playing over the P.A. system. From the time I arrived until closing, the sounds of WAEB, a local top 40 hits station, was filling the air. It was not unusual to hear songs like Zager and Evan's *In the Year 2525* or Tommy James and the Shondell's *Crystal Blue Persuasion* four or five times during the course of a day. Neil Diamond's *Sweet Caroline* started that summer as well along with the Stone's *Honky Tonk Woman*, Credence's *Bad Moon Rising*, and Presley's *In the Ghetto*. Countless other hits filled the air around Northwest Swim Club that summer.

I was barely aware of the music today as I debated how we should approach Linda's mother tonight. I had to come across as a guy she could trust with her daughter. I wondered if I should say that the girls would be sleeping in one tent and Trip and I would be in the other tent. I decided against that because I didn't want to insult Mrs. Smith's intelligence. She had been young once too, and I doubted she would believe it anyway.

I was off at five and raced home to shower and change. I spent a few minutes talking to mom and dad. I still valued my time with them given this amazing opportunity to relive this part of my life. Now with Linda in the picture, it was difficult to balance my time. There was only so much time in a day. Tonight, I was invited to have dinner with Linda and her family.

"So, are you ready?" I asked Linda as I got into the car.

"I guess so," she answered. "I don't want to do it at the table with my brother and sister sitting there."

"That makes sense," I said, realizing how awkward that might be.

Dinner was steak, mashed potatoes, and corn on the cob, some of my favorites. Conversation centered around the upcoming school year and what my plans were for beyond high school. Of course, Eddie and Susan, Linda's brother and sister, continued to bombard me with questions as they wanted me to like each of them better than the other. I helped Linda clear the dishes following dinner as Eddie and Susan disappeared to watch television in the den. That left me alone with Linda and her mother. We would never have a better chance than now to ask the big question. I tried to catch Linda's eye and give her a signal. As it turns out, she didn't need one.

"Mom, I was wondering if it would be alright with you if I went on a three -day camping concert sort of thing with Jason and a few of our friends?" I held my breath as I waited for her answer.

"When is it, honey?" she asked.

"It would be August 15th through the 17th," I answered.

"Where is it?" Mrs. Smith asked.

"Bethel, New York which is an hour above Scranton," I offered.

"How are you going to get there?" she asked next which worried me because the whole trip hinged on Linda being able to drive.

"I would be driving," Linda said with no hesitation. "You know I'm a good driver and would follow the rules of the road. You can trust me, Mom." Mrs. Smith was silent. We finished washing the dishes and Mrs. Smith still hadn't answered the question. I was about to assume that the silence meant no when Mrs. Smith spoke.

"I'm not crazy about the idea, not because I don't trust you, but rather because you'll be a long way from home if you have a problem."

"So, does that mean I can go?" Linda asked hopefully.

"Yes, you can go, but don't make me regret my decision."

"Thanks, Mom," Linda answered and gave her mother a big hug. I smiled. One step closer to the concert of my lifetime. Now I had to find a way to get the same answer from my parents.

We drove over to see Trip and share the good news. He had found out earlier that Bonnie was allowed to go too. That really put the pressure on me and my parents. Everybody had permission except for me, the person who had the idea to begin with. I tried to assure everybody that I would get the thumbs up from my parents, too. I prayed that I was right. Besides being embarrassing if they said no, it would be extremely disappointing. A chance to see what would become the defining moment of my generation; I simply could not miss it a second time. They had to say yes! On the way back to my house we decided tomorrow would be the day we would approach my parents.

It finally rained on Saturday, so I had off. Linda was working so it was the perfect opportunity to get together with the guys who all worked for the school district cleaning schools and had off every weekend. We decided to start the day at Greg's house because he had a pool table in his basement. It wasn't a very good table. It was made from pressboard not slate which meant it was warped. You had to learn to play the break on this table because the balls did not run straight and true. It didn't matter to us because everybody was at an equal disadvantage except for Greg since it was his home table. I found pool a hard enough game without throwing in a warped table, but we still had a great time playing until lunchtime. We headed over to Rob's house where his mother was kind enough to fix peanut butter and jelly sandwiches for us. Rob had a dart board in his garage. We played a few standard rounds of darts before we started inventing dart games. Our favorite was H.O.R.S.E. only with darts. One person made a shot and everybody else had to make the same shot or you got a letter. Once you failed to complete five shots you were out. Blindfold shots, left handed shots, behind the back shots, over the shoulder shots… we tried everything. We had a blast. We ended at my house where a dusty ping pong table stood in the basement. We cleaned it off and played doubles the rest of the afternoon. It was great day with Trip, Rob, and Greg, but all I could think of was Woodstock and whether or not I would be allowed to go.

The guys had all gone home. I took a quick shower and awaited Linda's arrival. She was coming directly from work. She and dad arrived at the same time. We had Swiss steak and noodles along

180

with green beans for dinner. The conversation was very similar to the conversation we had at Linda's house the night before…mainly what plans Linda had for after high school and how her summer was going. Connie was there, so we waited until after dinner to talk to mom and dad.

"We would like to talk to you both after we're done cleaning up," I announced. I saw an immediate look of concern pass back and forth between my mother and father. I wondered if they thought that Linda was pregnant. That might actually work to my advantage. They would be so relieved that Linda wasn't pregnant, that they would gladly give me permission to go camping with the group. Connie had overheard me apparently and she kept hanging around until my father finally spoke.

"Connie, you have a choice. You can either go watch television in the family room or go upstairs to your bedroom."

"Aww, Dad," she complained. "That's not fair."

"Fair or not, those are your choices." My dad stood waiting for her to make up her mind.

"Not fair," she muttered under her breath as she stomped toward the family room. Dad waited until she was gone and he heard the television come on before speaking.

"What is it you would like to talk about?" he asked. Mom looked like she was on the verge of tears as she wrung her hands together in her lap. The moment was here and suddenly I froze, not knowing the right way to start this conversation. My father sensed my discomfort.

"Whatever it is, we're both here for you," he said. "You can tell us anything. We'll figure it out together." He really did think I was going to tell him that Linda was knocked up. Before I could speak, Linda came to my rescue.

"There are a few of us are going to New York for a concert-campout sort of weekend. My mother has given me permission to drive.

Trip and Bonnie as well as Trip's sister, Corinne are going. We're hoping that you'll give Jason permission to come with us. It would be such a nice way to end the summer." I could almost see my mother sigh with relief. My father's wide smile gave away his feelings. I saw another look pass between them again.

"That sounds like fun," Dad said. "Just promise me that neither one of you will do anything stupid like underage drinking or drugs or other things that could ruin your future,"

"I promise, Dad."

"I promise too, Mr. Williams." Linda added. "Thank you so much. We'll be on our best behavior."

Later that evening as I walked Linda to her car, we were so excited that this trip was actually going to happen. Linda had no idea what she was in for, but I certainly did. Woodstock was going to be like nothing she had ever experienced. Me? I knew exactly what to expect and I couldn't wait!

CHAPTER 35

Sunday morning church proved to be much more interesting than I expected. It started out as any other service; prayers, scripture reading, and hymn singing. I was already staring at the stained-glass windows as Pastor Kopperman began his sermon.

"What would you do if Jesus walked in your door?" Pastor Kopperman asked to begin his sermon. He paused to let that thought settle into everyone's consciousness. It was an interesting question, but what he said next brought me to full attention. "According to Dr. Henry Cummings, a professor at Princeton University, time travel is possible and has been happening right under our noses." I could scarcely breathe. I was living proof that time travel was possible. Pastor Kopperman went on to explain that according to Dr. Cummings there were a number of documented cases of time travel. People had been able to predict events and inventions that they had no way of knowing or understanding long before they came to pass. The explanation was that these people had been transported back from the future. Sophisticated testing had proven these people were older than they appeared to be; in some cases, several decades older. The rest of the sermon used this information to suggest that Jesus could very well appear in the current time.

I didn't hear much else of the sermon. I was trying to wrap my head around the possibility that I wasn't the only person that had moved through time. I had moved back in time the same direction the sermon had suggested. Was it possible to also move forward in time? I needed to move forward to get back to Grace and my family. Then I had another disturbing revelation; in my dream where I was married to someone other than Grace, I had moved forward to a different point in time. Was that dream real? If it was, it meant that I had also moved forward in time...at least for the duration of my dream. Questions exploded in my head, one after another. Was there a way to return to my former life? Could I pinpoint how far forward I could move in time? Was the process precise enough for me to get right back to where I had come from? Speaking of a process...was there a definable process or was it just a random event? If it was random, I was in trouble. My dad had to tap me on the shoulder to stand for the singing of the hymn at the conclusion of the sermon. I had been so caught in all of this new information that I hadn't even realized the sermon had concluded.

We walked down Railroad Street to see Aunt Cile, Uncle Carl, and Grammy like we did every Sunday.

"Where are you?" Connie asked.

"What do you mean?" I replied.

"You've been in your own world this morning," she said.

"I guess it's just one of those daydreaming mornings."

"It must be a good one; you seem miles away," she said.

"Years away," I answered before I could catch myself.

"What does that mean?" Connie asked.

"Nothing...forget it."

"You're weird," she said ending the conversation. If she only knew!

Milk, cookies, and conversation followed for the next half hour. I spent more time talking to Grammy than anybody else. She was such a kind-hearted soul. It wasn't hard to see where mom had gotten her kindness. Grammy spoke in broken English, a mix of low German, Yiddish, and English. It was an interesting combination which I could understand much better now than I could fifty years ago. Words like schmutz, schlep, bissel, verklempt, shmaltzy, and oy vey were just a smattering of Grammy's vocabulary. Funny thing is that I still use some of those words many years later.

When it was time to leave, I gave Grammy a big hug which brought a big wide smile to her face. I hadn't done that nearly enough in the past. Connie had taken notice of the hug which she realized was out of character for me.

"What is with you today?" she asked again as we walked back to the car. "Seriously. Who are you?"

"I guess my weirdness is showing today," I said and laughed.

"You can say that again," she answered.

On the drive home I couldn't wait to research Dr. Henry Cummings. I needed to talk to him. Fifty years from now that would not be so difficult. Do a little search on the internet and find all kinds of contact information. Shoot him an email or a text message... no problem. The time I am living in now is 1969; this wasn't going to be so easy. The public library in town was closed on Sundays, but first thing tomorrow morning I planned on being there. Finally, I had a little something to go on, a place to look for some answers. For the first time since I had shown up back here, I had a sliver of hope.

Monday morning, I was out of the house early. I arrived at the library as they were unlocking the doors. I moved immediately to the card catalog and did a search for Dr. Henry Cummings and came up empty. I looked for time travel and found a smattering of fictional titles, nothing that would help me. Research was so much harder in this time period. Kids in the future would have no idea what a pain it was to do research this way. Next stop was the librarian's desk.

"Excuse me, I was wondering if you could help me?" I asked a woman sitting at the desk. She was an older woman with her gray hair pulled into a bun. She wore her reading glasses on a gold chain which dangled from her neck. Even though it was summer, she wore a solid beige, lightweight sweater. She was exactly what I pictured a librarian should look like.

"It would be my pleasure, young man," she answered in a soft high-pitched voice. "What can I do for you?"

"I'm trying to find information on a Dr. Henry Cummings. All I know is that he is a professor at Princeton University."

"I assume you checked the card catalog?" she asked politely.

"Yes, I did. I did not come across his name."

185

"Let me take a look," she answered and started looking through the card catalog that sat behind her desk. "I'm not finding anything either. Do you know what area of expertise he specializes in?"

"All I know is that apparently, he has done some research on time travel. Believe it or not he was mentioned in the sermon at my church yesterday."

"That is very interesting. Let me pull up some information on Princeton University. Maybe I can some reference to him there." She thumbed through the card catalog, jotted down a call number, and then disappeared briefly before she reemerged from the stacks with a thick book in her hand. "This is a college reference book. Let me find Princeton." She opened the large reference book and checked the index for a page number. A few seconds later she was scanning information on Princeton University.

"Here you go," she said. "Dr. Henry Cummings, Professor of Applied Physics. It's not much, but at least it's a start."

"If I wanted to contact him, does it have a phone number or address or anything like that?" I asked.

"No, I'm sorry. No phone number other than a general number for the university. Same with the address. I suppose you could write a letter to Dr. Cummings and send it to the main Princeton mailing address. Eventually it would find its way to him I would hope." She wrote down the address on a notecard and handed it to me. I thanked her for her help and set off for the pool, my mind going a thousand miles an hour. One other good thought I had was to stop in and talk to Pastor Kopperman. Maybe I could find out where he got his information about Dr. Cumming's research. Progress…for the first time since I had been transported here… actual progress!

CHAPTER 36

I arrived at the front gate to the pool at the same time as Debbie. She was sitting in an idling car that I did not recognize. She saw me. I started to wave and thought better of it. As I passed by the car, she leaned over and gave the driver a long passionate kiss. I had no doubt that the kiss was for my benefit.

She caught up with me later in the morning as I swept the deck over by the snack bar.

"I haven't seen you lately." she said and smiled.

"I've been around," I said.

"Still dating prom girl?" she asked and laughed.

"Which one?" I fired back. It was my turn to laugh.

"That was Mark dropping me off," she said. "We've reconnected."

"I figured it wasn't your father."

"You're just a regular comedian today."

"I thought it was funny."

"Do you know what else is funny?" she asked. "I am making Mark very happy…almost every night. That could have been you. Think about that."

"I don't think Linda would approve," I answered and tried not to smile.

"Your loss," she said and turned her back and walked back into the snack bar.

"Have a nice day," I called out behind her.

I thought back to my time with Debbie fifty years ago. She wasn't like this. Maybe her involvement with me had taken her down a better path. I guess I would like to think so. I had a good idea where she was likely to end up now; pregnant before she turned twenty. I wished there was something I could do for her to set her back on a better track, but I could see no way to do that where things stood now. She would have to find her own way back. I hoped she would before her father caught wind of her nightly dalliances with Mark.

I made my first rescue at the pool today. I was stationed at the baby pool which runs from three to twenty-four inches deep. There isn't usually much to do because the mothers sit around the edge of the pool and watch their little ones like hawks. Sometimes I sit on one of the benches and watch. Sometimes I walk around the pool. Today I was walking. Two mothers were having a lively discussion, laughing and jabbering away about something. One mother held the hands of her youngster as the child bounced up and down in the water giggling with delight. The child of the second mother was hanging onto the edge of the pool next to her mother's legs. As I watched, I saw the little girl slip underwater as she lost her grip. Neither mother seemed to notice. I waited for two seconds to see if the girl was going to bob to the surface. She didn't. I was on the far side of the pool. Rather than race around the outside edge, I simply stepped into the pool and cut straight across to where the child was still underwater. The mother's took notice of me just as I reached the little girl. The mother jumped up, reached down, and jerked the little girl to the surface. The toddler was coughing and spitting out water.

"I thought you are supposed to be guarding the pool?" she snarled at me.

"I was. That's why I'm standing here. I came to pull her out.'

"By the time you got here, she could have been dead," the mother was spewing pure venom by this point.

"I saw the whole thing. As soon as I saw she wasn't going to resurface by herself, I made a beeline over here."

"What's your name, young man?" she asked. "I'm going to report you to the manager."

188

"Be my guest," I said, my anger starting to rise. "Be sure to mention that you didn't see your daughter underwater until I was coming to her rescue."

"How dare you talk to me like that!" With that she stood up, picked her daughter and stormed over to the manager's office. The other mother looked at me.

"Don't worry. She'll calm down. She can get a little excitable when it comes to her daughter."

"Then I suggest she keep a closer eye on her," I said and moved on, not waiting for a response. A few minutes later, Susie, one of the other guards on duty walked over to me.

"Mr. Hutchinson wants to see you right way," she said.

"I figured," I answered.

"What happened?" Susie asked.

"Little kid slipped under the water because her mother wasn't watching her. I moved to pull the daughter out. Right as I got there, the mother realized what was happening and grabbed the daughter before I could. Then she went ballistic on me, accusing me of being derelict in my duty."

"Good luck," she said as I jogged over to the office. I knocked on the closed door and Hutchinson opened it and waved me in. Mrs. Hughes and her daughter were seated at the far side of the office.

"Have a seat, Jason," Mr. Hutchinson said. "Mrs. Hughes is upset with what just happened as well as your attitude. I think you owe her an apology." I couldn't believe this was happening. Hutchinson didn't even give me a chance to explain my side of the story. I weighed my options.

"Mr. Hutchinson, I would be happy to offer an apology if I thought one was in order."

"See what I mean?" Mrs. Hughes snapped. "This young man is one of the rudest people I have ever met. He should not be on the staff."

189

"Give me a minute, Mrs. Hughes. Jason, come with me." He led me out of the office and we walked over to the filter room.

"You could have handled that better," he said to me.

"Do I get to share my side of the story?" I asked.

"I already heard the story. Mrs. Hughes may have overreacted, but that doesn't give you the right to be a smart ass with her."

"I thought that you would be happy that I was paying attention to the kids in the pool. I saw the problem immediately and reacted appropriately. Half a second sooner it would have been me pulling her daughter to safety. She only realized what was happening because I was wading across the pool to get to her daughter. I guarantee if I had not gone into the water, there was no way she would have even noticed her daughter had slipped under."

"It still doesn't excuse you from giving her lip."

"I was very polite with her. I tried to explain that I acted appropriately. It was only after she told me that she was going to report me that things got a little heated."

"What exactly did you say to her?"

"I told her to make sure that she mention to you that she hadn't even seen her daughter until I was standing right in front of her." Mr. Hutchinson was quiet. "You can ask her friend. She saw the whole thing."

"Alright. Listen, it might be easier if you took the rest of the day off. I'll tell Mrs. Hughes that you are really shaken up and I sent you home."

"That's fine, but I don't want it to look like I did something wrong because I didn't."

"No, you didn't. I think she is probably angrier with herself than she is with you. You'll understand one day when you have your own kids." I almost said that I knew what he meant. I caught myself in a nick of time.

"I'll see you tomorrow, Mr. Hutchinson. And thank you."

"For what?" he asked.

"For believing me."

"There are always two sides to every story. Now get out of here so I can calm Mrs. Hughes down." I gathered up my stuff in the locker room and realized I had a couple of hours to kill before I was due home. I knew exactly where I needed to go.

CHAPTER 37

I stood in front of the church secretary.

"I was wondering if Pastor Kopperman is in? I asked. The secretary, who I recognized from Sunday morning church services, studied me, no doubt surprised to see a high school student asking to speak to the pastor.

"Could I ask what this is about?" she inquired.

"I was hoping to talk to him about his sermon this past Sunday. I found it very interesting." The secretary looked at me a moment longer, still trying to figure me out.

"Let me go check and see if he has a few minutes. You know he is a very busy man." I wasn't sure with an attitude like that, if she was the right woman for the job. When a parishioner comes to see the pastor, you don't discourage them by implying that he is too busy to tend to your problems. I remained silent. Finally, she rose from her desk and disappeared down the hallway.

Pastor Kopperman appeared a few seconds later with a big smile on his face.

"Jason, please come back to my office. I am happy to discuss my sermon with you." I followed him back, passing the secretary as I went. She did not look happy. I gave her a wink as I passed, which probably wasn't the right thing to do, but she could have been nicer to me to start.

"Come in, sit down," Pastor Kopperman said pointing to a chair across from his desk. "Now, what is it that I can help you with?"

"I am interested in where you found the information on Dr. Cummings and his research into time travel," I said, not sure of what kind of response I was going to get.

"Interested in time travel, I'm guessing," Pastor Kopperman said.

"I think the possibility is fascinating to say the least. Don't get me wrong, your sermon was great too," I said, not wanting to offend my pastor.

"I have known Dr. Cummings since I was an undergraduate at Northwestern University. We were in the same dorm for our first two years. We had a few classes together and got to know each other over that time. Anyway, we became friends and have kept in touch ever since."

"Was there a scientific journal article that you read about his interest in time travel?"

"There is although it isn't very in-depth. Most of my information came directly from the source. When I had the idea for my last sermon, I knew he would be the perfect person to talk to about time travel. I called him and he filled me in on his latest research."

"Is there any chance you could give me his phone number? I have so many questions."

"I would need to check with him first. I don't want to impose on his privacy or his time. He is a very busy man. Maybe you could ask me and I might be able to help you." Unbelievable... everybody is apparently too busy to be bothered by a high schooler. I weighed whether or not to say anything more. I decided to push it.

"What I'm about to tell you is completely off the record. I don't want this getting back to my parents. Will that work for you?" I asked.

"This sounds serious. Maybe you should get your parents involved. They could be a big help."

"Maybe I will discuss this with my parents eventually, but the time is not right. This has to be between us for now." I looked at Pastor Kopperman trying to gauge whether he was going to agree to my demands. He did.

"Alright, you win. Anything you say will be between us. Now, what is troubling you?"

193

"The reason I'm so interested in Dr. Cummings and his research is because I think I know someone who has traveled through time." Once the words were out of my mouth, I realized how lame they sounded.

"And?" Pastor Kopperman was looking for more of an explanation.

"That's it," I said not wanting to make this worse.

"What are you trying to find out?" Pastor Kopperman asked.

"I guess I'm trying to find out whether this person will be stuck here or will he eventually go back to where he came from... that sort of thing?" Pastor Kopperman, legs crossed, put his hands together and twiddled his thumbs as he weighed what to say.

"Jason, if you need help, I'm sure we can get it for you."

"What kind of help are you talking about?" I asked.

"Drugs are becoming a scourge of our young people."

"Hold on. Neither my friend nor I are involved with any kind of drugs. I am trying to be serious to be able to help my friend. Maybe I should go. I've taken up enough of your time."

"My apologies for jumping to a faulty conclusion. Maybe you seek a different kind of help. Maybe you would like to sit down and talk to a professional who can get to the core of what is bothering you."

"Who I need to talk to is Dr. Cummings. He, at the very least, is investigating the possible existence of time travel. If he thinks it's possible, would he not be interested in hearing about and possibly meeting a person who has actually experienced it?"

"I suppose he might. I guess my own personal bias is coming through when it comes to time travel. It made for an interesting theoretical sermon, but not one that I considered might come true."

"So, what would you do if Jesus came to your house?" I asked. I could see Pastor Kopperman was troubled by my question even though it was his question to begin with.

"I see your point," Pastor Kopperman responded. "Very clever to throw my own words back at me. So, what is it you would like me to do for you?"

"I would like you to get me some time with Dr. Cummings. I have my driver's license. I'm sure I could find my way to Princeton and back." Pastor Kopperman laughed although I wasn't quite sure why.

"What are you doing Sunday afternoon?" he asked.

"After church, I'm working until five."

"Would you like to come to my house for some iced tea and some snacks after work?"

"No offense, but why would I want to do that?" I asked, totally confused by his question.

"Because Dr. Cummings and his wife will be at my house for Sunday dinner. I'm sure I can arrange a few minutes for you to speak with Dr. Cummings… if you are interested."

"Seriously?"

"Absolutely," he answered. "I hope you are being honest with me. I would hate to waste Dr. Cummings time on his day off."

"Trust me," I said, "this will not be a waste of his time."

"In that case, I'll expect to see you on Sunday. Bring your friend if you would like. My secretary can give you my home address on your way out."

"Thank you so much, Pastor Kopperman. I can't tell you how much I appreciate this."

"Hopefully, your friend will too." I knew Pastor Kopperman didn't believe the friend angle, but there was nothing I could do about that. For that matter, he didn't believe the whole time travel angle so I guess it doesn't really matter.

I asked the secretary for Pastor Kopperman's home address as I reached her desk.

"Why would you need his home address?" she challenged.

"Because he was nice enough to invite me to his house on Sunday afternoon for some snacks and some lively discussion." I could see the doubt in her eyes. "You can ask him if you don't believe me," I added. With a huff, she pulled out a notecard and scribbled down an address and handed it to me.

"Thank you," I said. "I hope you have a good day." I didn't wait for a response. I snatched the card out of her hand and took a quick exit. Pastor Kopperman should really consider getting a new secretary.

On my ride home, I realized how everything had aligned just right for me. My run-in with Mrs. Hughes prompted me getting the rest of the day off. Pastor Kopperman was in his office when I got there. Dr. Cummings is coming to Pastor Kopperman's house for dinner on Sunday. This day could not have worked out any better. Hopefully, on Sunday I would get some answers how I might get back to Grace. Surprisingly when I said that, I had a little twinge of sadness because I knew when I went back, Linda would be out of my life. This was getting more complicated by the day.

CHAPTER 38

Sunday could not come any sooner. I was so excited about having a chance to talk to Dr. Cummings that I had a hard time thinking about anything else. Other people noticed. My parents asked me what was wrong. Linda wanted to know what was on my mind. I would love to be able to explain to them exactly what was happening, but obviously, I could not. They would never understand or believe my story anyway. More likely, they would have thought I was cracking up and needed help.

In the meantime, I was enjoying Linda's company. I wondered why I never met her fifty years ago. I guess there are so many random factors that lead your life one way or another that the chances of repeating anything from fifty years ago is very small. I knew that meant if I stayed in this time period, my chances of finding Grace again were almost non-existent.

Another question that was troubling me of late was the idea of a parallel existence. Just because I was living here in 1969, did that mean I wasn't living fifty years in the future? Did I simply cease to exist in that world because I was here now? What about my kids? Were they never born because Grace and I never found each other? I was driving myself crazy. There were so many things I wanted to know. Would Dr. Cummings be able to shed some light on my questions? Were there other documented cases of people traveling through time? If there were, did anyone ever make it back to where they started? What if you could only move through time in one direction? What if time was like a river and only flowed in one direction?

"Where are you?" Linda asked shaking me out of my malaise. "You have barely touched your ice cream sundae." Linda and I had come to the Big Scoop for a snack after we had watched some television at her house.

"Sorry," I said. "I guess I'm just tired."

"Do you want to leave?" she asked.

"No, not at all. I'll be fine." With that, I put on a big smile and attacked my ice cream. I tried to be more conversational the rest of the evening. I didn't want Linda to think that something was wrong.

Sunday afternoon finally arrived. I counted the minutes all afternoon. I had told my parents that I had run into Paster Kopperman and told him how much I enjoyed his last sermon. I told them that the pastor had invited me to his house to meet Dr. Cummings who was going to be there. I could tell my parents thought the whole thing was a bit strange, but I tried to be as honest as I could be.

As soon as the clock struck five, I took a quick shower and then rode to the pastor's house. I was practically shaking as I knocked on the door.

"Jason, I'm so glad you could make it," Pastor Kopperman said. "Come in. We're sitting on the back patio. I take it you could not convince your friend to come along?"

"No, I'm afraid he wants to remain anonymous," I said, wishing that I was comfortable enough to tell the pastor the truth. Hopefully, God will understand. I followed Pastor Kopperman through his house and out onto the back patio. There was Pastor Kopperman's wife and another couple who I assumed would be Dr. Cummings and his wife.

"Jason, I would like to introduce to Dr. and Mrs. Cummings. Dr. Cummings stood and I immediately realized that he was tall. He wore thick dark-rimmed glasses. The top of his head was bald, but he had plenty of hair on the lower half of his head including a full beard. He extended his hand.

"It's nice to meet you, Jason," he said. I met his hand and he gave it a strong shake.

"Thank you for taking the time to talk to me," I said.

"No problem. I understand you have a friend that might need my help."

"For sure," I answered. "You sound like the perfect person to talk to about his problem."

"Jason, before you men get too deep into any discussions, can I get you a lemonade?" Mrs. Kopperman asked.

"That would be great," I said.

"Help yourself to the cookies on the table," she said before she disappeared back into the house. Pastor Kopperman introduced me to Mrs. Cummings as I waited for the lemonade. A few minutes later, Mrs. Kopperman was back with the lemonade.

"We'll leave you to your discussion," Mrs. Kopperman said to the group. "Come with me, Doris. We'll give these men their privacy. I doubt their discussions would hold much interest for us." I was taken back by her somewhat subservient comments. Fifty years from now, women would never talk like that. The women headed to the kitchen.

"So, Jason," Dr. Cummings started, "Pastor Kopperman tells me that you have a friend who thinks he has traveled in time. Is that correct?"

"One hundred percent," I said.

"What makes you so sure?" Dr. Cummings asked.

"Because he knows things that haven't happened yet," I said.

"Your friend has traveled back in time I am assuming."

"Also correct," I answered.

"Do we know how far back in time he has traveled?"

"As close as I can tell, I am guessing fifty years… by what he tells me," I added to keep suspicion off of me.

"That means he has likely seen things that don't exist yet," Dr. Cummings stated.

"Many things… things that seem impossible, but according to him, they exist."

"Care to give me an example?" Dr. Cummings asked.

"A simple thing he mentioned was a remote control for the television. You don't have to get out of your chair to change the channel or adjust the volume."

"I could use one of those," Pastor Kopperman said and laughed.

"Anything else?" Dr. Cummings asked. I thought for a few seconds.

"An automatic teller machine. They are all over the country. You just put in a credit card sort of thing that has all of your information on it and you can draw money from your bank account wherever and whenever you need it. And another thing; everybody has personal computers that are small enough to sit on your desk or be carried in a briefcase." There were so many other things I could mention, but forced myself to be quiet.

"Interesting... very interesting," Dr. Cummings said. "Did your friend tell you exactly how he thought I could help him?"

"He has questions... lots of questions," I replied. And for the next twenty minutes I bombarded Dr. Cummings with all the questions that I had been tortured with over the last few weeks. I had no doubt that he was intrigued with my questions.

CHAPTER 39

"Jason, I think you've asked enough questions for one day," Pastor Kopperman said. "We'll be sitting down to dinner shortly so we need to wrap this up."

"Not a problem," I responded. "Thank you so much for this opportunity."

"Let me walk you out," said Dr. Cummings. I followed Dr. Cummings out the front door and down the porch steps.

"I'm hoping we could talk some more. I find your questions very interesting," he said.

"That would be great," I answered.

"I assume you know where Monocacy Park is," he said. We agreed to meet there at nine tomorrow morning to continue our conversation. "Oh, and by the way, bring your friend along if he would like to join us." Dr. Cummings winked at me. If I had any doubt whether or not he knew there wasn't a friend, it was erased.

I pedaled home, excited that I would have a chance to continue my discussion with Dr. Cummings. It was obvious that I could drop all pretenses about a friend. I couldn't wait until tomorrow. Linda was busy with some sort of family function all day, so I spent the evening with my family. I looked at my sister and my parents as we sat around the television. I had never appreciated how nice it was to have a nice quiet family night at home. It's funny how fifty years can change your perspective, especially when you realize that those important people in your life won't be there forever. If only I had understood that the first time around. I realized how lucky I was because most people don't get a second chance.

The next morning, I was up early. I couldn't wait for the meeting with Dr. Cummings. My parents didn't ask any questions about why I was leaving earlier than usual. I guess they assumed I was heading off to the pool. As I rode to Monocacy Park on my bike, I began to think how much had changed in fifty years. Meeting an adult in a park early in the morning could lead onlookers to believe only that something inappropriate was going to happen. In 1969, that wasn't the case. There was an innocence that was sorely missed in the future.

I realized Dr. Cummings and I had not established exactly where we would meet in the park. I headed to the most obvious location; the pavilions by the falls. Halfway to the pavilions I spied Dr. Cummings sitting on a park bench in the sunshine reading a newspaper. I rolled to a stop and hopped off my bike.

"I'm glad you came," he said. "I assume your friend wasn't able to make it?"

"I'm sorry about that," I started. "I was uncomfortable talking about this topic in front of Pastor Kopperman."

"I figured as much," he answered. "So, tell me your story."

"I'll cut right to it," I said. "I was living in 2019 until a few weeks ago."

"How do you know it wasn't a dream or a vivid imagination?"

"Because I remember everything."

"Tell me what you mean when you say everything," Dr. Cummings said.

"I remember my whole life…growing up, my college years, my adult life, my wife, my kids, my friends…everything."

"Do you have any way to know it's real?" I had to think about that for a few minutes.

"Actually, I do. A few weeks ago, I went to find my wife in her younger days. I knew where she had grown up. I convinced a friend of mine to drive me to New Jersey. We found her house. I knocked on her front door and she answered the door. We talked although I didn't tell her that we would be married years down the road. She would have thought I was crazy."

"Yes, I can imagine that might have been awkward."

"How would I have known her and known exactly where she lived if I hadn't been there before?"

"That is a very compelling argument. Let's assume that you have truly come back from the future. Tell me exactly what led up to your arrival back here and why you think you came back."

"I had received an invitation to my fiftieth high school reunion which led to discussions about what were the best years in our lives. I had been thinking a great deal about the past, especially my high school years. Then one morning I feel someone tapping my shoulder to wake me up. I open my eyes to see my mother who has been dead for a number of years. I am back in my old room, and I come to realize that I am back near the end of my junior year of high school."

"That must have come as quite a shock," Dr. Cummings said.

"You can say that again. I thought I was dreaming. I kept waiting to wake up, but so far, I haven't."

"Do you have any thoughts on why you came back to this particular point in time? Were there events that you wish you could redo? Was there some big traumatic event which you wanted to make right?"

"Not really," I said. "I mean I think everybody probably has things that they would do differently given the chance, but there were no big regrets that I wanted or needed to atone for."

"Since you have been back, are there things you have done differently?" Cummings asked.

"A few minor things like attending a sports banquet and my junior prom, neither of which I had attended, but nothing major…well at first."

"What does that mean?" Dr. Cummings asked.

"When I realized I wasn't waking up from a dream, I was trying to figure out how I was going to get back to my life. I was afraid that If I changed my past, it would change the future and my chance of getting back to my wife and kids would be compromised. I found out quickly that it wasn't going to be so easy to follow the same path that I had taken fifty years ago. It wasn't long before my girlfriend from fifty years ago and I broke up a full year ahead of schedule. I am seeing someone else that I hadn't known well at all fifty years ago. It worries me every time something happens to me that didn't happen to me fifty years ago, that I am jeopardizing my chances to get back to where I belong. I am afraid that every change now makes it more unlikely that I will return to my past life. Does any of this make sense?"

"It makes perfect sense and I wish I had an answer for you," Dr. Cummings said. "In my research I have come to the conclusion that others before you have traveled through time. Actually, traveled might not be the right word."

"If I haven't traveled through time, what do you call it?"

"Keep in mind what I'm about to tell you is a theory," Dr. Cummings said. "There is no definitive proof and I'm not sure there ever will be... at least in my lifetime." I was practically quivering in anticipation of what Dr. Cummings was about to tell me. Maybe at last I would have some kind of explanation for this strange turn of events.

"Am I going to like this?" I asked.

"I think you will," he answered. "Have you wondered what might be happening in the life you left since you have been gone?"

"I think about it all the time. I mean do I even exist or has my life as I knew it been erased? Or is everything the same except I am missing or dead? I have been driving myself crazy with all the possibilities. Does what I am doing here and now determine where I will end up in the future? See what I mean... nothing but questions."

"I can certainly understand your fears and frustrations. I would be surprised, given your circumstances, if you didn't have lots of questions. If my theory is correct... and understand that is a big if... I think you will like what I have to tell you. Do you understand the term déjà vu?"

"That's where you feel like you've seen or done something before… right?" I asked.

"Exactly," Dr. Cummings answered. "What if you have seen or done something before but not in this life?"

"How could that be possible? I don't understand."

"What if you are living several lives simultaneously? What if in each of those lives there were some similarities but also some differences? You would not have the same experiences from life to life. Keep in mind when I say lives, I'm not talking about one life after the other; I'm talking about simultaneous lives… living multiple lives at the same time."

"I'm really confused… multiple lives at the same time?"

"Same time frame, but not the same place in space," Dr. Cummings said as he grinned from ear to ear.

"You're just having fun with me… right?" I asked.

"Not at all. It excites me to meet a person like you who has jumped between lives. It makes my theory even more credible."

"I still don't see how I can be living different lives at the same time. And what did you mean by not the same place in space?" I asked more confused than ever.

"To understand my theory, you need to accept the existence of parallel universes. In the time-space continuum, I believe it is possible to exist in several different planes at the same time. You questioned it yourself when you said you were afraid that you might change the future by what you do now in the past. Think of all the infinite choices we make every day; choices that affect our future even if only in little ways. What if each time you reach a junction where you make a decision, instead of going down only one path, you go down two? On one side you continue to live the life with the choice you made, but on the other side you continue down the path with the choice you didn't make... parallel lives... same time, different place in space."

"But with so many choices that a person makes throughout their lives, there must be hundreds or even thousands of parallel lives."

"That would be correct. Now understand when I say choice, I'm not talking about every little decision we make. I'm not talking about what you chose to eat for lunch today, but rather bigger choices... like breaking up with a girlfriend for example."

"So even though I broke up with Debbie a few weeks ago, in some parallel universe I am still together with her?"

"That's the general idea."

"So, according to you, déjà vu is a memory of something we've experienced in one of our parallel lives?"

"It makes sense, doesn't it?" Dr. Cummings asked. My mind is going a thousand miles an hour. New questions are popping up at an incredible rate.

"If I am living all these parallel lives, why can I only remember two of them?"

"Most people only remember one. It has to do with our consciousness. We only get one of those. Even though our body can seamlessly exist in multiple places, our mind does not. It exists in only one place. You are one of the rare cases who have memories of another consciousness from a parallel existence."

"Alright... so let's say I get what you are saying. How does your theory account for the difference of fifty years? I am fifty years younger than my previous existence. How does that fit into your theory?"

"That is an excellent question," Dr. Cummings says. "You need to understand that your mother and father and your grandparents and your great grandparents also lived in parallel universes. Decisions about when to have children generation after generation could have delayed your birth by years… maybe even fifty years. That's my best explanation. Like I said, it is a theory."

"So, you are saying that I still exist in my former life. It's not like I disappeared. I still have a wife and two kids, but my consciousness is in this life right now?" I ask still trying to come to terms with the doctor's theory.

"That would be my assessment of the situation," Dr. Cummings answered.

"How do I get back into my former consciousness and return to the life I remember?" I asked, hopeful that Dr. Cummings would be able to offer an explanation. I could tell by the change of expression on his face that I wasn't going to like the answer.

"I wish I had an answer for you, but I don't. I'll know when it happens because if my theory is correct, you will still be here physically but will have no memory of your former life. Your consciousness will be somewhere else… hopefully back to your former life."

"Is there anything I can do to make it more likely to happen?" I asked.

"I can't say for sure, but you told me you were thinking a great deal about your high school years when your consciousness shifted. Maybe, if you think about your former life, your consciousness will shift back to that place. I'm sorry I don't have any better ideas."

"Actually. I'm relieved. I was so afraid that my wife never knew me and we didn't have our kids. At least I feel better knowing that I still exist in their world, even if I am not currently sharing it with them consciously. Thank you."

"Thank you for being willing to share your story with me. Every little piece of information I can gather on this topic gets me one step closer to unraveling one of the great mysteries of the universe."

"I have one more question for you," I said. "Is it unusual that I remember everything that happened to me in another life?"

"Not as unusual as you might think," Cummings began to explain.

"If people didn't have at least some memories of other lives, they would have no way to know they had shifted into a different universe."

"Is there anything else I can do to shift back into the universe I remember?" I asked.

"Nothing other than what I already told you. "I'm sorry I don't have anything more concrete for you."

We shook hands and I was on my way to the pool. There was a great deal to consider with the information that Dr. Cummings had dropped on me this morning… a great deal.

CHAPTER **40**

I knew today was going to be a very difficult day to focus on lifeguarding. I considered asking Mr. Hutchinson for the day off, but I decided against it. I would need to concentrate on the pool when I was in the lifeguard chair and not my conversation with Dr. Cummings. I was as relieved as I could be given my situation; at least I still existed in my former life if his theory was correct. I wondered how many other places I existed.

"Where are you today?" a voice asked from behind me. I turned to see Debbie coming up behind me.

"What does that mean?" I asked trying to cover up the daze I was in.

"I said hello three times and you didn't respond," she said. "You seemed a long way off."

"You have no idea," I answered more truthfully than she could ever imagine.

"Is everything alright?" she asked. I was caught off guard by her concern. We hadn't really spoken much since our breakup.

"Just tired, I guess," I said. "Thanks for asking though.," I added for good measure.

"You know, even though we aren't together anymore, I don't hate you." Danger signs were flashing in my head. I couldn't help but believe that she was probing to see if there was any chance that we could get back together.

"Thanks. I don't hate you either. We had a good thing going; it just didn't work out." I figured that would answer any further questions she had about where she stood. It didn't.

"I'm not sure what your status is with prom girl, but I want you to know that if things don't work out with her, I would love a second chance to make things right." I wasn't sure how to respond to that. I didn't want to encourage her, but I also didn't want to hurt her. It was a fine line.

"I thought you had a boyfriend?" I questioned.

"I do for now, but if the right opportunity came along, I wouldn't hesitate to make a change if you get my drift."

"I get your drift and I hope you find what you are looking for," I said again trying to cool things down.

"I already found it, but I let it get away," she said. "Now I need to find a way to get it back." Debbie wasn't holding back. She put her heart out there. Just as I was about to stomp on it, Mr. Hutchinson saved me.

"Williams, I'm not paying you to gab with the snack bar help. And Gravely, don't you have things to get ready in the snack bar?" Hutchinson said. Debbie and I looked at each other. I knew she wanted to continue this conversation. I didn't.

"We'll finish this conversation later," she said before heading back to the snack bar. I hustled to finish sweeping the deck before the pool opened. My conversation with Debbie gave me two things to worry about instead of one. Of all days to be working until closing time, it had to be today.

I did manage to keep my eyes on the people in the pool, although my mind wasn't always engaged. At least nobody drowned on my shift. I avoided the snack bar the rest of the day, even going so far as to walk down to the 7-11 near the pool to get some dinner. Since the snack bar closed before the pool, I figured that Debbie would be gone before I finished for the day. I was wrong.

As I exited the pool gates, Debbie was sitting on the hood of a red Ford Fairlane that I didn't recognize.

"Like my new wheels?" Debbie asked.

"This is yours?"

"I finally convinced my dad that I needed my own car. I must have gotten him in a soft moment because we went out car shopping last weekend and came home with this."

"Congratulations. You are now free as a bird."

"Want to go for a ride?" she asked.

"Maybe another time. I have my bike here."

"Come on… let me take you for a short spin." I knew this was a bad idea, but I knew how much getting a car meant to her.

"Fine, but just around the block. I need to get home. It's been a long day." I climbed in and Debbie drove out of the parking lot, her smile beaming from ear to ear. It actually made me feel good that she was so happy with her new car. What could go wrong?

I realized I was in trouble when she kept driving further and further away from the pool with no indication of heading back there.

"I thought you said this was going to be a quick little trip? How about we head back," I suggested.

"Just a little bit further," she answered. We drove on. As we drove by Monocacy Park, it dawned on me where she was taking me; Atwood Lane, the best parking spot in the whole town. I knew I should never have gotten into this car. What if somebody I knew saw me and reported it back to Linda. I wasn't sure she would believe how I got there. If the roles were reversed, I wouldn't believe me either.

"Debbie, I don't want to do this."

"Do what? I just want to talk." She turned onto Atwood Lane and parked.

"Take me back to the pool or I'm going to get out and walk home." I reached for the door handle.

"Just wait a minute. Why do you have to be so dramatic?" she asked.

"Because I don't want to be here," I answered honestly.

211

"You used to like to come here with me. Wouldn't you like to be able to do that again? Having my own car changes everything."

"It doesn't change anything for me... I'm sorry." She sat quietly. It looked like she was about to cry.

"Just hold me for a minute," she pleaded as the tears started to come.

"I'm not going to do that." She started reaching for me leaving me no option but to open the door and step out.

"Get back in the car," she begged. I turned and started walking down the road. I heard the car start up behind me. She pulled up next to me and kept pace with me.

"Get back in this car now." Her demeanor had completely changed. I kept walking.

"It's over," I said.

"Get in the car...I mean it. I don't want to do something that we'll both regret." She revved the engine and steered the car into me giving me a nudge with the fender. I didn't think she would actually hurt me, but now I wasn't so sure. I cut across the tree line that separated Atwood Lane from the field adjacent to the cemetery. My walk turned into a jog and then a sprint. I wanted to cross over Center Street before she got there because I knew I could cut through Monocacy Park and the golf course and make my way home without giving her the chance to do anything stupid... like run me over.

I had just turned into the park and hid behind the old mill when I saw her car go flying by on Illick's Mill Road. If she would have hit me at that speed, I would be dead. This never happened to me fifty years ago. I needed to get back to the future and soon before something untimely happened to me.

I made it to the last big street I would need to cross; Shoenersville Road. I looked up and down the street. I saw no red Ford Fairlane waiting for me so I sprinted across the street. I took smaller streets that I wouldn't normally take to get home. It took me twenty minutes longer, but I was almost home without spotting her car. Unfortunately, she was sitting in front of my house, the car idling. I walked a block out of my way and cut through my neighbor's yard behind my house. I was never so happy to be home as I was at that moment. I can honestly say in all my years I have never had someone try to do serious bodily injury to me with a car until now.

"I think there is someone waiting out front for you," my mother said as I walked into the kitchen. My parents, to their credit, didn't miss much.

"I think it's a group from the pool. They talked about going out to eat."

"Isn't it a little late for that?" my mother asked.

"Probably," I responded. "I'm not going anyway. I'm tired." I walked to the front door and stepped out onto the front porch. I smiled and waved toward the car. The only response was the engine revved up and then the car pulled away from the curb and disappeared up the street.

Thirty minutes later, I flopped down into my bed. What a day I had just had. Starting with the conversation with Dr. Cummings and ending with a kidnapping and attempt on my life by a spurned girlfriend. I was still trying to process it all as I fell asleep.

CHAPTER 41

I knew today at the pool was going to be interesting. I wondered how Debbie would act toward me. I still couldn't believe that she threatened to run me over with her car. Mom drove me to the pool because my bike was still there from the night before.

I purposely avoided getting anywhere near the snack bar to avoid Debbie. I did not want to start the day with a confrontation. Unfortunately, it didn't take long for her to track me down.

"I wanted to apologize for last night," she said looking embarrassed.

"Forget it," I replied trying to keep this conversation as short as possible.

"You didn't have to walk home. I would have driven you."

"Would that have been before or after you ran me over with your car?"

"I wouldn't have done that," Debbie said and laughed.

"Let's just forget the whole thing. It will be our little secret."

"About that… I wanted you to know that somebody did see us last night," she said.

"Who? Is it going to be a problem?" I asked with a feeling of dread growing in my gut.

"I don't know who it was, but whoever it was couldn't wait to tell Mark. He called me this morning and he is very upset."

"I'm sorry to hear that, but I don't see how that is my problem."

"He told me that next time he sees you, he is going to beat you to a pulp."

"That's just great. Thanks so much for getting me put on your boyfriend's hitlist."

"I'm sure he'll calm down. Just try to avoid him for the next few days," Debbie said.

"Do me a favor… stay away from me. I don't need these problems." I stalked off, annoyed that I was put in this situation. I had only myself to blame. I should have never agreed to go for a ride with Debbie last night.

I went through the day in a miserable mood. I just kept replaying last night and how I could have made better choices. Now, because somebody had seen us at lover's lane, I had to come clean with Linda. I didn't want her to hear about it from somebody else.

At five, my shift was over. I walked out to find Linda waiting for me.

"What are you doing here?" I asked hoping that news of last night hadn't already reached her.

"I just wanted to see you, and invite you to dinner at my house tonight."

"I'll have to ride home and make sure my mom doesn't mind," I answered.

"We can throw your bike in the trunk and I'll drive you home."

"Sounds great," I answered. I walked over to the bike rack to retrieve my bike only to find that things had just gotten worse. Overnight, somebody had apparently tried to steal my bike. Unable to cut through my bike lock, they settled for slashing my tires to shreds. Linda pulled the car around and saw the condition of my bike.

"What happened?" she asked as she popped her trunk.

"It's a long story which I'll share with you after dinner." I lifted the bike into her trunk and climbed into her car. As she drove to my house, I was wrestling with how I was going to bring up the mess from last night. I was even more angry with myself now that my bike needed two new tires on top of everything else. I wondered if my bike was payback from Debbie.

Mom had no problem with me going to Linda's for dinner. I took a quick shower while Linda talked to Connie and Mom. Ten minutes later I was ready to go. As we drove to Linda's house, I still didn't have a clue about the right way to explain last night. Would she believe that I was kidnapped? I doubted it. There was no choice; I had to tell her the whole story.

Dinner was barbequed chicken, corn on the cob, and potato salad. Eddie wanted to know if I had saved anybody. His eyes grew big as I related my save in the baby pool. I didn't bother to mention the unappreciative parent that came with that story.

"Have you given any thought to your plans after high school?" Mrs. Smith asked. "I know you still have a year of high school to get through, but it's never too early to start thinking about the future." I had to stifle a laugh when she mentioned the future. Not only had I planned for my future, I had lived it.

"Nothing definite other than I'll be going to college somewhere," I answered.

"Do you have any idea what field you might be interested in?" Mrs. Smith asked.

"Not for sure. I have always been interested in things like paleontology and oceanography so I guess those areas are possibilities. I love history, too, but I'm not sure what I could do with that. My dad is pushing something in the business area.

"I keep telling Linda that she needs to start thinking about college," Mrs. Smith said.

"Mom, really… do we have to do this now?" Linda asked, obviously embarrassed.

"Just promise me that before the summer is over, you'll start thinking about what kind of major might interest you."

"I will, Mom. I promise. Now, can we get off that topic?"

"Tell me about another rescue you made," Eddie jumped into the conversation not a moment too soon. I laughed.

"Eddie, there isn't much to tell. If I am doing my job properly, I shouldn't have to make rescues. I try to keep people safe and out of situations which might require rescuing."

"That's boring," Eddie said. "It would be way more exciting to make rescues every day. When I grow up to be a lifeguard, I'm going to rescue someone every day."

"I feel sorry for the people you would try to rescue. You would probably both drown," said Susan, Linda's younger sister.

"Would not!" Eddie challenged.

"Both of you… knock it off," Mom said.

Dinner finished with a delicious slice of watermelon. Linda helped wash the dishes and I dried which was amusing because I never did that at home… either now or in the future. After the dishes were done, Linda suggested sitting on the back patio. I knew the time had come to share the twisted tale about last night.

"Linda, I have something to tell you."

"This sounds serious," she said.

"You saw my bike. That didn't happen today. I'm guessing that it happened last night."

"Last night?" Linda asked. "How did you ride home last night if your tires were slashed?"

"I didn't ride home last night. The bike stayed locked to the bike rack outside the pool all night."

"So, how did you get home if you didn't take your bike?"

"Eventually, I ended up walking home," I said.

"From where?"

"From Atwood Lane, but before you say anything, please let me explain."

"Just tell me what you were doing at Atwood Lane," she pushed.

"Debbie was waiting for me when I got off work last night. Her father had bought her a car and she wanted to show it to me. She asked me to go for a quick ride… you know… just to get a feel for the car. I told her no, but she persisted. She was so proud of the car; I didn't want to burst her bubble."

"So, you ended up at Atwood Lane… an interesting choice," Linda said, now clearly upset.

"It wasn't supposed to be like that. I told her that she could drive me around the block, but that I needed to get home. It didn't take long before I realized that we weren't going around the block. I told her to turn around and take me back to the pool. She kept driving until eventually we ended up at Atwood. I told her we had to leave immediately. She insisted that she just wanted to talk."

"Talk… yeah, I'm sure that's what she wanted to do."

"I'm telling you the truth. She told me how she wanted to get back together. Next thing I know she is trying to hug me. That's when I jumped out of the car and started walking home. She yelled at me to get back in the car. I continued to walk at which point she actually nudged me with the front bumper of her car. She told me to get in or the next time it would be more than a nudge. That's when I took off through the trees. I cut through Monocacy Park and the golf course to get home. When I finally got home, she was waiting for me in front of the house. I actually cut through our neighbor's yard behind us and came in through the back door." I let my story settle to see what kind of reaction I was going to get from Linda.

"She actually hit you with her car?" she asked in disbelief.

"It was just a tap, but yes… she hit me with her car."

"She's a psycho," Linda stated.

"It gets worse," I said.

"Seriously?" Linda asked in disbelief.

"Apparently someone saw us at Atwood Lane and reported it back to her boyfriend. Now he wants to rearrange my face."

"Are you going to report this to the police?" she asked.

"No… what would I say? That my girlfriend kidnapped me and took me to Atwood Lane and then tried to run me over with her car? It would be her word against mine which doesn't usually work out well for the guy."

"What about the boyfriend?"

"I guess I'll deal with that when the time comes."

"Jason, I'm really glad that you shared this with me."

"I'm so sorry that it happened at all."

"I'll tell you one thing… the next time I see psycho Debbie, I'm going to give her a piece of my mind." This is just great. Now my current girlfriend is gunning for my old girlfriend while at the same time my old girlfriend's boyfriend is gunning for me. I should write a book!

CHAPTER 42

The clock was ticking and there wasn't much progress on Woodstock. I decided it was time to get together with Trip and Bonnie to talk about logistics. Linda and I picked them up and headed to the Big Scoop. I wasted no time.

"So, is everybody still good for Woodstock?" I asked.

"I can't believe we are really going to do this," Bonnie answered.

"Look out Woodstock…here we come," Trip interjected.

"What about your sister, Trip?" I asked.

"Yeah, unfortunately she's still coming," he replied. "Maybe she can sleep with you and Linda in your tent one night."

"Nice try, Trip," I replied. "Your sister…your tent… your problem."

"I thought you were my friend," Trip said.

"I am…I'm just not going to chaperone your sister so you can have alone time with Bonnie."

"You don't have to chaperone her. Just keep her busy for an hour or two here and there so Bonnie and I can be alone."

Linda nudged me in the ribs and looked toward the door. She wasn't laughing. I followed her gaze and found Debbie and Mark stepping through the door. Suddenly I wasn't laughing anymore either. Trip picked up on the change in Linda and me.

"Is there going to be a problem?" he asked.

"There might be," I said. "It's a long story, but there is a good chance that Mark might think that I was parking at Atwood Lane with Debbie."

220

"Were you?" he asked.

"Like I said, it's a long story." Trip looked at Linda and then back at me.

"You didn't say no," he said.

"It's not what you think," Linda came to my defense. "His ex is a psycho."

"Would somebody please tell me what is going on," Bonnie said.

I watched as Mark started toward our table. Debbie grabbed his arm and tried to hold him back. I began to rise from the table. Linda grabbed onto my arm and wouldn't let go.

"I'm here for you, brother," Trip said and started to rise from his seat as well.

"What is going on?" Bonnie asked.

Mr. Gemmi, owner of the Big Scoop, saw trouble developing and stepped out from behind the counter still wearing his apron.

"I don't want any trouble in here," he warned. "Settle down now or take it outside. Anything starts in here and I'll be calling the police. Any damage will be your responsibility," he stated pointing first at Mark and then at Trip and me.

"This isn't over, Williams" Mark said shaking his fist at me. "You think you can fool around with my girl and get away with it; you got another thing coming."

"Is that what she told you?" I asked pointing at Debbie. "Did she tell you how I ended up there? Did she tell you that she was begging me to get back with her?"

"That's bs," Mark sputtered, a vein in his neck bulging.

"Don't listen to him, Mark," Debbie said. "He was the one who was begging me to get back with him!" Linda had enough.

"Listen you psycho, keep your hands off Jason. He is with me and he doesn't want anything to do with a nutjob like you."

"What's the matter, Jason? Prom girl has to fight your battles?" Debbie asked and began to laugh.

Linda stood up from the table, the anger in her eyes blazed like hot coals. Now it was my turn to hold her back.

"Don't!" I said. "She's not worth it." That really threw Debbie into a rage. She charged Linda. Mark did not try to stop her. Trip intercepted Debbie before she could reach Linda.

"Calm down," Trip said as he held onto Debbie. Debbie continued to struggle, but Trip held onto her.

"Get your stinkin' hands off my girlfriend," Mark shouted.

"Tell your girlfriend to chill," Trip answered as he continued to struggle with Debbie.

"I warned you guys," Mr. Gemmi shouted above the fray. "The cops are on their way."

"Debbie, move it. Let's get out of here before the cops show," Mark yelled. He reached for Debbie and pulled her away from Trip. "You guys are toast. You'll both be sorry…soon… real soon. Be seein' you around." With that he exited, pulling Debbie behind him. He pushed her into his car and the two sped off.

"I'm sorry, Mr. Gemmi," I said. "Those two have some issues."

"I can see that," he said. "Listen, I don't want to get you and your friends in trouble. You better scram before the cops get here."

"Thanks, Mr. Gemmi," I said. "Let me settle our bill and we'll be out of here."

"Pay me next time you come in. There's no time right now. You need to go." On cue, I could hear the police sirens coming closer.

"Thanks," I said. The four of us wasted no time exiting. We were pulling out as the cops were pulling in.

"Well, that was interesting," Linda said.

"Will somebody please tell me what is going on?" Bonnie asked.

"Yeah, I'm kind of curious myself," Trip added. Then Linda filled them in on the whole story as we drove back to Linda's house.

"You do lead an interesting life, my friend," Trip said.

Later that evening, after we took Trip and Bonnie home, Linda and I had a discussion.

"What do you think is going to happen now?" Linda asked.

"It's obvious that Debbie isn't going to tell him the truth," I responded. "I guess we'll just need to watch out for the two of them unless I can talk some sense into Debbie."

"Do you think that's possible?"

"Before tonight, I would have thought so. Now… I'm not as convinced. Somebody that knew Mark saw us at Atwood Lane and that messed up her whole plan. She was only going to ditch Mark if I agreed to get back with her."

"I feel sorry for Mark. He doesn't get that Debbie is only using him until something better comes along," Linda said.

"You're too nice," I joked. "I can't feel sorry for someone who wants to pound my face into hamburger."

"That's understandable," Linda agreed. "By the way, should I be worried about getting ambushed by Debbie?"

"I doubt she'll come looking for you, but if you happen to run into each other anytime soon, I would keep my guard up."

"You know what… Trip is right."

"About what?" I asked.

"That you lead a very interesting life." It was my turn to laugh as I thought about the events of the last few weeks.

"You have no idea," I said. "Since we're out driving around anyway, do you want to go to the scene of the crime?"

"You mean Atwood?" Linda asked.

"That's exactly what I mean."

"That sounds like a good plan," Linda said.

CHAPTER 43

The next day it was my turn to find Debbie at the pool.

"What was that last night?" I asked when I found her in the snack bar.

"Mark is a little excitable," she said and laughed.

"You need to reign in your attack dog," I said.

"What's the matter? Are you afraid?" she asked.

"One thing I never took you for was a liar," I said. "I guess I was wrong."

"You could have made this simple," she said.

"You mean get back together with you?" I asked.

"You say that like it's the most terrible thing in the world."

"After seeing what kind of person, you are the last few weeks, I have zero interest of getting back together with you."

"You think you and prom girl are so perfect. Let me assure you, that's far from the truth," she said.

"Why are you doing this? Accept the fact that I'm with Linda, and you and I are officially through."

"I hope I'm there when Mark catches up with you," Debbie said, venom dripping from her tongue.

"Have a great day," I said and walked away, not wishing to continue this conversation any further. She was a hopeless case.

I was done guarding at five and I had arranged to have Linda pick me up. She was waiting in her Chevy Nova as I exited the pool gate. We drove by the 7-11 which stood in front of the pool.

"Turn in," I yelled. Linda jerked the car into the parking lot and came to a quick stop.

"What's the matter?" she said looking at me with concern.

"I just saw Mark go into the store," I said.

"Isn't that a good reason to get out of here?" she asked.

"I'm going to do the big lug a favor. I just hope he sees it the same way."

"I hope you know what you are doing," Linda said shaking her head slowly back and forth. I climbed out of the car and leaned against the fender. It didn't long for Mark to emerge from the store with a Slurpee in his hand.

"Look who it is," Mark said. "You want to get your beating over with now?" he asked and laughed and then took a big pull on the straw extending from his drink.

"Want to take a ride with us?" I asked.

"Why would I do that?" he asked.

"Because I think you'll want to hear what I have to say."

"What if I don't?" he asked.

"Then I guess I'm going to get that knuckle sandwich sooner than I was hoping." I held the door open so he could crawl in the back seat. Linda looked at me like I was crazy. Maybe I was.

"Where to?" Linda asked.

"It doesn't matter just drive around," I answered.

"Get to the point, Williams. Why am I here?" Mark asked.

"Look, I don't know you well at all, but you seem like a decent guy… a guy that deserves to know the truth."

"The truth according to who?" he asked and snickered.

"There is only one truth. It is true as you already know that I ended up at Atwood in Debbie's car."

"So, you admit it," Mark said.

"I never denied it, but you need to hear the whole story. Did Debbie ever tell you how I ended up in her car in the first place? Did she ever tell you what she told me that night? Did she ever tell you how she tried to run me over that night? Did she ever tell you how I got home from Atwood? And for that matter, did she ever tell you where she went after she left Atwood?"

To Mark's credit, he sat and listened as I laid out the truth of that evening. After I finished up with the whole sordid tale, he sat quietly in the back seat. I figured either he was getting ready to pound me into mincemeat or maybe…just maybe, I had said something that hit a chord with him. Another minute or two passed before he spoke.

"Take me back to my car," he said. Linda glanced over; worry etched in her face. We drove back to the 7-11. Linda pulled into the parking lot, pulled into an empty space and shifted the car into park. I climbed out and pushed the seat forward to let Mark out. He stood and turned toward me.

"Williams, you got guts," he said. I stood and waited for whatever would come next. "I guess I knew Debbie was only stringing me along until something better came along. I didn't want to believe it, but I can't say I didn't expect it. Even after you two broke up, I could see that she was still crazy about you. I was jealous and hoped I could change her mind over time. I can see now that she was only using me to make you jealous and when that didn't work, she lied about what happened so I would rough you up."

"What now?" I asked.

"I guess it's time to call it quits with Debbie. She is going to bail on me sooner or later anyway so it's not like I'm losing anything that wasn't going to be lost anyway." To my surprise he reached out his hand in my direction. I hesitated just for a second before I reached my hand toward his. We shook hands right there in the parking lot officially ending his vendetta against me.

"Good luck," I said and meant it.

"No luck needed," he answered. "I'm done with her. Let her go find some other sucker." With that he turned and climbed into his own car. Linda waited for him to leave the parking lot before she left. We watched as he turned toward the swim club. Apparently, he wasn't going to wait. He was bringing the hammer down on Debbie tonight. One side of me felt sorry for her; the other side felt like she was getting exactly what she deserved.

"Any other passengers we need to pick up before I take you home?" Linda asked.

"Nope, that was the last one for today." We both laughed as Linda steered her car out of the parking lot and toward my house. As we drove, I wished I could be present for the discussion between Debbie and Mark. I would have loved to hear how she would have tried to lie her way out of this situation. I was fairly certain that there wouldn't be anything that Debbie could say that would change Mark's mind.

"After I change and we get dinner somewhere, are we still going over to your mother's house. You mentioned that she had some questions for me."

"I'm not sure it's a good time," Linda said and looked away from me.

. "Woodstock starts in ten days. If she is having second thoughts about allowing you to go, we need to find that out now."

"What if she asks about the sleeping arrangement?" she asked.

"I don't want to lie to your mother," I answered. "She would never trust us again if she found out that we lied to her. It's not worth the risk. Hopefully, she trusts us enough to let me take you camping for a long weekend. There is nothing we could do on the camping trip that we couldn't do on Atwood Lane if you really think about it."

"I hope you aren't going to say it that way," Linda said, somewhat alarmed with my choice of words.

"Of course not," I said. "I'm hoping she will realize that on her own. It still comes down to how much she trusts me. I guess we'll find out later tonight."

I knew this wasn't the only thing that could ruin our trip. My parents had said yes almost too easily. I felt there was still a chance that they might change their minds. I wondered if they had thought about the sleeping arrangements. Although the summer of love had passed two years earlier, I'm not sure my parents were big fans of it. My biggest fear was that Linda's mother would stay true to her original decision, only to have my parents change theirs. That would be horrible. To make it worse, I was certain that the first time I passed through this life there is no way my parents would have permitted me to go to Woodstock; even less of a chance if it involved camping out with a girl!

CHAPTER 44

We settled on Dempsey's Restaurant for dinner. I knew that the restaurant would close in 2005 for good. It had sat empty ever since its closing. Tonight, however, there was a good crowd enjoying the food. I settled on a turkey club while Linda went with the grilled shrimp salad. We ate quickly, nervous about the upcoming discussion we were going to have with Mrs. Smith. I'm sure neither Linda nor her mother would have any idea what Woodstock was going to turn out to be. Very few people did. Of course, I knew because I saw it all go down on the nightly news and in the newspapers. Fifty years later a museum and concert venue sit on the site of the original festival.

Once at Linda's house, no time was wasted on small talk. Linda jumped right in.

"Mom, you mentioned that you had questions about Woodstock. Fire away."

"I need a few more details," she answered. "Where exactly you are going for starters as well as when are you leaving and when can I expect you back home?"

"It's out in the country in Bethel, New York, a quiet farm community. It would be August 14th to the 18th. There is going to be a concert taking place there with some really good bands," Linda answered.

"Is the plan still for you to drive?" her mother asked.

"Yes, it is. I'll be careful. You know I'm a good driver."

"We're all chipping in for the gas," I said feeling the need to get involved in the conversation.

"Where is Bethel, New York?" she asked. I was prepared for this question.

"It is an hour and a half north of Stroudsburg. Total driving time would be about two and a half hours," I responded.

"Are there going to be a lot of drugs and hippies there?"

"I'm not going to lie to you; I'm sure there will be some drugs and hippies there, but most people will be there for the music and the beautiful countryside," I said. "Besides, none of us do drugs. I don't want to get mixed up in that whole scene."

"And Trip and Bonnie are still going along?" she asked.

"Yes, plus Trip is taking his sister, Corinne," I answered without elaborating because I didn't want sleeping arrangements to be part of the discussion.

"Are you sleeping in tents?" So much for avoiding the issue.

"Yes, we are."

"And how many tents will there be?" There it is. She was worried about inappropriate behavior.

"Two tents," I said again without elaboration. I was going to let her draw her own conclusion as to the sleeping arrangements. If it made her feel better to think that the guys would sleep in one tent and the girls in the other... let it be.

"No funny business... right?" she asked. I really didn't want to lie, but this would be a deal breaker if I answered truthfully. Linda saved me.

"Mom, really... what kind of girl do you think I am?" Linda asked.

"You forget... I was young once too," she replied.

"If we wanted to fool around, we wouldn't need to go to New York to do that," she said. I wasn't sure how her mother would respond to that. I held my breath. Mrs. Smith looked from Linda to me and back to Linda before answering.

"I guess that's true enough."

"So, any other questions?" Linda asked.

"No, that will do it. Just don't make me sorry that I gave you permission."

"Thank you, Mom." Linda gave her mother a big hug.

"Thanks, Mrs. Smith," I added. "You can trust me."

"I hope so," she answered.

We left to tell Trip and Bonnie the news. We found the two of them at Trip's house. We spilled our news and then they spilled theirs; Bonnie's parents were having second thoughts. Just when it looked like everything was good to go...now this. I wasn't sure what would happen if Mrs. Smith found out that Bonnie wasn't allowed to go.

"Do you want us to talk to your parents?" I asked.

"I don't think it would make any difference," Bonnie replied.

"Are you sure? Peer pressure can be a wonderful thing." I suggested.

"I think it's worth a shot," Trip said. "It can't hurt...at least I don't think it can."

"What do you think Bonnie?" I asked. "Would it be better if we went to talk to your father?"

"My dad isn't any fonder of the long hair hippie types, their music, their drugs, or their free-wheeling lifestyle than your father is. I think he is worried that I'll be influenced by the hippies."

"Lets' go talk to them. We need to find out either way." I said.

"So, you really want to go over to my house now?" Bonnie asked.

"Might as well get it over with," I answered.

232

The four of us walked into the Rootman's residence, knowing that the Woodstock trip could very well be hinging on what happened in the next few minutes.

"To what do we owe this unexpected pleasure?" Mr. Rootman asked.

"We're hoping we can convince you to let your daughter come with us to Woodstock, sir," I said.

"Why is it so important to the rest of you?" her father asked.

"Because we really were hoping to do this together," Trip said.

"I see," my dad said. "That's the way the rest of you see it as well?" We all nodded our heads in agreement.

"How can I be sure that there won't be bad decisions being made on this camping trip?" he asked.

"Because you've known us for years," I answered. "I would hope that you consider us to be decent, law-abiding, reasonable people that know right from wrong."

"How are you getting there?" her father asked.

"I would be driving, sir," Linda replied. "I am eighteen and have my senior license. I have never had a ticket of any kind and I don't expect that to change anytime soon."

"And your parents are fine with you driving?" Mr. Rootman asked.

"My mother is. My father doesn't live at home anymore because my parents got divorced." Mr. Rootman turned toward his wife who had been silent up until now. "What do you think?"

"I can't say that I'm crazy about the idea. New York is so far away," she said.

"It's only a little over two hours," I stated. "There are places at the Jersey shore that are further away than that."

233

"It's still far," Mrs. Rootman answered. "What if something goes wrong?"

"First off, we'll be very careful. With five of us going, we can help each other out if any problems arise," I answered.

"Please Mom, I really want to go," Bonnie spoke. I hated to see her resort to begging, but she knew her parents better than we did. Her mother was on the fence and I knew whatever side she came down on, her father would agree with her. She had to say yes; she just had to.

"Well, I suppose it's aright as long as your father agrees." All eyes turned back toward Mr. Rootman. He didn't answer right away. It was almost like he paused for dramatic effect.

"As long as you promise to be careful and not do anything stupid. You said there would be live music. Does that mean some of those long-haired hippies will be there doing drugs?"

"Probably," I answered.

"But it doesn't matter because none of us mess around with drugs. You can trust us," Trip said. There was another pause as Bonnie's father looked at each of us before answering.

"Alright, you can go. Just don't make me sorry I said yes." It was almost the same warning that Mrs. Smith had given us. Adults must learn that in parenting class or something. I thanked Mr. Rootman and we filed back out of the house. I didn't want to give them a chance to change their minds. As it stood right now, everybody was going to Woodstock; a lifelong dream would be fulfilled.

Later that evening as I lay in bed, I could not believe that I am this close to attending Woodstock. It was surreal on so many counts, but mainly because it had happened fifty years earlier. I hated to admit it, but I was beginning to enjoy my time in this parallel universe or whatever it was. I felt guilty because I should desperately be wanting to get back to Grace and my kids, but ever since my meeting with Dr. Cummings earlier in the week I was relieved that my "being" still existed in my former world. It wasn't like Grace and the kids were missing me because the truth of the matter was that they didn't even know I was gone. I wondered if anybody else in the entire history of the world had experienced what was happening to me now. If there were others, I wonder if any of them made it back to their former lives. That was really the question that mattered; would I ever go back to where I was or was I destined to live my life over again from this point forward? Surprisingly, I realized that I was beginning to believe that it wouldn't be so terrible if I ended up staying here. I was still with friends and family. Currently I was seeing a great girl in Linda. Most of my life was still in front of me which I certainly could not say about my former life. I had managed to "fix" a few things from my past and now Woodstock would be the icing on the cake.

CHAPTER 45

Things at the pool had slowed down considerably. Even the numbers on weekends were down. It seemed many people that had been coming to the pool, took their vacations in August. Days at the pool had become boring. Thankfully, Debbie had left me alone. Other than saying hello when we passed, there wasn't much other conversation. I did hear through the grapevine that she and Mark were finished. Either he dumped her or she dumped him depending on who you heard it from. I wasn't sure if she blamed me for their breakup or she blamed herself. Truthfully, I didn't care. I had more important things to worry about.

Every hour that I wasn't at the pool, I was thinking about Woodstock. I knew exactly what issues the four of us would face over the course of the weekend, and I wanted to make sure I was prepared for them. The three primary problems were the traffic getting there, the shortage of food once we were there, and the stormy weather. I worked those issues into my conversations with my traveling partners.

"I think we should leave early because I think by Friday the traffic is going to be snarled beyond belief," I said as the four of us sat around a pizza which was quickly disappearing.

"You really think it's going to be that bad?" Trip asked. "There hasn't been a ton of publicity for this concert. I bet most people don't know anything about it."

"For sure the locals know about it," I answered. "I bet more people know about it than you think."

"What time do you think we should leave?" Linda asked.

"I would really like to leave after work on Thursday," I replied.

"You really think that's necessary?" Bonnie asked.

"Would you rather have a nice, easy drive up to New York on Thursday night or be stuck in traffic on Friday?" I asked. "Besides, if we get there Thursday night, we get our choice of campsites and parking closer to the event," I replied.

"It doesn't matter to me," Trip said. "I can go whenever you want to go."

"I'm not sure my parents are going to be excited about me leaving even earlier than I first said," Bonnie said.

"I think the same is probably true for me," Linda said.

"Maybe the two of you to need to have a sleepover," Trip suggested.

"How is that going to help our situation?" Bonnie asked.

"Bonnie, you tell your parents you are staying at Linda's house Thursday night," Trip explained. "Linda, you tell your parents you are staying at Bonnie's house. No one will ever be the wiser." I looked back and forth between the two girls, not sure how Trip's idea was going to fly.

"I haven't lied to my parents about this weekend and I'm not going to start now," said Bonnie. "Giving me permission to go at all was a big step for them and if they find out I lied about when we are leaving, it would ruin all the trust they have in me."

"I feel exactly the same way," Linda said. "Furthermore, since I'm driving, I guess I get to call the shots on when we leave." The look on Trip's face was pure shock. It was obvious he wasn't expecting the girls to stand up for each other. I laughed silently to myself; wait until Trip sees how women and their position in society changes in the next fifty years. He ain't seen nothing yet in the words of Bachman, Turner, Overdrive who hadn't hit the big time yet.

"I guess we're going when you say we're going," Trip replied to Linda.

"What's the latest you think we can leave and still beat the traffic? Linda asked me. Not leaving until Friday morning probably meant we weren't going to beat the traffic. I get Linda's position with her mother. I tried to be diplomatic in my answer.

"What's the earliest you think you can leave?" I asked.

"Truthfully, I would say not until the sun starts to come up. I'm fairly certain my mother would not be comfortable with me leaving in the dark," she answered.

"That sounds fine," I said. "Since we'll all have stuff to carry, do you mind picking each of us up?"

"Not at all," Linda said. The traffic problem was handled. We still had two more problems to discuss.

"I have a tent," I announced. "It could sleep four, but it would be crowded and it wouldn't give us much privacy." Trip laughed.

"We definitely need privacy, don't we Bonnie?" he asked. Linda and I laughed. Bonnie wasn't as amused.

"I swear, that's all you think about," Bonnie said.

"Can you blame me?" Trip asked. "I mean, really it's your fault for being so hot." Bonnie was even less amused by that comment.

"Keep it up, and I won't even be in the same tent as you," Bonnie said. Trip got the message and made no further comments on that topic.

"Does anybody else have a tent?" I asked.

"I have one. I'll need to get it out and see if all the pieces are there," Trip said.

"Can't we just sleep out under the stars?" Linda asked. "That would be so romantic." I had to admit that it did sound nice, however I knew that the weather was not going to cooperate.

"I figure we should take the tents just in case of bad weather... or in case somebody needs their privacy," I answered.

"Hey, you're going to get me in trouble," Trip said.

"It's too late for that," Linda replied. "You're already in trouble." We all laughed, except for Trip. Now it was his turn not to be amused.

"Final thing we need to talk about is food," I said,

"Won't they be selling food there?" Linda asked.

"They will, but I'm afraid the lines and the prices will be ridiculous," I answered. "I think we should plan on backpacking some of our own food in to cut down the cost for starters. That way if they do run out of food, we won't starve."

"What kind of food are you thinking about?" Linda asked.

"Just basic stuff and nothing that has to be cooked. I'm not sure building a fire would even be permitted." Of course, the weather was going to make fires impossible, but I kept that to myself.

"You're talking stuff like beef jerky and granola bars," Bonnie said.

"Exactly," I replied. "Stuff that isn't too bulky and doesn't spoil easily. Maybe some cheese and crackers."

"Maybe peanut butter and apples," Trip added.

"Maybe some pretzels and chips," Linda added. "Maybe we could all go to the grocery store on Thursday night and stock up."

"That sounds like a plan," I said.

By the time our discussion had ended, the pizza was gone. I felt like we really made some progress. We had addressed the major issues that I knew we were going to face. I was sure there would be other problems that would need to be dealt with once we got there. Parking was an issue that I didn't bring up. Many cars were just left along roadways and in fields. I wasn't sure how Linda would feel about leaving her car in the middle of nowhere. I also knew that we would need to carry everything we needed into the site. Between tents, sleeping bags, raincoats, food, and a change of clothes for when we got soaked, this was not going to be an easy proposition. I was beginning to regret that I knew so much about the festival. The rest of the people going to the concert had no idea what they were in for... maybe ignorance was better. Even knowing everything I know; this is going to be an adventure... an adventure I wouldn't trade the world for.

Later that evening I lay in bed still thinking about Woodstock. Then I had a terrible thought; what if I was transported back to my former life now? Plain and simple; that would suck. I immediately felt guilty saying that. I still loved and missed Grace and my kids more than ever. The problem was that going to Woodstock was the opportunity of a lifetime. It was an opportunity that I never expected I would have. How could I have ever imagined that this was going to be possible? What if I was presented with an opportunity to go back to my former life now? I mulled that over for a bit, but it didn't take long to realize that I would go back to where I belonged; Woodstock or no Woodstock. I lay in bed in my childhood home saying a silent prayer that if I went back, please make it after Woodstock.

CHAPTER 46

Monday morning started off as a beautiful day; warm and sunny. Unfortunately, it didn't stay way for long. The first thunderstorm rolled in around 1:30 in the afternoon. The small crowd scattered quickly to the safety of their cars leaving only the staff at the pool. The storm passed quickly and the sun was out a half hour later. A few people began to trickle back into the pool. They barely got wet when the second storm of the day blew in. This one was big. High winds, bolts of lightning, loud booming peals of thunder, and torrential rain. Again, the pool complex emptied out except for the staff. We all gathered in the manager's office to ride out the storm. Even Debbie and Joyce from the snack bar joined us. I made a point not to anywhere close to Debbie.

This storm lingered on with thunder rumbling in the distance ninety minutes later. By four, Hutchinson made the decision to close the snack bar for the day. Debbie and Joyce closed up the snack bar and made a dash for Debbie's car in the parking lot. He also gave any guards who were off at five the option to leave an hour early. I was one of those guards and gladly accepted the option. I ran to my bike and sprinted home in a light rain. I had thought of something earlier today that I definitely wanted to take to Woodstock; my Kodak Instamatic camera.

I knew there was good chance that photos of the event would be in big demand. I might be able to sell some to newspapers and magazines. Maybe eventually, I could turn them into a book somehow. There were certain iconic photos of Woodstock that existed even fifty years after the event. I was hoping maybe a few of my photos could join the list.

Photography changed drastically in the fifty years that followed Woodstock. Film cameras were replaced with digital cameras. Whereas the number of photos on a roll of film was limited to twelve or twenty-four, the memory cards of digital cameras could hold thousands of photos. With film, you had to pick and choose your shots. With a digital camera you could shoot away with little regard for numbers. The chances of getting a good shot or two multiplied immensely when you were shooting a couple of hundred shots instead of twenty-four. My plan was to take a bunch of film with me and shoot lots of pictures. It would cost a small fortune to develop all the film, but it would be worth it if I captured some amazing photographs that would be in demand by the media.

I was soaked by the time I got home, so I took a quick shower and changed into some dry clothes. The search for my camera did not take long. I found it in the bottom drawer of my desk. Even better, according to the shot counter, I still had eighteen shots on this roll of film. I hoped to find more film, but had no luck on that count. I would need to buy some film before we left. The camera used the Kodak 126 Instapack film cartridges. Kodak knew what they were doing; they sold the film cheaply, but made a fortune on the developing. What I kept in mind was that I didn't need to get all the film developed at once. I could take it slow and do a couple of rolls at a time, spreading out the hefty cost.

I started calculating how much film I was going to need. Given the state of photography in 1969, I knew I didn't need to worry about night shots; that would just be a big waste of film. That eliminated the Friday night and Saturday night portions of the concert. That left the daylight portions of the concert cutting my film cost in half. Besides the performers, I also wanted to focus on the people, the storm, and the aftermath of the storm. That's where the best shots were likely to be found. Eighteen rolls of 24 print film would give me four hundred thirty-two shots. That, hopefully would be enough. At $1.25 per roll, I would need to spend $22.50 plus tax on film. That was a good chunk of change for a high school kid making $1.30 an hour lifeguarding...like me.

I was getting more and more excited as the big day neared. Not only would I be seeing many of my favorite bands, I would possibly be in a position to profit handsomely from it. It might even launch me into a career of photojournalism. I realized right at that moment that I hadn't really thought about where my life might lead if I

242

didn't get back to my other consciousness. Here I was, with a chance to redirect the course of my life. I could atone for my lackluster effort in college, this time paying more attention to my studies instead of fraternity parties. Even if my career as a photographer didn't pan out, I would still have a chance to get into law which I realized far too late that I might like. Everybody I knew always said I liked to argue. It was appearing unlikely that I would end up with Debbie in this life given all our trouble this summer. Much more likely was the possibility of ending up with Linda. At the moment, that seemed like a great idea. I could see myself spending the rest of this life with her. The chances of ever meeting up with Grace in this life seemed remote at best. I realized the possibilities of where I wanted this life to go were endless. This world was still in front of me. Almost on cue, a loud crack of thunder and flash of lightning split the air. It was like the gods were sending me a message; they were not happy with me. I didn't understand why they would be displeased with me; I didn't choose to come here and apparently; I had very little say whether or not I would ever go back.

"Dinner," Mom yelled from the bottom of the stairs. I snapped out of my daydream and hustled down the stair taking two at a time.

"Honestly Jason, you're going to break your leg one day if you insist on coming down the stairs like that."

"I doubt it," I answered. I never had fifty years ago so why would I have an accident now. Then I realized my mistake; there were a number of things that had not gone as they had fifty years earlier. Because it hadn't happened before did not mean it might not happen now. In that instant I knew I had to avoid any unnecessary risks over these next few days; I did not want to screw up my chance at attending Woodstock.

"How are your plans for the camping trip coming along," my dad asked.

"I can't believe you are letting him go," Connie interrupted. "He always gets to do the fun stuff. It's not fair."

"I am older than you," I said. "Do you think that might have something to do with it?"

"Alright, you two," Mom replied. "Let's not ruin dinner."

"But it's not fair," Connie repeated.

"Connie, you heard your mother," Dad said. "That will be enough." Connie folded her arms against her chest, closed her eyes, and huffed. Mom and Dad chose to ignore her.

"We came up with a plan for what we need to take the other night. I think we have everything covered," I answered.

"Good, I'm glad to hear that. I would hate to see you get all the way up to New York and realize you forgot something," Dad said.

"Thanks, Dad," I said and meant.

My sister was still fuming and said nothing else at dinner, barely eating a thing. Mom and dad shared their news of the day with each other. I was only too happy to sit back and enjoy their conversation. It was still hard for me to believe I was sitting here with my parents all these years later. It was a gift to be able to spend this time with my parents. I cherished every extra minute of time I got to spend with them, the most important people in my life... now or ever.

I called Linda after dinner and told her that I wanted to spend some time at home tonight. She completely understood. Connie stayed in her room the rest of the night, still miffed over me being allowed to go on this camping trip. Mom, Dad, and I settled in front of the television for the rest of the night. We didn't talk much, but it didn't matter. It was just nice to be there with them.

CHAPTER 47

The next three days went by as fast as any three days in my life…either life. The anticipation I felt for Woodstock was off the charts. Feeling guilty every morning, I was grateful and relieved that I was still in 1969. I checked in with Trip each day after breakfast to make sure that he and Bonnie were still good to go. They were.

The days at the pool were quiet. Attendance was down as the magic of the pool had worn off by this point in the summer. Kids were already thinking about the next school year. Parents were trying to fit in vacations before school started. The guards that were heading off to college were down to their last few days working at the pool. Then they were off to their next big adventure. I doubted if any of them truly understood how different their lives would be after starting college.

Thursday, I was finished at five. I had arranged for Linda to pick me up from the pool. We had shopping to do. I walked out of the pool to find her Chevy parked right outside the gate.

"Right on time," I said as I climbed into the car.

"At your service," she replied and laughed. "Where to first?"

"I want to buy film for my camera first so let's go to Almart first." Almart was Bethlehem's version of Kmart or Walmart. They sold a wide variety of products including the film I needed. I headed right for the camera section on the first floor.

"I need eighteen rolls of K-126 film," I said to the clerk behind the counter. He was an older gentleman dressed in a white shirt and a bowtie, very old-fashioned looking.

"Eighteen rolls?" he questioned. "That's a lot of pictures. Are you sure you need that much?"

"Positive. I'm going to a really big event. I am hoping I can sell some of my photos to the newspapers and magazines." The old-timer tried to suppress a chuckle.

"So, you're going to make money selling your photographs," he repeated.

"Yes sir. That's the plan." He laughed again.

"Well sonny, I see two problems with your plan," he said. "Want to know what they are?"

"Sure," I answered.

"First off, if this event you're going to is this big, chances are that the newspapers will have their own reporters and photographers covering the event. I doubt they will be buying photographs from amateurs such as yourself."

"I guess I have a little inside information; there won't be that many photographers in attendance," I said.

"If that's true, I doubt that this event is as big as you think," he commented.

"It's a secret," I replied. The old-timer laughed.

"You mentioned two problems," I said. "What's the second one?"

"I only have twelve rolls of that film in stock at this time. I should have more coming next Tuesday."

"Next Tuesday will be too late," I said. "I need it now."

"I'm sorry. The best I can do is to sell you ten rolls."

"I thought you had twelve?" I asked, now confused.

"At Almart, we try to be considerate of all our customers. If I sold you all twelve rolls, there wouldn't be any left for anyone else. I can only sell you ten rolls." I was so angry at myself for not taking care of this detail sooner. I would have had the chance to scout around for additional film. I paid for the ten rolls and walked out. My mind was working overtime to try and think of another place I might be able to purchase film. Thrift Drugstore might be one option and they might have a few rolls at the grocery store. Acme and Thrift Drugs were at

246

opposite ends of the same shopping center where I was. I handed Linda the grocery list.

"You can start with the groceries. I'll check the drugstore and then meet you at Acme to help you finish up there," I said.

"Make it quick," she answered. "You have the money."

I jogged one direction while she headed in the opposite direction toward Acme. I checked at the counter in the drugstore. They had two rolls of the film I needed. I immediately purchased them and took off on a sprint to Acme.

By the time I found Linda, she was already halfway through our list. We finished the rest of the list up in no time. They had a small area where they sold camera film. Unfortunately, I could only find one roll of K-126 film. I added it to our groceries. None of the food was going to spoil so we left everything in the trunk of Linda's car. I was disappointed that I was five rolls of film short of what I originally wanted. It would have to do. I had to be a little more selective in the shots I took.

We spent the rest of the evening on Linda's back porch. Trip and Bonnie joined us a little later. Talk centered around our big trip, although I suspect none of them realized the enormity of the event that they were about to witness first-hand. Bonnie put a little damper on things with a question that none of us had considered previously; one that I should have.

"How much extra clothing is everybody taking along?" she asked. We all looked at each other. Apparently, neither Linda or Trip had thought much about this.

"I want to remind everybody that whatever we take, we'll need to carry into the site and depending where we park, that could be a long walk."

"What are you taking?" Trip asked me.

"I figure a couple pairs of clean underwear and a clean shirt. And I'm taking my raincoat just in case." Everybody agreed that my packing list wouldn't add much weight to my load. I reminded everybody to bring a backpack tomorrow so that we could divvy up the food that we had bought. I figured Trip and I could handle the two tents. I knew going in would be easier than coming out when everything was going to be wet. Wet sleeping bags would be heavy to carry not to mention the tents. I put those thoughts out of my head. We would worry about the return trip to the car when the time came.

Trip and Bonnie left first a little before ten. I hung around for ten more minutes before heading home myself. Tomorrow was going to be a big day. On the way home, I thought about my camera and film; I needed to find a way to keep the camera and film dry. As soon as I walked in the door, I went to the kitchen and pulled out half a dozen plastic sandwich bags. Hopefully they would do the trick. I realized that my plan for getting some fantastic photos at Woodstock rested on six cheap plastic sandwich bags. It would have to do; I didn't have a better solution at this late time.

I knew sleep was going to be difficult, if not impossible. I wasn't sure that was a bad thing. To go back to my former life now would have been devastating. I just wanted to get through the weekend right here in 1969. After that, the powers of the universe could send me to any parallel universe that they wanted; just let me stay here for the next three days... a mere three days.

Impossible as I thought sleep would be, apparently my body did not agree. The alarm clock that I had set just in case, woke me. I was afraid to open my eyes. Please, please, please... let me still be in my parent's house. I opened my eyes and rolled over. I was alone. I was still here. I was going to Woodstock.

CHAPTER 48

Linda pulled into the driveway in front of my house a little before six. I peeked into my parent's bedroom and whispered goodbye to my mom who was sitting up in bed reading a book with a little nightlight.

"Be careful and stay out of trouble," she whispered back to me.

"Got it," I said and gently closed their door.

I gathered up my stuff which I had left by the front door. With the tent, my sleeping bag, and extra clothes and my raincoat stuffed into my backpack, it was a challenge to get out of the front door. I managed to get my stuff to the car. Linda had already popped the trunk and I dumped everything into the trunk.

"The adventure begins," I said as I slid into the front seat.

"I get the feeling that somebody is excited," she said.

"Aren't you? I mean we're going to see some of the biggest names in rock history."

"To be honest, I'm more excited to be spending the weekend camping out with you," Linda said. I reached over and kissed her on the cheek.

"That's a really nice thing to say," I said.

"You're a really nice person," she replied. The weekend was off to a good start and we hadn't even left my driveway yet. We picked up Bonnie next before driving to Trip's house. I was surprised to see only Trip waiting out front. Originally his sister was supposed to come with us.

"Where's your sister?" I asked.

"Corinne is sick," Trip answered. "She started tossing her cookies last night."

"I'm sure you're heartbroken that she won't be coming," I replied.

"You can't imagine," Trip answered as the four of us broke into laughter.

The trunk was filled to the max by the time Trip finished jamming his stuff in it. I glanced at the contents of the trunk one last time before I shut it. It was going to be a challenge to carry all that stuff from the car to the venue. I sure hoped we would be able to find a parking place close to the action. From stories I had read about Woodstock, I knew that people had started to arrive Thursday night.

Linda took Route 512 to Wind Gap where she picked up Route 33. In 1969, this was as far south as Route 33 had been finished. We followed 33 to Marshall's Creek where she took Routes 209, 434, and 55 to the turnoff at Dr. Duggan Road. My excitement grew the closer we got to Woodstock. It wasn't until we turned onto Route 17B West that the traffic really picked up. There was a steady stream of cars heading toward the concert site. We weren't moving fast, but at least we were moving. A few miles later we turned onto Hurd Road which meant we were close. Traffic really slowed down as cars were crawling along looking for a place to park.

"What do you think?" Linda asked. "Should I pull over and find a place to park?" I knew we were still a few miles from the actual site. I didn't want to have to lug all that stuff that far.

"Keep going," I suggested. "Let's see what happens." Linda inched along, each foot another foot we didn't have to carry our stuff. Cars were just pulling off to the side of the road and stopping. We drove on, barely moving. People were walking along the side of the road faster than we were driving. Another five minutes and we had seemed to come to a virtual standstill. People were parking in a large field just off the road.

"I think this is about as far as we're going to get," I said. "You might as well pull in here." We followed the cars in front of us and parked. There didn't seem to be any real pattern to how people were parking. It would be a nightmare to get out of here. We'd have to worry about that when we left.

"Do you know where you're going?" Trip asked as we started to unload the trunk.

"Just follow the crowd," I replied. "They're all going the same place that we are."

Like I suspected, the loads we had to carry were a challenge. It was only a little after ten in the morning when the sun came out from behind the clouds and warmed up the day. The temperature rose steadily as we trudged along, following the line ahead of us.

"Bad time to ask," Trip started. "What are we going to do about tickets?"

"We'll sneak in with the crowd," I answered.

"Seriously… that's your plan," Trip responded.

"That's it."

"We came all this way and your plan is to sneak in. Are you for real?" Trip asked, his irritation obvious.

"Trust me…you'll see… it will all work out." I continued climbing the hill in front of me. The four of us walked on in silence, growing warmer by the minute. History told me tickets would not be a factor. It was so cool to have this kind of information ahead of time.

We came up over a rise and there it was: I was looking at the Woodstock stage from the top of the hill. The bowl below us was filling with people all the way down to the stage.

"Where are we going to set up camp?" Trip asked. I surveyed the situation. There were no trees and no water up here where we were. Just behind the stage there were some woods, and I knew there were some ponds and lakes back there too. The shade from the trees would certainly help us stay cooler. The ponds would come in handy to cool off and after the rains came, to clean off all the mud that would soon cover us.

"Down there," I answered and pointed to the woods just beyond the left side of the stage.

"That's a long way down the hill and keep in mind, we'll need to climb back up when we leave," Trip said. The girls looked from Trip to me. I could tell that they saw the wisdom in what Trip had said.

"I know what I'm doing," I said and began walking down the hill, threading my way through the crowd. I didn't turn around; I didn't want to give them the chance to argue with me. A few minutes later, I was pleased to see that they were right behind me. The walk down had been easy, and I knew the walk back wasn't going to be fun, but the advantages of being down in the woods outweighed the con of climbing back up the hill.

When we passed by the stage, I was surprised to see a beehive of activity as they raced to finish the stage so it would be ready for the performers. Once again, history told me the first performer wouldn't take the stage until a little after five this afternoon.

I found a nice clearing just inside the woods a little way beyond the stage. It was perfect. We were close enough to the stage to hear everything. It would only take us a minute or two to walk over to the stage and get a view. The clearing gave us a little privacy away from the horde that would descend on this site over the next three days. I knew from pictures that I had seen that we were close to two ponds and a larger lake if we wanted to cool off or attempt to bathe.

Trip and I began to unpack the tents. Both were small dome tents and as long as we had all the poles, they would not be hard to set up. Trip and I struggled more than we should have much to the amusement of the girls. Thirty minutes later, sweaty and embarrassed, the two tents stood next to each other.

The girls threw the sleeping backs, food, and other miscellaneous gear into the two tents. Trip and I headed to find one of the ponds to cool off. It didn't take long as we followed the sounds of laughter and splashing. The pond came into view along with something I should have been prepared for; naked bodies frolicking in the water.

Reading about it and seeing pictures is different than witnessing it for yourself firsthand.

Trip surprised me. His shirt was already off and his pants weren't far behind. He even dropped his underwear and spread them out in the grass to dry before charging into the pond.

"What are you waiting for?" he asked. "The water feels great!" I looked around. Nobody was paying any particular attention to anybody else. I shrugged my shoulders and began to disrobe. Thirty seconds later I was in the water up to my chest enjoying the coolness. It had been a long time since I had skinny-dipped and when I did, it was at night with a small group of friends. Here I was, in the middle of the day with a crowd of strangers, without a stitch of clothing on.

"Do you think the girls will skinny-dip?" Trip asked.

"I doubt they would come in here now with all these people around. Maybe tonight, after it got dark. They might consider it then," I said. I soaked in the water wondering how this weekend was going to play out with Linda. We hadn't really done anything other than neck. I laughed to myself with my use of that word. Neck... I hadn't used that word since high school. Certainly, being alone this weekend gave us the opportunity to take things further. I still was troubled by doing anything with anyone other than Grace. I was still trying to wrap my head around the whole thing with parallel universes. Assuming Grace wasn't with me in every parallel universe, it meant I was probably sleeping with multiple women. Even so, it didn't make me feel any more comfortable with the idea of becoming more physical with Linda this weekend.

Ten minutes later, we waded back to the edge of the pond, retrieved our clothes, and began to dress. A woman sitting in the grass wearing only a towel around her waist was the only person to comment.

"Very nice... maybe I'll see the two of you later," a twenty-something woman whispered to me as I pulled on my pants.

"I don't think my girlfriend would approve," I answered and laughed.

"Bring her along," she said and smiled at me. "It could be fun." I made no further comment and continued walking.

"I guess the summer of love isn't over," I said to Trip.

"I'm beginning to think I should have left Bonnie at home," he said. "Don't tell her I said that. She would kill me."

"Your secret is safe. Besides, I'm guessing after a night in the tent alone with her, you might feel differently."

"Good point." We arrived back to find the girls sitting on a fallen log near the tents.

"Why are you guys wet?" Bonnie asked.

"We found a pond and cooled off," Trip answered.

"What does everybody want to do this afternoon?" I asked.

"I actually was thinking I could use a nap," Bonnie said. "It was an early morning."

"That sounds good to me," Trip said.

"Hold on, buster. When I said nap, I meant nap. Don't go getting any ideas."

"Me? Never," Trip said. Three of us laughed. Bonnie did not.

"I'm going to take a walk around. Maybe I'll get some good shots with my camera," I said.

"Mind if I come?" Linda asked.

"I wouldn't mind at all." By the time I found my camera, the other two had disappeared inside the tent and closed the flap. I was betting that before the end of the afternoon, other things besides napping would be going on inside of that tent.

"The crowd was swelling larger and larger, minute by minute. The heat was building. Work on the stage continued at a frantic pace. It was becoming evident to anyone who was paying attention, that this event was going to exceed the attendance estimates. I took a photo here and there, trying to capture shots that I thought would help define the experience. Long hair and tie-dye were everywhere, both men and women. My father would have hated this crowd and the large number of hippies. As we walked, the smell of marijuana wafted up from place to place. Everybody was chilling and just having a good time despite the crowds and the heat.

A number of things became apparent as we walked. First the food supply was going to be totally inadequate for the number of people that would be here. Second, the bathroom facilities which consisted of several dozen port-a-potties were not going to be sufficient either. Long lines at the food tables and the bathrooms stretched for a hundred yards. This was exactly why I insisted we bring some of our own supplies including a couple of rolls of toilet paper.

Linda and I made our way back to our tent. The flap was still closed on the other tent. I suggested that we take a walk down to the pond. I was interested to see what kind of reaction I would get from Linda when she saw all the naked bodies.

"Are we going in?" Linda asked after one glance at the pond.

"It's up to you," I said. Without another word, Linda disrobed completely and slid into the water. I admired the view for a few seconds before I dropped my shorts and followed her into the water. We both moved to chest deep water where she wrapped her arms around me and pulled me into a big hug. My hands wasted no time exploring the treasures hiding in the dark water below.

"This is going to be a fun weekend," she said before she leaned in and gave me a long, intense kiss. Indeed, it was shaping up to be a great weekend.

CHAPTER 49

Thirty minutes later I was cooled off enough to emerge from the water without any anatomical protrusions. We sat in the grass for a few minutes to dry off before pulling our clothes on and heading back to our campsite. Trip was sitting outside the tent. He barely acknowledged us when we returned.

"What's wrong with you?" I asked.

"I'll give you three guesses," he answered. I guessed that napping was the preferred activity in his tent, although I didn't verbalize that thought.

"The music should be starting soon," I said. "Do you and Bonnie want to come with us?" I asked.

"Let me check with Sleeping Beauty." Trip disappeared back into his tent. He reappeared seconds later.

"It will just be the three of us," he said.

We left Bonnie at the campsite and took the short walk to the corner of the stage. It was obvious that the stage still wasn't completely ready. I looked at my watch and it was a few minutes after five. I knew that Richie Havens was going to walk out on that stage in less than five minutes to kick off the music... and he did. Woodstock had begun and I was here to see it for myself. Unbelievable!

Richie Haven and his band minus his bass player who was stuck in traffic, performed for three hours. He did three encores because no one else was ready to perform. Included in his third encore was the song *Freedom,* which he made up on the spot. From our vantage point, we could see the hillside in front of the stage continue to fill with people.

Trip returned to the campsite to see if he could rouse Bonnie. Linda and I enjoyed music from John Sebastian, who wasn't even scheduled to perform. Country Joe McDonald stepped up to the microphone next to lead his famous Fish cheer, only it wasn't fish that he spelled. The crowd loved it. Hearing a couple hundred thousand people shouting out the f-bomb in unison was an experience in itself. As Sweetwater was finishing their set, Trip and Bonnie reappeared, although the two did not appear to be speaking to one another.

The show rolled on with a couple of folk acts, Bert Sommer and Tim Hardin, before Ravi Shankar and his sitar music took the stage. The first rain of the weekend began to fall as Ravi was wrapping up his set. Trip and I walked back to the tent to grab raincoats and some apples and cheese. It was more difficult than I expected to find our tents in the dark woods.

Melanie took the stage around eleven. The rain was steady now. The best part of her set was actually when the public address announcer asked everyone to light candles. The hillside lit up with a soft glow. Linda and I held each other in the rain, swaying to the music and watching the ethereal vision on the hillside. It was a beautiful moment, one of many I would experience this weekend.

Trip and Bonnie headed back to the campsite during Arlo Guthrie's set. Linda and I opted to stay. Joan Baez concluded the night with a twelve-song set ending at 2:15 A.M. on Saturday morning. We almost missed our campsite in the dark as the rain continued. Eventually we found our way back.

We quietly slid into our tent and stripped off our wet clothes. I started to pull on some dry stuff.

"Don't," Linda whispered.

"Don't what?" I asked.

"Don't put on your clothes." Linda lay down on top of her sleeping bag and pulled me down next to her. We kissed and let our hands roam freely, but that was as far as it went. I wasn't ready for anything else and neither was Linda apparently. I pulled my sleeping bag over us before we fell asleep in each other's arms.

I woke to the sound of arguing. Trip and Bonnie were going at it. From the gist of what I could hear, Bonnie wasn't interested in Trip's early morning advances. Linda and I pulled on our clothes and emerged from our tent.

"Good morning, you two," I said acting like I hadn't heard them arguing. The morning was gray and foggy. At least it wasn't raining.

"You missed some good performances last night," I said.

"We may not have seen them, but we could still hear them," Trip replied. Bonnie hadn't spoken a word to us.

"How did you sleep?" I asked Bonnie to break the ice.

"Sleep? What's that?" she answered in a huff. "Trip doesn't believe in sleep."

"I like sleep," Trip answered. "It's just that I like other things better."

"You're an ass," Bonnie replied. "I'm going for a walk…alone." She grabbed her raincoat and left our campsite.

"She can be a bear in the morning," Trip said. Neither Linda nor I responded to his comment. We grabbed some peanut butter and crackers and an apple for breakfast. The ground was wet and muddy so we ate standing up.

"I guess I better go look for her," Trip said and disappeared through the woods.

"It's too bad they're not having a better time," Linda said.

"It really is," I responded. "Last night was magical."

We finished our breakfast and headed toward the lake. We both thought a dip in the lake was just what we needed. The lake was more difficult to find in the fog. We did eventually find it and far fewer people were there. I guess many people were sleeping in after the late night. We disrobed and waded into the center of the lake. It felt chillier this morning so we didn't stay in very long. We sat in the grass just long enough to get somewhat dry before pulling on our clothes.

"Let me get my camera and then we can walk up the hill to see what is happening," I suggested.

"If you don't mind, I think I'm going to get a little more sleep," Linda replied.

"Not a problem. Before I go… give me a smile." She looked at me as I snapped off a couple pictures of her with big smile on her face with the fog swirling around her.

"Don't' waste your film," she said.

"Trust me… they may be my favorite photos I take all weekend." She reached up to me and kissed me.

"Listen, I'll be back to join you after I walk around a bit." I grabbed my camera and headed to the hillside. At first, I couldn't see very far in front of me, but as the fog started to burn off, I could see just how enormous the crowd had grown. I stepped around people sleeping in the mud and made my way up the hill. Everybody I saw was wet and covered in mud. I was glad that we had brought along the tents. I snapped a few pictures; soggy sleeping bags, people huddled together under make-shift tarps, others lying sound asleep in the mud, and even a few people passing around a joint to get their day off to a good start.

I made my way into a few of the parking areas. A number of VW busses were parked in the fields. I took a few pictures of those covered with their peace signs and psychedelic paint. Nothing was more iconic for the hippie movement than those busses. People were everywhere. As I walked, I couldn't believe the number of people that were here and the number of people still pouring in. Reading about it was a lot different than experiencing it first-hand.

The day was turning warm and muggy as I headed back to our campsite. More people were stirring on the hillside as I returned. For such a loud crowd, it was surprisingly quiet. Everything was hushed.

259

There was action at our campsite when I got back.

"Come on, Bonnie… you can't be serious," Trip was pleading.

"I'm not changing my mind," she replied as she pulled her backpack and sleeping bag out of the tent.

"I'm not letting you drive back home with strangers," Trip argued.

"It's not your choice. The rain, the mud, the humidity, your constant pestering… this sucks," she said. "I'm going home."

"Then I'm coming with you," Trip said.

"Do what you want." Trip pulled his stuff out of the tent and began to take the tent down. I had no idea what to say so I helped Trip pack up his tent. It was obvious Bonnie wasn't waiting for him. She was already stalking off as we packed up the tent.

"Keep the food," Trip said. "We're not going to need it."

"Thanks," I said. "Sorry, this didn't work out."

"Not your fault. For what it's worth, I had a great time while I was here. I wish I could stay."

"Why don't you?" I asked.

"Believe it or not, I do care for that girl. If I stay, it would probably be the end of us. I don't want that to happen." Trip finished grabbing his stuff and jogged off to catch up to Bonnie.

"Think they'll make it?" Linda asked.

"I think they will," I answered knowing that they would eventually get married although ten years later they would be divorced.

I knew the music wasn't starting for a few hours yet, so we crawled back into the tent and tried to nap. I had a hard time sleeping as guilt crept into my consciousness. What the hell was I doing? I was a married man… wasn't I? Here I was lying next to a beautiful young woman who was not my wife. Last night we had come dangerously close to making love. I wasn't sure if I would be able to resist tonight. All of the previous questions about what I should or shouldn't be doing in this situation filled my head. I tried to rationalize what I was doing using Dr. Cummings logic. It wasn't working. I finally came to the conclusion that there wasn't anything I could do. I was here and I might as well enjoy it. If things reached the ultimate physical conclusion tonight, then I would deal with it. I heard the first notes of music from the stage officially signaling the start of day two at Woodstock before I nodded off.

CHAPTER 50

We finally pulled ourselves together a little after 2:00P.M. We snacked on a couple of apples and some Slim-Jims as we walked to the stage. The skies were cloudy, but it was extremely warm and muggy. We watched as they set up for the next band. Few in the crowd knew the band, but I knew we were in for a treat. Santana put on one of the best performances of the weekend. *Evil Ways* and *Soul Sacrifice* made Santana an instant legend.

We hung by the corner of the stage for sets by Mountain and Canned Heat. The afternoon had been a mixture of sun, heat, humidity, and short showers. We walked back to our campsite to find more food only to find that our tent had been ransacked. The only thing taken was the food and water. Luckily, I had my camera in my pocket. The extra film in my backpack was untouched.

We decided to head to the top of the hill where the food stands were. We wound our way up the hill through the crowd now over a quarter of a million strong. Just beyond the top of the hill was an area of booths giving away all sorts of things from drugs to blankets, but no food. We walked through the camping area where several campfires were burning with crowds huddled around each.

"Anybody know where we can get some food?" I asked one of the groups we passed. The group pointed us in the right direction. It didn't take long to find the area where volunteers were whipping up something that reminded me of oatmeal. People were waiting in line to get a scoop or two. They even had milk to go over the top of it. Paper bowls were available but no spoons. We waited our turn, bowls in hand. The line snaked forward and soon the mush was being scooped into our bowls. I looked up and saw none other than Wavy Gravy who played such an integral role at the concert. He and his traveling commune, the Hog Farm, had been given the job of concert security. He did everything he could to help the festival-goers have a good time. Now, here he was making sure that the food distribution was running smoothly. I reached out my hand as I neared him.

"I just wanted to thank you for everything you are doing," I said. He looked at me a little puzzled at first trying to gauge if I was being serious or not. He tentatively took my hand and shook it.

"Groovy man, thanks!" With that he turned and jogged off, probably to check on some other problem. Linda and I took our bowls and moved to a quiet spot. I tilted my bowl and poured some into my mouth. The taste was surprisingly good, although my hunger may have accounted for part of that.

Linda and I finished up and headed back down the hill. Canned Heat was finishing up their set. I snapped pictures as I went, looking first toward the stage and then back up the hill. We came across a steeper section of the hill that had been turned into a mudslide. People would run and dive onto the slope and slide down the hill in a spray of water and mud. I snapped a few pictures and decided I wanted to try it myself.

"Hold my camera," I said to Linda.

"You're not," she said to me with a big smile on her face.

"I am." I waited for an opening and then took off at a sprint and dove down the hill. I slid, mud flying everywhere. I raced back up the hill, winked at Linda as she took my picture, and did it again. After the third time, I had had enough. It was tiring as I slogged back up the hill covered in mud after each slide.

"I think it's time for a dip in our favorite lake," I said.

"The way you look, you might want to go in with your clothes on," she said and laughed. That is exactly what I did including my shoes. Linda, not being muddy like me, opted for skinny dipping. I tried to rinse as much of the mud off my clothes as I could. Then I disrobed and spread my clothes on the grass before rejoining Linda in the lake.

"This whole thing is so cool," she said.

"I couldn't agree more, although I don't think our parents would approve," I answered. We both laughed, knowing our parents would be apoplectic if they knew what was going on here. We stayed in the water until we heard the next band start up. I wanted to catch at least part of their set. It was Credence Clearwater Revival banging out the opening chords of *Born on the Bayou*. There was no way my clothes were going to be dry so I pulled on my pants and carried my soggy shirt and shoes.

We managed to get back to our corner of the stage, although that was getting harder to do as the crowd had grown even larger. I snapped some pictures as the gray day turned darker. I wasn't sure if it was night time coming on or another storm. Credence finished off with *Suzie Q.*, bringing a huge ovation from the crowd.

I decided to head back to the tent before it became totally dark. I wanted to pull on a dry shirt and grab my raincoat. I knew before day two was over the rain would return. I opened the tent flap to find a white rear-end in my face. The young lady beneath the white rear-end tried to cover herself.

"Hey man, what are you doing?" asked the bare-assed guy I had interrupted.

"What am I doing? You're in my tent."

"Really? This is your tent?" he asked.

"My tent," I repeated. I need to get a dry shirt and my raincoat from my backpack."

"Just hand out the backpack and you can get back to your business," Linda said.

"Sure man. That's cool," the intruder said. He found the backpack and handed it to me. I pulled out a shirt and my raincoat and tossed my backpack back into the tent.

"We'll be back later," I said. "I would appreciate if you weren't here when we got back."

"No problem, man. Thanks." He pulled the tent flap back and I hadn't even finished putting on my raincoat when the amorous activity in the tent began again. Linda and I smiled at each other and headed back to catch the next act; the legendary Grateful Dead. Although I wasn't a big fan of their music, it would be fantastic to see them perform here.

By the third song of their set, the rain had begun again. I looked around and people were scurrying to get under cover anywhere. Plastic sheets, cardboard boxes, and soggy blankets were used as shelter from the storm. Some people were too stoned to even care. They simply sat and stared as the Grateful Dead revved it up on stage. The rain continued to come down. Things could not possibly get muddier and yet they did.

That night the music just went on and on. Sly and Family Stone came on around 1:30A.M. followed by Janis Joplin. Despite the rain, her set blew everyone away especially when she launched into her encore of *Piece of My Heart* and *Ball and Chain*. Unbelievably the Who came on after Janis. It was 3:30 A.M. I was running on fumes.

"I can't stay awake," Linda said. "Do you mind if we go back?" I was torn. I knew that Jefferson Airplane would follow the Who to conclude the music of day two. They had long been a favorite of mine. I was exhausted too, and I knew we could still hear the music from our tent. We headed back.

The couple that had previously occupied our tent were gone. I stripped off my raincoat and disrobed. I collapsed on top of the sleeping bags as Linda finished getting out of her clothes. She lay down and snuggled in next to me. A few kisses later, it was apparent that we had more energy than we thought. The Who had finished their set with *Summertime Blues, Shakin' All Over*, and *My Generation*. Our lovemaking was as energetic as the music.

There was only the silence of the rain hitting the tent as we recovered. I refused to feel guilty. I was here in a different life. I had nothing to feel guilty about… or so I kept telling myself. The music started up again as the first light of the new day started to appear in the sky. Jefferson Airplane strummed a set that included *Somebody to Love, Wooden Ships*, and *Volunteers*. The lovemaking was unhurried the second time around. It was tender and beautiful among the rain, the mud, and a half a million of our closest friends as the strains of Jefferson Airplane swirled through the mist.

CHAPTER 51

We slept until noon. Considering how many people were in the area, it was very quiet as we stepped out of the tent. We walked to the lake hand in hand. There must have been one hundred people or more in the lake already. Everybody appeared to be in a daze, the combination of the heat, the lack of sleep, and the effect of the drugs for some.

We disrobed and waded into the lake without breaking the silence. The water felt great, invigorating us which we definitely needed. We didn't stay in the lake vey long as hunger became an issue. After we air-dried, we headed back up the hill, hoping they were still dishing out the oatmeal concoction from yesterday. We trudged up the muddy hill. I was snapping a photo here and there as we went. People were sprawled everywhere still recovering from the long night of music. Mud covered everything including tarps, sleeping bags, blankets, and people. Those that were awake were just sitting in a daze staring off into space. It looked like something from a refugee camp.

There was more activity at the top of the hill as people were lined up for the bathrooms. A little farther on, we found the line for the food. I took more photos as we waited in line. In addition to the oatmeal, volunteers were also passing out oranges. Thirty minutes later we were eating in the shade of a big elm tree. I had a big decision to make considering what the rest of the day would hold. I knew that a huge storm was going to blow in around three in the afternoon. There would be torrential rain and heavy winds at the height of the thunderstorm. If we left now, we could miss it all. I also knew that if I stayed, I would get some incredible photos.

"I wouldn't be surprised if we had a thunderstorm today with all this heat and humidity," I said as I peeled my orange.

"You think so?" Linda asked.

"I do," I said. "It will be a mess when it happens."

"You seem pretty certain. How can you tell?" I realized my mistake. I had to be more careful.

"Just a feeling," I said trying to cover my mistake.

"Do you want to go?" Linda asked. Decision time. I threw the ball back in her court.

"What do you want to do?" I asked. I had decided if she wanted to leave, I would leave.

"I'm having a blast. I'd like to stay for the afternoon. I did promise that I would be home tonight so we can't be too late. I don't want my mother to worry." Her comment made me realize how life would change after cellphones became commonplace. A quick call to mom could assure her that everything was fine. The only news our parents were getting was what they were seeing on the nightly news. I'm sure they were worried out of their minds.

"Whenever you want to go, just give me the word," I replied. I snapped a picture of Linda as she popped an orange slice into her mouth. With the sunlight filtering through the branches, she looked beautiful. We sat and watched people stroll by us, a few were totally naked and didn't appear to have a care in the world. Either they were supremely confident or stoned out of their heads. I was almost certain it was the latter. The smell of campfires and marijuana sifted through the air.

Eventually we headed back down the hill trying not to slip and fall in the mud. I hated to admit it, but I was getting tired of the mud. Even though I was a teenager again, certain parts of my brain seemed to remember that I was really much older. More of the hillside was stirring. Mudslides were in full operation at several places on the hill. I snapped more photos as we walked.

We had just reached our little corner near the stage when Joe Cocker took the stage. Not many people knew of him before Woodstock. His career was launched into the stratosphere with his incredible performance this afternoon, the highlight being his rendition of the Beatles tune, *A Little Help From my Friends*. As Cocker continued ripping through his set, the wind picked up noticeably and dark clouds started to appear. The storm was on its way.

"Looks like you were right about the storm," Linda said.

"Yeah, it looks like it's going to be a bad one." I could see the crowd paying as much attention to the sky as they were to the stage. Everybody could see it coming. For many there was simply nowhere to run. They covered themselves in whatever tarps and soggy blankets they had at their disposal. I started snapping pictures as the first raindrops started to fall.

"Do you think you can find your way back to the tent?" I asked.

"You're not coming?" she looked at me in disbelief.

"I want to capture at least part of this storm on film."

"I'm not going back without you," Linda replied. "I'm staying with you."

The speaker towers began to sway in the wind with people hanging on. The public address announcer was begging the people in the towers to get down because a collapse or a lightning strike could be catastrophic. People were running to find cover wherever they could. The rain was coming down heavier. Thunder was echoing through the fields. Lightning was flashing everywhere. I snapped and snapped and even managed to change the film in my camera a few times while running from place to place to capture the moment. Linda stayed close on my heels. The stage crew was doing their best to cover speakers, soundboards, and various other equipment with plastic tarps. It was chaos as I continued to take photo after photo.

The storm continued to intensify. Rain was coming down in sheets. The wind was howling and lightning flashed all around us. It was time to take cover. I grabbed Linda's hand and slogged back to our tent. I threw open the flap and we tumbled into the tent in a soggy heap.

"That was intense," I said as I started to remove my wet clothes.

"Oh my god... that was insane," Linda replied. "I have never felt more alive in my life." She pulled me down on top of her. "Make love to me now." Wet clothes were thrown to the corners of the tent as our bodies entwined. The storm continued to rage outside while our own private storm raged inside the tent. In my entire life I had had never had more passionate lovemaking than I had in that tent on Sunday afternoon at Woodstock.

Afterwards, we just lay in each other's arms as the storm ebbed. Being here this weekend was amazing enough, but to get to share it with a beautiful young woman put it on a whole other level. I knew there was one more picture I wanted before this weekend ended.

I pulled on my clothes and grabbed my camera. Linda opted to stay in the tent and pull herself together. The hillside looked like a disaster zone. People were starting to emerge from under their blankets and tarps. The stage crew was starting to uncover the equipment as the storm moved off, thunder still rumbling in the distance. I got as close to the stage as I could. I didn't want to miss what came next.

A few minutes later, a special guest was ushered onto the stage and placed in front of a microphone. It was the man who made this all possible by agreeing to allow the organizers of the festival to use his alfalfa field. Max Yasgur was about to address the crowd. I knew what he was going to say, but I couldn't wait to hear it directly from him. He began to speak.

"I'm a farmer, I don't know how to speak to twenty people at a time, much less a crowd like this. But I think you people have proven something to the world. This is the largest group of people ever assembled in one place. We had no idea there would be this size group, and because of that you've had quite a few inconveniences as far as water, food, and so forth. Your producers have done a mammoth job to see that you're taken care of... they'd enjoy a vote of thanks. But above that, the important thing that you've proven to the world is that half a million kids- and I call you kids because I have children that are older than you are- a half-million young people can get together and have three days of fun and music, and have nothing but fun and music, and God bless you for it!"

270

The roar from the crowd was deafening. I snapped photos of both Max and the crowd reaction to his words until I ran out of film. His words had captured the spirit of Woodstock; three days of fun and music.

I walked back to the tent, knowing my time at Woodstock was coming to an end. I wasn't going to get to see another band that launched their career here, Crosby, Stills, and Nash nor was I going to see Jimi Hendrix close the festival on Monday morning with his rendition of the *Star-Spangled Banner*, but it didn't matter; I had been to Woodstock.

Linda had managed to pack up all the wet clothing into our backpacks. She had actually managed to find a few dry things for us to wear on the ride home.

"Who was that speaking?" she asked. I explained who Max Yasgur was and what a great speech he had made as we began to take down the tent. I stuffed it into its bag as best I could. It was soaked and it was going to be much heavier carrying it out than it was carrying it in. It was worth it; the tent had served us well. I took one last look around the clearing that had been our home for the last three days. I hoped one day I would get back here. I turned and we started our long trek back to the car as the first strains of Country Joe and the Fish blasted from the speakers that were still standing on top of the towers despite being pummeled by the high winds and heavy rain; a symbol of resiliency of the crowd that survived everything nature threw at us this weekend.

Chapter 52

The crowd had thinned appreciably when the storm hit. It took close to an hour to get back to the car. I feared that we would be parked in with no chance of getting on the road. Much to my surprise, many cars had already departed. We threw our stuff in the trunk and Linda began to pick her way around the worst of the muddy ruts until we were back on Hurd Road. There was a steady stream of cars joining the exodus, but at least it moved at a steady pace.

I did my best to keep up conversation because we were both tired and I wanted to help Linda stay awake as she drove. We found a little diner about an hour into our ride home. We pulled in to get some food and coffee.

"Were you kids at that big festival this weekend?" the elderly woman behind the counter asked.

"We were," I answered.

"Wasn't it just horrible?" she asked. "I saw it on the news… all the rain and the mud."

"It was actually kind of fun," I said.

"It was the best weekend of my life," Linda added.

"Hmmpf," the waitress grunted not expecting that answer and probably not approving of what she imagined went on there.

We wolfed down some burgers and fries followed by big pieces of delicious apple pie. Considering how scarce food had been this past weekend, it was like a feast at a fancy restaurant. We took two large coffees to go, paid our bill and left a big tip for the waitress before getting on the final leg of our journey home.

The coffees did the trick and kept us wide awake. I smiled to myself as I thought that maybe I should invest in a five- hour energy drink loaded with caffeine. I had no doubt it would be big in the future.

As we neared home, Linda took a slight detour. Much to my surprise she pulled into the parking lot at Monocacy Park.

"I don't want the weekend to end." She took my hand and we started walking toward the falls. It was dusk and night was coming on fast. We stood by the railing in one of the pavilions holding onto each other, watching the water slide over the falls, each of us lost in our own thoughts.

"I really meant what I said about this being the best weekend of my life," she said before pulling me into a kiss. After suppressing it all weekend, the guilt I felt was coming on like a tidal wave. I wanted to respond to her, but I just couldn't find the right words.

"Jason...I love you." I froze at hearing those words. It wasn't that I didn't have strong feelings for her, but things were so complicated. She had no idea the crazy ride I had been on these last weeks. I knew she wanted to hear something in return. I kissed her again to buy some time. In this time and place, I did love her. It was amazing how close we had become in this short time. It wasn't right for me to hide my feelings from her. She deserved better; especially since my feelings for her were genuine. I broke the kiss and looked into her eyes.

"I love you too," I said and meant it. I prayed Dr. Cumming's theory about alternate universes was correct otherwise I was going to hell. We kissed again and watched as the darkness took hold. We made our way back to her car, neither of us speaking. Everything that needed to be said had just happened; no other words were necessary.

A few minutes later we pulled up in front of my house. We both sat there, neither of us making a move to open the door. At that moment I would have given anything to be back in that tent in our own private clearing listening to the music at Woodstock. I think she felt the same way.

"I'm so glad we got to share this weekend together," I said.

"Me too," Linda answered. "I have never had a feeling like this in my life."

"Poor Trip and Bonnie," I said. "They have no idea what they missed."

"I hate to say it, but I think I liked it more being alone," Linda said and laughed.

"We can't tell them that, but I think I did too." We both laughed and agreed to keep that little fact a secret. I pulled all my soggy stuff out of the trunk.

"Am I going to see you tomorrow?" I asked.

"If you want to."

"I want to," I said. "I'm working until seven tomorrow. The last few weeks of the season, closing time is at seven."

"Want me to pick you up?"

"That would be great." With tomorrow's plans to see each other settled, I wrapped Linda into a big bear hug. She looked up and we kissed.

"The greatest weekend of our lives," I whispered in her ear.

I watched as Linda drove away, sorry to see this whole experience come to an end. I gathered up my wet stuff and walked into the house. The whole family met me at the door.

"You're alive," my mother shouted. She pulled me into a massive hug. "I was so worried. The news showed the crowd and the weather and they talked about all the drug use. People died this weekend from drug overdoses."

"It wasn't like that," I said. "There were a few bad apples, but most of the people were just enjoying the music. Everybody was helping everybody. It was beautiful."

"You sound like a hippie," my dad said and shook his head. "I think you have been indoctrinated. Next thing you know, you're going to run off and join a cult."

"Why would I do that?" I asked. "I have it too good here."

"That's certainly true," Dad said. "You didn't do any drugs, did you?"

"Dad, if I had wanted to, I could have. Drugs were readily available, but you taught me better than that. Neither Linda or I did any drugs."

"Well, I'm glad to hear that," Dad said seemingly satisfied with my answer.

"Are you hungry?" Mom asked. "I can reheat some of the hamburger casserole left over from dinner."

"Linda and I stopped at a diner on the way home. I'm fine."

"Weren't Trip and Bonnie with you?" Mom asked.

"They actually found another ride home," I replied.

"Did you guys have a fight?" Connie asked hoping that we did.

"No. Actually Trip and Bonnie did and they left a little earlier than us. That was fine with me because I really didn't want to listen to them bicker all the way home."

"That's too bad," Mom said. "I hope they can patch things up. They're such a nice couple."

"I hope so too," I answered. With the questions answered, I headed to my bedroom after first dropping all my wet stuff in the laundry room. Next stop was the shower. A long hot shower was going to feel great.

I was getting ready to call it a night when I remembered my camera. I hadn't seen it when I unloaded my wet clothes. I remember stuffing it in my backpack before we started the climb up the hill. I walked to the laundry room and checked my backpack carefully... no camera. I retraced my steps from the curb where Linda dropped me off to the laundry room. No camera. I checked my room. No camera. I was getting a bad feeling. My only hope was that it was in Linda's car somewhere. It was too late to call her now and find out. It would need to wait until the morning. All those great photos I had taken... the thought of losing that camera was almost unbearable. It had to be in Linda's car... it just had to be.

I lay in bed. I tried to focus on the incredible weekend I had just experienced, but my thoughts kept returning to the missing camera. I prayed that my memories of Woodstock would be more than the memories

CHAPTER 53

I had a dream about Grace and the kids. When I awoke, I thought that I was back to my old self. A quick glance around told me that I was still in my childhood bedroom. I wondered if the dream was a sign that I would soon be returning to my former life. The thoughts of Grace had me judging my behavior over the last few days. I missed her and now after the intimate weekend with Linda, when things were said and done that maybe should not have been, I felt terrible. I was in complete inner turmoil. Did I really love Linda or was it just the result of a great weekend? Could I love Linda here and still love Grace there? Was I living in an alternate universe that existed in its own time and place and had no connection to other lives that I have been living? Was it wrong to get involved with another woman even though I still had a conscious memory of Grace?

The thought of my missing camera got me out of my whirlwind of emotional confusion. I was positive I had some photos that people would want to see. I just had to find what I did with camera and the rolls of film. All I remembered was placing the camera and film in a plastic bag to try to keep everything dry and then stuffing it in my backpack.

After my shower, I had some breakfast and then called Linda.

"You didn't happen to find my camera in your car, did you?" I asked.

"Don't you have it? she asked.

"I searched my bag and retraced my steps from your car into the house. I can't find it anywhere."

"I'll check as soon as Mom gets back from grocery shopping. I'm sure it will turn up."

"I hope so. I think I took at least a few good photos."

"Do you want me to drop it off at the pool once I find the camera?" Linda asked.

"No, you don't need to go out of your way. Just bring it along when you pick me up tonight," I said.

I felt better after talking to Linda. She seemed very confident the camera was somewhere in the car. She remembered me packing it too. By seven tonight, I was confident that the camera would be back in my hands.

Band camp started at 10A.M. Monday morning. I pulled my trumpet, which I hadn't touched all summer, out of the closet. I took it out of the case and practiced a few scales after applying some oil to the sticky valves. It would be fun to see everyone that I hadn't seen all summer. Other than Trip and Bonnie, Rob and Anna, and Greg and Vicki, I hadn't seen any other band buddies. It would be fun to catch up with Tom and Mike, fellow trumpeters. Patti, a clarinetist and Lynn, a flutist were always fun to talk to as well.

Trip picked me up and we arrived at the field in front of the high school ten minutes before practice started. Everyone was greeting each other with hugs and handshakes. It didn't take long to find Patti and her infectious laugh. Our group of friends watched as the newbies arrived at the field. The tenth graders would become the butts of our jokes for the duration of the football season. It was a rite of passage for them as it had been for us in our sophomore year.

Mr. Demkee, our young band director, blew his whistle and summer band camp had officially begun. He laid out his expectations of us during the upcoming season which included being at all summer drills and practicing the music on our own time at home. Then he began with some basic marching drills to break in the tenth graders. For the next hour plus, we marched and played the Freedom fight song over and over. Just before noon, our first day of summer band camp was done. Trip dropped me off at home so I could grab a quick lunch and change into my bathing suit. Next stop was the pool.

Mom dropped me off at the pool after I explained that Linda was going to pick me up at the end of my shift. I had only been gone for three days and yet I felt like a stranger back at the pool. Some of the older staff were on their way back to college, so there were a few younger kids replacing them.

The crowd was light as it usually is in the last few weeks of the pool season. It made the day go slowly. I was so bored that on one of my breaks I walked over to the snack bar to say hello to Debbie only to find out that she had left to start college too. That was really too bad. I felt badly about the way things had ended between us. I had no interest in getting back together with her, but I did want to wish her well on the start of her college career and let her know that I still considered her a good friend. Sitting in the lifeguard stand later, I wondered if Debbie and I were together in some parallel universe. I suppose it was possible... if you believe in that sort of thing. I smiled to myself as I considered how many other women I might be living with in my other existences. I realized that I must be a real Casanova to juggle all those different women and keep them all happy.

Seven finally arrived. I did my closing chores quickly before racing out to meet Linda. I jumped in the car. She did not look happy.

"I searched everywhere; I didn't find your camera. I'm really sorry."

"You saw me pack it when we were in the tent, right? I asked.

"Yes, I remember clearly that you put it in your backpack," she said.

"Then it has to be here somewhere. After we get a bite to eat, we'll search the car again."

"Sounds like a plan," Linda replied. "I'm sure it will turn up."

It was a good plan, and we searched her car thoroughly after dinner. We checked along the sides of her seats, under her seats, the entire trunk...twice and found nothing but a few random coins. We went to her house and she checked her backpack. We went to my house and checked my backpack. We checked out front of the house and inside the house. Everywhere it could possibly be, we checked, but it was to no avail.

"Where can it be?" I muttered to myself.

"I can only think of one other possibility," Linda said.

"Go ahead and say it," I answered, already knowing what she was about to suggest.

"Is it possible that it fell out of your backpack as we hiked back to the car?" I did not want to consider that possibility because it would mean my camera with its award-winning photographs were irretrievably gone.

"I don't see how that would be possible, but considering we can't find it, I need to at least consider that possibility."

"Could you have left it at the diner?" Linda asked, looking for some small ray of hope to grasp onto.

"I didn't take the backpack into the diner so I'm almost positive that I didn't leave it there." Having no other ideas, we both sat silently on my back patio. After the thought of losing my camera sunk in, I really wasn't much in the mood to do anything. Linda left me sitting on my back porch still hoping that my camera would show up somewhere although I knew in my heart that it was gone.

I had another dream about Grace. It was almost as if my parallel universe was trying to call me home. I woke in a sweat in the middle of the night. I expected to find Grace next to me, but she wasn't there. I was still a teenager. I lay in bed, wide awake thinking and thinking. I realized that I wasn't in as much of a hurry to get back to my previous life as I thought. Linda and I had made a real connection in these last weeks. She was young and beautiful. I was young too, and didn't have all the aches and pains that came with almost seventy years of life. There were definite plusses of staying right where I was. Unfortunately, there were minuses too. Even though I was there for Grace in a parallel universe, I wasn't experiencing life together with her consciously. That saddened me to think I was missing out on the tender moments that the twilight years would bring us. I am a conflicted mess.

CHAPTER 54

I finally did drift back to sleep and had no more dreams. When I arose, I felt much better. I had rationalized that even though the camera was gone, I still had managed to experience Woodstock and would always have the memories of that special weekend. I sat at breakfast running through the possibilities of where my camera could be one last time. The only possibility was that I had dropped it somewhere as we walked to the car. Someone else probably found it and will enjoy my photographic memories of Woodstock. I would hate to think that it got buried in the mud and my photos will never be seen.

My weekdays had fallen into a pattern of band camp in the morning, lifeguarding in the afternoon, and seeing Linda at night. I was not spending much time with my family which bothered me. If and when I got back to my previous life, I knew I would be angry with myself for not carving out more time to be with them. Sunday mornings were still church and time seeing my Aunt Cile, Uncle Carl, and Grammy; something else I would miss dearly if I returned to my old life.

Somehow, I sensed my time in this universe was drawing to a close. I would continue on here, but my consciousness would be somewhere else. I prayed that I would remember my time here in this world when I returned to my previous life. There were too many good memories to forget; too many things I did differently than my first time; the awards banquet, the junior prom, my relationship with my family members, and meeting and growing close to Linda. Then there was Woodstock; one of the most amazing weekends in any of my lives… at least the ones I could remember.

Linda and I were parked at Atwood Lane once it grew dark. We kissed and professed our love for each other. The radio was playing *Crystal Blue Persuasion* by Tommy James and the Shondells. We just held each other and watched the moon rise through the trees. Heat lightning flashed in the distance and we heard an occasional rumble of thunder a long way off.

We sat and talked about our upcoming senior year. There were so many exciting things to look forward to in the next year including college visits, the senior prom, and graduation. It would be a big year; however, I doubted that I would be here consciously to enjoy it. I stared at Linda and wished I could explain everything to her. I knew I couldn't. I was afraid that she wouldn't understand and all it would do was ruin the beautiful relationship we had. I hoped that it would continue long after my consciousness departed this world. I would need to be satisfied knowing that I would still be here with her. We would go through this life together even though I would have no conscious memory of it.

We sat and kissed and talked and listened to the music late into the night. We hadn't made love since Woodstock. Somehow it seemed that we both knew that it would pale by comparison to that beautiful moment we shared at Woodstock.

Reluctantly, we headed home. We were still teenagers and our parents expected us home at a reasonable hour. We parked in front of my house. I looked deep into Linda's eyes.

"I am so glad we met," I said. She looked at me with a puzzled look on her face.

"It's not like you're never going to see me again," she said.

"I know, but I want you to understand how much you mean to me."

"What a nice thing to say," Linda said and reached across the center console and kissed me. "I truly love you, Jason. I have never felt this way about anybody in my life until you."

"I love you too like I have never loved before." We kissed one more time and held onto each other, never wanting to let go. If this was the ending, it was perfect. Neither of us spoke as I climbed out of the car and shut the door. We took one long look into each other's eyes before she shifted the car into gear and slowly pulled away from the curb. I watched her car until it rounded the corner at the end of the street.

I walked into the house feeling down. Surprisingly, my parents were still up watching a late movie. I sat with them until it was over, knowing I wouldn't be seeing them again when I returned to my old life. We talked about the upcoming school year and my relationship with Linda. Before I went off to bed, I spoke to them from my heart.

"I just want to tell you both how much I love you and appreciate everything you do for me."

"Alright, what trouble did you get into tonight?" my dad asked, suspecting I was kissing up to them.

"No trouble at all. I just don't tell you enough how much you both mean to me." My father looked like he still didn't believe me. My mother looked like she was about to cry.

"Give me a hug before you go to bed," Mom said. We did and she kissed me on the cheek before we broke the hug. I took one last look from the top of the stairs at my parents. I wished I could stay forever and do it all over again, but I knew it wasn't to be.

The last thing I did was peek into Connie's room. I tiptoed over to the side of the bed where she was sleeping. I leaned down and gave her a peck on the forehead.

"I love you, kid. Stay out of trouble." She stirred, but did not wake. I tiptoed back out of her room. I got ready for bed, reluctant to go to sleep. I knew this was it. I could feel it. I took one last look around my childhood room before I turned off the lights and crawled into bed. I tried to stay awake. I didn't want to leave this world yet. Eventually, I closed my eyes for the final time in this consciousness.

CHAPTER 55

I did not open my eyes when I first awoke. I listened for familiar sounds, but heard none. The first clue as to my whereabouts was the familiar pain in my right shoulder, too many years of tennis and pickleball. I opened my eyes fairly certain that I was back to my old life. The bedroom I saw was no longer my childhood bedroom. The Apple watch on my wrist confirmed that I was indeed, home.

I walked over to the bathroom and brushed my teeth and showered. I pulled on clean clothes and headed downstairs. The smell of fresh-brewed coffee was unmistakable.

"There's Danish on the counter," Grace said.

"Thanks," I said as I stared at the beautiful woman sitting at the counter. I poured myself a cup of coffee and took a cherry Danish and sat down next to Grace.

"What's on your schedule today?" she asked.

"I haven't decided yet," I answered truthfully.

"You have lunch at noon with the guys according to the calendar. Are you still planning to go?"

"Of course.... it's been a while since I've seen them." My first mistake, I realized a beat too late.

"You mean since last week?" Grace teased.

"It was a long week," I replied. We both laughed at my joke. If she only knew the truth.

"What's on your schedule?" I asked.

"Are you alright?" she asked. "You seem a little off this morning. It's Thursday; you know I have my golf league every Thursday morning."

"I guess I'm not awake yet. I forgot it was Thursday." I wanted to tell her about my adventure, but I knew it would raise too many questions. How do you explain what I just had experienced especially the part about sleeping with another woman? My alternate universe would need to stay my secret.

"Do you want to go out to dinner tonight? Then you don't have to cook after a long day on the golf course."

"That would be lovely," Grace answered. "Where do you have in mind?"

"I'm not sure, but it will be somewhere nice," I replied.

"Oooh, I love surprises."

I finished my Danish and coffee. I stood as Grace did. I embraced her and held her tight. I kissed her like I hadn't kissed her in a long time.

"You are acting strange. Don't get me wrong… I like it, but why are you being so nice?"

"Can't a guy show his beautiful wife how much he absolutely adores her?"

"Alright… let's have it. What did you do?" she asked. I laughed thinking back to a similar encounter with my father when my show of affection brought the same response. I really needed to show more affection on a regular basis to the people that were special to me.

"I didn't do anything. I guess I just have had a recent epiphany about how lucky I am to be your husband."

"This is good stuff. I guess you're hoping to get lucky tonight."

"I really hadn't thought about it, but I'm not going to say no."

"You expect me to believe that? You forget… I have been living with you for a long time."

"Wow... I try to be nice and all you can think is that I am angling to get sex later tonight." We both laughed. I don't think anything I was going to say was going to change her mind. She went to get changed for golf. I had a little time to kill before I had to meet the guys for lunch. I knew exactly what I was going to do with that time.

Once Grace left for golf, I settled in front of my computer. I was surprised that the date on the screen read September 14th. My last conscious memory in this universe had been late May. Once I was over that surprise, I got down to business. I debated whether or not I should do this. Even though I knew this was probably a bad idea, I couldn't resist. I typed in a search for Linda Smith. It was unfortunate that her last name was Smith. That complicated the search. I started adding qualifiers to the search; Linda Smith from Bethlehem, Linda Smith from Freedom High School, Linda Smith born 1951 or 1952.

The search was frustrating because it was likely that she had married and had a different last name. I had no idea what that name might be. Her former boyfriend was named Darren and he was two years older than she. I had no idea if he went to Freedom High School or not. He would have been in the class of 1968, the first class to graduate from Freedom. If my memory was correct, I think they gave students going into their senior year the option to finish high school at Liberty. So, he could have graduated from Liberty or Freedom. It would not matter if she didn't end up marrying him.

I eventually was able to track down Darren. He did graduate from Freedom in 1968. Once I found an online copy of the 68 yearbook, it was an easy job to match his face with a name; Darren Talman. Next, I searched the local newspaper archives for wedding announcements. Was there a Smith-Talman wedding? Bingo! There it was. An article from June 17th, 1973. Linda Smith married Darren Talman. Weirdly, I was jealous even though I had barely known her in this universe.

I checked records to see if I could find an address. I hit on an address in no time; the 1500 block of West Union Boulevard, just a half dozen blocks west of my junior high school, Nitschmann. Now that I had this information, I wasn't sure what I was going to do with it. I couldn't just walk up and knock on her door and say that we were in love in a parallel universe. Besides, what would be the point? I wasn't going to try and start up a relationship. I was back with Grace… where I belonged. Despite that, my curiosity was not satisfied.

Now that I had a last name, I searched Facebook. There were lots of Smiths and since there were fewer Talmans, I started there. It didn't take long to exhaust that list. I started wading through the Linda Smiths. It took twenty-five minutes, but I found her. According to her profile she had worked as a music teacher in the Bethlehem Schools. There were no recent posts, but the posts on her Facebook page made it clear that she was no longer with Darren. There was another man by the name of Bob that seemed to have taken Darren's place a few years ago. I am not surprised. My first and only impression of Darren was not a good one. I hoped for Linda's sake that Bob was a nice guy. She deserved that.

I wasn't sure what to do now that I had this information. For now, I had to go meet the guys for lunch at Perkins. Driving over to the restaurant, I realized that the reunion I had signed up for more than three months ago was this Saturday night. I almost ran off the road as I considered the possibility that Linda might be there.

There wasn't much new with Don, Jimmy, and George. Truth was that I was having trouble concentrating on the conversation. I couldn't get the reunion and the possibility of seeing Linda out of my mind. It was going to be an interesting Saturday night!

CHAPTER 56

Saturday morning Sarah and the grandkids stopped in for breakfast.

"So, tonight is the big night Mom tells me," Sarah said as Grace tended the bacon and eggs on the stove.

"Nothing big about it." I answered. "Just some old friends getting together to reminisce about old times."

"The key word there is old," Sarah said and laughed.

"Grandpa's old... grandpa's old," Bobby, my four-year old grandson chirped over and over. Sarah couldn't contain her laughter.

"See what you started," I said as Bobby kept up his chant running through the house.

"Don't be so sensitive," Sarah said to me.

"I wish I could see you at my age. Maybe then you would have a better understanding of old age."

"Somebody got out of the wrong side of the bed this morning," Sarah teased. Grace managed to corral Bobby on his latest dash through the kitchen. She gave him a cookie to munch on to quiet him. I picked up my coffee cup and headed to the screened-in porch to get some peace and quiet.

A few minutes later, Sarah joined me.

"I'm sorry if I upset you," she said. "I was just teasing. I think you and Mom are amazing for your age. I hope I am as active as the two of you when I am your age."

"Thanks. I appreciate you saying that. I guess I have been a little sensitive about my age lately. This fifty-year reunion thing made me realize just how old I am."

"You're only as old as you feel…isn't that what you always say?" Sarah asked.

"I do say that and there are days I feel way younger than my actual age, but there are also days that I feel every bit of my age. It's all part of the journey. You need to take the good with the bad. I have a little motto that has served me well through my life."

"Care to share these pearls of wisdom with me?" Sarah asked.

"Expect the best, prepare for the worst, and take whatever comes with a grin," I replied.

"I like that," Sarah replied. "I'll have to remember that."

I finished breakfast without having to suffer any additional age-related digs. Sarah and the grandkids took off. I puttered around the house the rest of the day, not being able to concentrate on anything. I was more nervous about this reunion than I thought possible. It all revolved around one person; Linda. Would she be there? What would happen if she was?

The reunion started at five for cocktails with dinner to follow at 6:30. I pulled into the Lehigh Valley Steel Club dressed in a nice black suit with a paisley tie that I owned for years. It seemed appropriate for the occasion. Inside the front door there was a reception table where you had to pick up your ID badge complete with your high school graduation photo and name just to prove to people how fifty years had ravaged you. Trip was a few spots ahead of me.

As I waited my turn to sign in and get my badge, I scanned the other ID tags on the table looking for one specific name. It didn't take long to find it. Linda's graduation photo looked just like she had when we had been at Woodstock together. My heart started to race a bit, and I seriously considered leaving.

"Hey man, this is going to be fun," Trip said as I stepped up to the table.

"I hope so," I answered trying to calm myself down. Trip and I moved toward the bar to get a drink. I recognized other high school friends immediately. Rob waved us over. He was standing at the far end of the bar.

"Seems like nobody brought their spouses," he said and laughed.

"Grace told me straight out she thought I would have more fun if I went by myself," I said.

"Considering Bonnie and I have been divorced for many years, it is probably best that we came separately," Trip replied which brought another round of laughter. We were soon joined by more of our band friends including Patti, Lynn, and Sue. So far, the record was perfect; no spouses were in attendance. We were soon joined by Greg and Vicki breaking our perfect record, but since they had both graduated in our class, we decided that it didn't count. They had become an item in high school and were still together after all this time. Rob and Anna could say the same thing, although Anna was in the class behind us.

Our group talked and talked about our high school days, especially the band which played such a big role in all our lives. I kept one eye on the table to watch for Linda's arrival during the conversation. I was about to give up hope as dinner was about to be served when she walked in looking just as beautiful as I remembered.

"You look like you have just seen a ghost," Trip said to me.

"No, not at all. I was just trying to place who that woman is that just walked in." I pointed toward Linda.

"That's Linda Smith if I'm not mistaken. She was in my English class." Trip had an amazing memory for the past. He could tell me what period and in what room he had each of his high school classes. "I think she was in your Trig class during first semester."

"How do you remember all this stuff?" I asked.

"I have a weird memory for things like that. I wish my memory had been as good for my schoolwork."

Dinner was being served so whatever was going to happen with Linda, if anything, would need to wait until later. I sat at the band table which included Trip, Bonnie, George, Vicki, Rob, Patti, Lynn, and Dave. It was amazing that after all these years the conversation flowed easily, like fifty years had never intervened in our friendships. I stole several glances toward the table where Linda was sitting. I recognized a few faces, but certainly did not know anyone well enough to go over and start a conversation. I couldn't just walk up to her and say that we went to Woodstock together in another universe. Dinner finished and various groups were called to get their photos taken in front of the reunion banner.

The band started playing and a few people started dancing. More and more mingling took place as table groups spread out to say hello to other friends and acquaintances. Linda headed to get her picture taken with the Buchanan neighborhood group. This was my chance. I waited until the picture was taken before I walked up to her. I made a show of looking at her name tag.

"Linda Smith… I think we were in the same Trig class in our junior year."

"What a good memory. I'm impressed." She took a closer look at my nametag. "Jason, of course. I remember you."

"So, what have you been doing for the last fifty years?" I asked.

"For most of that time I was teaching music in the school district," she answered. Small talk continued for a few more minutes before it started to become awkward. It was time to wrap it up.

"Our high school years were really something, weren't they?" I asked. "Maybe the best times in our lives, but I won't speak for you."

"There were big events for sure, but most of them were bad when you really think about it," Linda replied.

"Bad?" Like what?" I asked.

"Martin Luther Ling and RFK being assassinated. The Vietnam War and all the protests and demonstrations. The Kent State shootings. Sharon Tate murder by Charles Manson. The Beatles broke up. Should I go on?" Linda asked.

"There were a few good things," I countered. "The first Earth Day. Landing on the moon. Great music."

"That's true," she began. "And who can forget Woodstock?" My head jerked up and I searched her face for some hidden message.

"Woodstock indeed," I answered. "Were you there?" Time seemed to stop as I waited for her answer.

"It's a strange thing," she said. "I wasn't there, but on occasion I have had some very vivid dreams of the event. There's a part of me that feels like I was there."

"In your dreams, do you see anybody else?" I ask, my body coursing with electricity. She closes her eyes and seems to be thinking. She opens and bends forward to look at my ID badge.

"This is crazy, but I think that it's you in my dreams," she answers. I feel like my head is about to explode. Somehow, some way she remembers our time at Woodstock. Dr. Cummings would have a field day with this information.

"I hope we had a good time," I answer and laugh.

"Don't tell anyone, but in my dreams, we had a great time." She smiles and laughs.

"It will be our secret," I assure her. I don't have anything else to say. It is enough that she remembers. I don't understand how any of this is possible, but it is and I'm glad it happened. We talk about our current lives for a few minutes before we head back to our respective tables.

293

The rest of the evening is a blur. My head is still reeling over the Woodstock connection. The party starts to thin out as the evening draws to a close. One by one, my friends take their leave. I wonder if I will ever see some of these people again. Soon I am one of the last ones left. I look around to see if Linda is still here. I can't find her. It's time to leave. I head to the door and into the parking lot. Suddenly a person comes up behind me. It's Linda. She pulls me into a hug and gives me a kiss.

"That's for Woodstock," she says. Before I respond, she turns away and disappears into the dark parking lot. I stand frozen. The whole magical weekend comes rushing back into my head. Somehow, I know that this will be the last time I see Linda. I am back in this life with Grace which is where I want to be. I get into my car and drive home, smiling all the way.

Epilogue

A month after the reunion, my life has returned to normal. Grace and I talk about the news of the day as we share meals together. Sarah and the grandkids visit a few times a week. Sarah was glad to hear that I was able to reconnect with some of my old friends. She avoided any age-related jokes which I appreciated.

One thing had changed for sure; my appreciation for the great life I had right here. Skipping back to my youth was fun, but I missed Grace, my kids and grandkids, and my friends. Even though I was here the whole time physically, I missed the conscious interaction with all of them. I supposed that I was still there physically in the alternate universe with Linda. At least I hoped I was. On some level I wish I knew how things turned out in that life. I wondered if Linda and I would spend the rest of our lives together there.

I wasn't quite ready to let go of my alternate universe completely. My curiosity was as strong as ever. I wondered if Dr. Cummings lived in this universe. He would be quite old by now if he did. There was no guarantee that he worked at Princeton if he did exist here, but at least it was a starting point. I searched current professors, although I didn't really expect to find him. I didn't. Next, I searched Princeton's records for professor's emeritus, a title given to retired professors of note. That's where I found a brief bio of Dr. Cummings. He retired in 1982, thirteen years after we met. The most interesting thing I discovered was that a building was named for him upon his retirement; Cummings Hall dedicated to the time-space continuum and the theory of relativity. I was in the presence of a brilliant man when we met fifty years ago. Unfortunately, Dr. Cummings passed away in 1996, at least in this universe. I had no way of knowing if the length of time you lived remained consistent from universe to universe. There were many questions about parallel universes for which I would never know the answers.

One thing I wanted to start doing on a regular basis was to visit my parents' graves. My chance to see them again made me miss them even more than I had before my trip through time. I bought a bouquet of yellow roses and drove to the cemetery in Allentown that overlooked the Lehigh River. During the summer, if the wind was blowing in the right direction, you could hear the announcer at the Iron Pigs' games calling the play-by-plays. Being October, there were no ball games today. I was the lone visitor to the cemetery on this day. A cool wind was blowing from the north giving a hint of the colder weather to come. I stepped out of the car near my parents' graves. I divided the bouquet in half and placed the roses in the built-in urns on either side of their gravestone. I said a little prayer thanking my parents for everything they had done for me. Mom had been gone for eight years and Dad had been gone for seven. Being back with them, even for the short time I had been, was priceless. Tears began to form in the corners of my eyes. I knew I would never see them again until I crossed over to the other side one day down the road.

After the cemetery, I took a drive by some of the places I had been in my alternate life. I drove by my childhood home on Bonnie Drive. The color was different, but nothing else had changed much. Then I drove by Linda's childhood home. It looked unchanged although I'm sure there were new owners. Next, I stopped at Monocacy Park. I parked the car and walked the path to the pavilion where Linda and I had bumped into each other the day after our junior prom. I stood at the railing and watched the stream cascade over the falls. So many memories came flooding back to the times I had spent here. Atwood Lane, my favorite parking spot, was next. Homes lined both sides of the street now. Most of the trees that lined the lane were gone. I doubted that anybody was using this as a lover's lane anymore. My final stop on my tour was Freedom High School. There were additions to the building that weren't there in 1969. Memories of summer band camp came rushing back. Things were so simple then. We were so innocent.

By the time I arrived back home, I was feeling melancholy. I missed the people and places that weren't here anymore. The passage of time was inevitable. Things had to change. Looking back on my life, I am happy with the choices I made. Hopefully I still had a number of good years left to enjoy it. My somber mood passed quickly. There were too many good things happening to be worrying about things I could not change.

Over the next few days I moved further and further away from my jaunt through time and space, but there was one more thing I wanted to do; I wanted to visit Woodstock. They had built a concert venue and museum on the top of the hill at the original site. According to what I had read, the museum was supposed to be outstanding; a true tribute to those days in August of 1969 when half a million kids descended on Max Yasgur's farm to celebrate peace, love, and music. I brought up my plan to Grace as we sat at dinner.

"I'd like to take a trip to see the museum at Bethel Woods. Any interest?" I asked.

"Sure, that could be fun." she answered.

"We'll take a drive through the country and spend the day touring the museum. On the way back we can find a little place to get some dinner."

"That sounds nice," Grace said. "When are we doing this?"

"I checked our calendar and we have nothing this Saturday. Does that work for you?" I asked.

Saturday morning arrived and we left around eight. I stayed to the back roads much like my previous trip to Woodstock. We pulled into the parking lot a little before eleven. We paid the admission fee and entered the museum. There were photos and videos and displays everywhere. Music that had been recorded at the festival was playing from all corners of the museum; Hendrix, the Who, Credence, Crosby, Stills and Nash. I paid particular attention to the bands I hadn't been able to see on that Sunday evening so long ago.

There were many different alcoves in the museum, each depicting a different band's performance at Woodstock. I studied the photos and videos intently, wondering if it was possible that Linda and I might actually show up in a photograph. With a half million people, it was unlikely. The afternoon drifted by as we went from exhibit to exhibit. There was one more section of the museum to see. It was entitled Memories of the Past. It was a miscellaneous collection of personal items that people had left behind at the concert including an actual VW bus. Display cases were filled with miscellaneous shoes, articles of clothing, and various pieces of jewelry. There were assorted pipes that had undoubtedly had been used to inhale marijuana. Umbrellas, tarps, a motorcycle helmet, a broken guitar, jewelry, and a rusty harmonica filled the cases. Photos filled the cases depicting many of the scenes from the concert.

It was the last case that I looked in that blew my mind. There was a Kodak Instamatic camera sitting among a number of Kodak 126 Instapack film cartridges. And behind the camera was a picture of a beautiful girl smiling into the camera shrouded by the fog. I found it difficult to breathe as I stared at the face looking back at me from the photo. It was Linda. It was my camera and I had taken the photo. Somehow, which I could not begin to understand or explain, my long-lost camera and the picture I had taken of Linda so long ago had found its way into the museum. Linda and I were officially part of the history of Woodstock. If only that camera could talk; I would have loved to hear its story and how, after all this time, it had ended up here at the museum.

Walking out of the museum, I took a look from the top of the hill down toward where the stage had been in 1969. I could imagine Linda and I standing near the corner of the stage just beyond the woods. Somewhere off to the left there had been a pond. I wondered if it was still there. Deeper in those woods was a clearing where a young couple had pitched a tent fifty years ago. It was a beautiful moment in time that I could never share, but would remember forever.

The End

July 9, 2023

****Notes on Woodstock:

The depiction of Woodstock is accurate as far as the order and times of the musical acts. Timing of the rain and thunderstorms is accurate as well. Wavy Gravy was a real person at Woodstock as described. Max Yasgur's speech to the crowd is verbatim.

Made in the USA
Middletown, DE
30 July 2023

35982976R00166